RONALD FRAME

The author was born in 1953 in Glasgow and was educated there and at Oxford. He has written five other books including the novels SANDMOUTH PEOPLE and the prize-winning WINTER JOURNEY. He has also written a collection of short stories, WATCHING MRS GORDON. He has recently received the Samuel Beckett Prize for his first television play, *Paris*, and he has also won PYE's 'Most Promising Writer New to Television' award. His latest published collection, a novel and fifteen stories, is called A WOMAN OF JUDAH.

Ronald Frame

A LONG WEEKEND WITH MARCEL PROUST

Seven stories and a novel

sceptre

Copyright © 1986 by Ronald Frame

First published in Great Britain in 1986 by The Bodley Head Ltd.

Sceptre edition 1988

Sceptre is an imprint of Hodder and Stoughton Paperbacks, a division of Hodder and Stoughton Ltd.

British Library C.I.P.

Frame, Ronald
A long weekend with Marcel Proust.
I. Title
823'.914[F]

ISBN 0-340-42891-0

Printed and bound in Great Britain for Hodder and Stoughton Paperbacks, a division of Hodder and Stoughton Ltd., Mill Road, Dunton Green, Sevenoaks, Kent TN13 2YA (Editorial Office: 47 Bedford Square, London WC1B 3DP) by Richard Clay Ltd., Bungay, Suffolk.

For my mother and father,
and for Euan Cameron

CONTENTS

ACKNOWLEDGEMENTS

The title story was broadcast on BBC Radio Three, as was 'The Blue Jug' (read by Dame Peggy Ashcroft). 'The Lunch Table' appeared in *Company* and 'Incident in Le Lavandou' in *Scottish Short Stories* (Collins). The story of 'Prelude and Fugue' has been filmed for Channel Four as 'Out of Time'. The source of 'The Camelhair Jacket' is an incident recounted by Gabriel García Marquez in 'The Fragrance of Guava' (Verso, London, 1983).

The extracts from Noel Coward's songs, 'London Pride' © 1941 Chappell & Co. Limited and 'I went to a Marvellous Party' © 1939 Chappell & Co. Limited, are reprinted by permission of the Noel Coward Estate and Chappell Music Limited.

The extracts from the Rodgers and Hart song 'Spring is Here' are reprinted by permission of Belwin Mills Music Limited.

'Good night, good night. You go this
way?'
'Alas. I go that.'
  VIRGINIA WOOLF, 'The String Quartet'

'We are, each one of us, our own
prisoner. We are
locked up in our own story.'
  MAXINE KUMIN, 'Address to the Angels'

A Long Weekend with Marcel Proust

for Patrick Rayner

We've come to Normandy, to Cabourg. Proust called it 'Balbec'.

Checking us into the hotel on the promenade, Martin enquired, which was Proust's room—where he wrote—might he please see it?

'And your wife, also?' the girl at the desk asked, but I drifted out of hearing range.

Martin's got down to his research straightaway. I can't find my third volume. I must have left it behind in Paris. I haven't said.

I like Cabourg—for what it is, not for the 'Balbec' Proust made it. The Empire villas are like scaled-down city mansions spelled here to the seaside from Neuilly; others are bizarre hybrids, crossed with Normandy 'traditional'—the most outlandish are latticed on their upper floors with wooden beams painted brown and their towering gables give them a gaunt, ludicrously lumbering look that reminds me of the spooky house in 'Psycho'. Some of the names on the gateposts seem too fortuitous to be real: 'L'Ancrage', 'La Sauvegarde,' 'Alice', 'La Résidence Odyssée'. One garden I saw into was a tangle of giant lilies. In others monkey puzzle trees cast deep Edwardian shadows. Tanned Finzi-Contini children on whirring bicycles pedal along sandy roads. There's a creek with a tilting boardwalk and yachts resting high-and-dry on their keels in the mud, waiting for the tide.

The nip in Paris's air has gone. Suddenly there's a heavily scented, drowsy atmosphere. Everywhere smells of lavender bushes and umbrella pines, and the sea.

*

There's a party of English Proust devotees staying here: the tweedy well-to-do kind hob-nobbing with the inevitable wall-flowers, single women who look as if they'll have jobs in local government or make invaluable school secretaries; there's also a buttoned-up bachelor who might work anonymously in hospital administration, perhaps disappointed to find the hotel doesn't have a lift-boy as it did in Proust's time. They walk around carrying Painter's biography tucked tightly under their arms.

The tweedy ones speak in loud, superior voices. What brings them here? Is reading Proust for them like—like opening a door into a sunny, fragrant garden? In the books people know their place, the order of things hasn't collapsed? They can disregard the degeneracy and sexual adventuring because gentlemen in the end are always gentlemen and Proust's world was the same one—more or less —which fathers and uncles and elder brothers traded their lives in Flanders mud to preserve?

*

At night Martin and I sit in the dining-room with its high windows and I follow the progress of the ships out in the Channel, passing each other with their private language of lights and sirens.

'This room,' Martin reminds me, 'Proust said it was like an aquarium.'

I smile—smile tiredly—through our reflections, out into the darkness.

The 'truite Albertine' and 'gâteau au chocolat Odette' have been rather disappointing.

Cheeky French schoolchildren cock snooks through the glass at the English party, who are exchanging their stiff-jawed politesse.

Along the coast, on the hairpin road, I see the lights of cars. Martin sees too.

Proust liked to be driven by night, Martin tells me, sometimes for dozens of miles. I know the story. Proust would ask to see a particular building—a chateau usually, one he remembered, or which he thought he remembered, or persuaded himself he did—and when they'd found it, his chauffeur would negotiate the driveway and sweep the track of the car's headlamps across its front.

The experience of reading Proust is like that, I feel—nocturnal, muffled, subterranean, like travelling in another element. Like handling fine porcelain wearing padded boxing gloves.

I don't tell Martin that.

Outside the windows, on the esplanade, lovers stroll arm-in-arm.

It's odd—I don't suppose it's in Martin's nature to be a romantic.

He can write lucidly about the condition in other people's lives and when it manifests itself in books. Maybe he thinks he's quite complete as he is?

*

So. Here we are.

If Professor Brinkley hadn't died, probably we wouldn't be.

I looked through Brinkley's notes in Paris: boxes of index cards, marshalled into order by Martin. Martin said the book was to have been called 'The Skein of Memory'. He thought he'd change the title when he's licked the book into shape. To 'A View of Delft', after the Vermeer painting Proust saw in Paris. Martin showed me a photo of it—a harbour on a perfect summer's evening, the fiery water glassy and still, sailing boats at rest, neat cleanly starched figures motionless on the quayside, belonging to the scene. Memory and time transfixed. Seeing it made Proust swoon.

I've given up telling Martin he's not obliged to finish the book: just because it was asked in the will doesn't mean he *has* to. 'I owe it to him,' Martin keeps saying. 'For old times' sake.'

I think he was happy then, in his Cambridge days. There's another Martin who belongs to that time and I'll never know him. He only lives inside *this* Martin's memory.

*

When dinner's over, Martin writes a postcard to Jennifer, in his tiny, exact academic's script. He curves his arm, so I can't see—a schoolboy's gesture, or an earnest student's who knows the rightness of his exam answers.

I don't think I've ever realised how close they must have been, Martin and Jennifer. People either overlook brother-and-sister relationships, or they dread the worst of them. Martin loved Jennifer: in the purest sense, of course. He still loves her, although she now has a husband and a baby is due.

At dinner he said, 'It was in Trouville Proust met Marie Finaly. Albertine. "Mysterious Albertine outlined against the sea". Remember? With the "sea-green" eyes?'

I immediately thought of Jennifer's eyes, which are green. My eyes are green too, not by accident.

I think I've always been a surrogate for Jennifer. When she married, and then Martin married me—the term after I graduated—maybe he was subconsciously becoming *her* husband?

I don't look very like her, not enough for people to confuse us—but I do have green eyes, and dark brown hair which he encourages me to wear piled up like hers, and we both have noses a little on the long side. My ears are smaller: Martin bought me pearl and filigree studs for our first anniversary in February— Jennifer had received the same present from *her* husband on *their* anniversary.

Did I catch him on the rebound? I wonder. Whenever he talks about it, in his version it's *I* who did the pursuing.

In Paris it struck me for the first time, maybe I've married a bachelor . . . ?

*

Morning.

The wind's churning the sea to froth and thumping punches on the orange canvas awnings all along the beach side of the white hotel. From our balcony I watch as the walkers struggle and pitch themselves forward at twenty degrees.

I like windy days like this. They empty me of myself. At home they blow people's conversation my way when I want to eavesdrop, and away from me when I'm being expected by the other university wives to listen. They play havoc with other women's tidiness and make me feel what I've never had the daring and folly to be, a domestic rebel, clothes rumpled and hair messed.

Albertine—what did Proust call her?—'a domesticated wild animal'. 'Mysterious Albertine', whose real home was the 'horizon of sea', whom no one could ever quite tame . . .

Behind me Martin's papers are tossing themselves around the room; they sound like the fluttering of paper wings, wings that cannot fly.

*

He's correct, of course, Martin. I *did* pursue him.

Students have always tipped their caps at their teachers: I wasn't unusual in that respect. We merely took the game several stages further, and we married.

I blame Martin for Professor Brinkley and the obligation of finishing the book. But *I*'m not blameless either.

I wonder if it's not my father I'm trying to find? Because I'm married, he seems *nearer* to me even though he's dead: he isn't in a chasm of black time.

It's not the blustering, successful businessman I remember as my father, but the guilty, unfulfilled man I knew he was too. Even when I was a child—getting over the sadness of my mother leaving us—he told me then that the life of books and quiet, contemplative thought was the perfect one, his ideal. If only, he said, if only he could have his life over again . . .

So maybe I felt I *had* to grow up clever? I *had* to shine? I think I did make him proud. And he lived to see me go to university, which was as much as I could do.

I try to imagine him doing the things Martin does. I persuade myself, it's an ideal life—Martin's university terms, our long holidays, conferences in comparative literature I accompany him to. Even the other university wives who let me know they think I'm stand-offish have their part in it, and are to be suffered.

It's becoming more difficult for me to have that faith, that it *is* a proper life. Maybe it's because everything you're dealing with is dead. A novel's nerve and life is sapped out of it by locating it in a certain historical milieu. A poem ceases to be valuable for the emotions it contains, its purpose is to be placed inside a specific context of ascertain-able persons and incidents.

Martin sees how I feel. He guesses my dissatisfaction: that all is not with us as it was. Maybe he imagines this is only temporary, I shall recover my equipoise?

He's used to dealing with lives that are finished, which assume a pattern in the factual re-telling.

But surely the pain and mystery of living your life—and potentially its happiness—must be . . . contriving your own destiny for yourself?

*

To Illiers this morning. I couldn't remember and looked up the entry in the guidebook. It said: Illiers, called 'Illiers-Combray', the market-town where Proust spent holidays at his uncle's house when he was a boy, which became 'Combray' when he turned memories into fiction decades later . . .

Poor Proust.

We saw the little brown house in its undistinguished side-road. We were shown the boy's bedroom with its magic lantern and hard bolster-bed. The hypochondriac aunt's room was directly opposite: among the lemonwood furniture there was a bedside cabinet, equipped on top with books of devotion and bottles of tonic, like a church altar cum pharmacist's counter. A notice said it was from there that the famous lime-tea and madeleines were dispensed.

'It's like the table beside Proust's bed, in Paris,' Martin whispered to me. 'Remember? The medicines and the drafts of the novel?'

I nodded. I didn't remember, but there were only the two of us in the bedroom and I felt I could tell an untruth and not be caught out.

I liked the cosy kitchen, the boy's den where the cook entertained him with stories of her life: Ernestine who became Françoise in the books. But I also understood why anyone should have wanted to escape from the ritual of existence in the house: the rooms were 'comfortable' but over-furnished and cramped, I could stretch up and touch the ceilings with my fingertips, the ticking clocks and twitching floorboards became a strain after half-an-hour. I noticed the fanlights of clear glass above the bedroom doors, which must have made complete privacy impossible. The panes of stained glass in the hall introduced a religious light on things which I felt vaguely disquieting—perhaps because in this age we've lost the consolation as well as the fear of God.

It started to rain. While Martin pored over the artefacts in the museum downstairs I watched the drizzle from the window of Proust's bedroom.

Escape and bondage. It was these rooms and the lives they held which Proust made it his life's work never to have to return to —living in Paris, living by night, cultivating salon society— but he was trying to find them again in his books, through the associations of words. He tried to recreate what had been, *but in a perfect form.*

Art when it's self-conscious like that is destructive too. People and places and happenings are how the artist wants them to be and how he wants them to stay, for ever—he selects his own final version of events.

It's not to say things were really like that—*truth* doesn't seem to be the object. Not at all. Surely it's immaturity, not only being unable to accept something as past, but having to re-devise it over and over again in your own image. (As if you're trying to convince yourself, yes, despite my doubts, I did make the best choices possible in my life, I did, I did.)

Martin bought sepia brown-and-white postcards of the quiet, decent rooms and wrote one to Jennifer and husband in Edinburgh, snug as bugs in their terribly decent villa in Barnton.

I walked outside, into the walled garden, thickly green and still. The vegetation dripped, politely.

I savoured the quiet. I noticed the thrushes—heads cocked—hunting for snails.

I picked my way across the damp grass to the glass-roofed summer-house. Inside, the walls were lined with photographs. I took my time studying them. Faces of society hostesses and boulevard beauties of the 1890s. Agostinelli the loving chauffeur was included, and Daudet's effeminate teenage son, and the Count de Montesquiou with pomaded hair and wearing an astrakhan coat with a white rose buttonhole. Proust's chameleon features were there too: able to adjust to placate any rich woman's—or rich man's—ego. His chin rested in his cupped hand, his moon eyes swam in his languorous olive-skinned face.

At the very moment in a troubled weekend when I was wanting to assess myself, to be *honest*, I felt I couldn't. I wanted to know —about *me*—but it was like wading in quicksands. The posed expressions on the walls all seemed to hold some sly knowledge of the world's ways, there in the sleepy sensuous come-hither eyes. *Let be, let be* . . .

Outside in the garden the wood-pigeons chortled contentedly. Up in the trees the branches squeaked and the leaves rustled as the ghost of a breeze ran through them. Thrushes pecked—and snails in shells, as is the order of such things, surrendered. The front door bell rang in the house, sounding far, far away. From a gurgling roan-pipe water dripped, dripped, dripped into a rain-barrel . . .

I felt Illiers-Combray was suffocating me: it was like being smothered by a dead weight of feathers . . .

I thought, how *could* Proust have been content with this after the Bois and the Boulevard Haussmann and the Ritz Hotel? He wasn't just duping us, he was tricking himself. It was because he couldn't decide what to do with his life that he let the past hold him in its clutch.

At twenty-five or twenty-six he was writing in letters, *now* his life was going to begin in earnest. But he continued to postpone: till he would be thirty, till his beloved mother would have passed away, till his fantasies would be in print (paid for by himself)—when it was he started turning his clumsy life into a story, making conclusions and sequence where in life they don't exist, they never exist.

*

Martin suggests, let's see Chartres on the way back.

The cathedral with its bleached stone and green roofs is visible across miles of flat fields and poplar breaks. Approaching it through the dog's leg alleyways of the old town, its proportions are dizzying. Pigeons wheel about its height like cliff birds.

The afternoon light begins to go; a battery of floodlights makes an unearthly theatre of spires, pinnacles and buttresses.

Martin quotes Ruskin. ' "Trees of stone".'

Inside the cathedral is humbling, it's like walking into the belly of a whale. The glass is a deep rich crimson or blue, eliminating what daylight's left. Furtive figures scurry off into angles of shadow. The medieval darkness is pricked with lighted candles.

Martin says it's like Debussy's 'Drowned Cathedral'. 'La Cathédrale Engloutie'. I don't know it, but he's right, exactly right.

The weeping wax smells cloyingly sweet. While a priest intones, worshippers kneel and pray in whispers—and it seems to me that what they're begging from the Mother of God is hope, and luck, and to be spared this survival game, living from minute to minute to minute.

It's what drowning must be like. You find you've somersaulted head-over-heels and upside-down and you're travelling backwards through a vast, lightless place.

So much sweet, lulling darkness in the middle of the world, it *is* a kind of dying . . .

*

The next morning—tired—we drive from Cabourg along the switchback coast road. Through Houlgate, clinging to its wooded shoulder of hill; past the villages where the Narrator and Albertine and 'the little band' feasted in farmhouse kitchens. Through Deauville and Trouville. And on to Honfleur, which Baudelaire and the Impressionists came to visit.

Dozens of sleek white pleasure-craft bob in the harbour, straining on their hawsers, pulling them taut. In the channel nearer open sea, battered fishing smacks chug in and out. The tall, teetering, grey-slated buildings on the Quai Sainte Catherine remind me of home, of the towering lands of Old Edinburgh.

We walk through the cobbled alleyways at the back of the town—past fusty lugubrious parlours, murky workshops no bigger than walk-in cupboards, past fat cats asleep on window-sills among chipped pots of geraniums. Dull, matter-of-fact existence.

Martin says, isn't it like Balzac? He can only see it as a book, not as these people's lives. I nod and have a vague memory of lecture-room notes about the 'Human Comedy' and characters propelled by their individual obsessions, fighting society and the age for the freedom to be *themselves*.

*

Coming back we took the wrong road at a cross-roads. I wasn't attending to the map, so I suppose the fault was mine.

The road turned away from the sea; it narrowed, and we realised then it wasn't the right one. It became a leafy lane, but we continued following it. Martin was muttering some lines from Proust, from one of his letters maybe, about a flinty lane with trees interlacing overhead like a tunnel.

Two children jumped out of the trees in front of us and ran ahead for several seconds before disappearing back into the undergrowth. As the car passed the spot where they'd vanished, I had a picture in my head of Martin and Jennifer scampering up the driveway of the house in St Andrews I went to once to meet his father. Then the two children became a child and an adult: my father in his holiday clothes and myself—in the blissful days before his new wife, my new mother—the two of us walking together down a shady Cornish lane between lush grassy banks of campion and willow-herb, to a secret sandy cove among rocks.

The car engine strained, but Martin kept going. At the top of the lane we both saw at the same moment the *reason* for the stony track: behind a crumbling honeystone wall—an old but restored farm-house.

Blue shutters were pulled across the windows, siesta-fashion; white doves fluttered on the high, steeped roof. The sun came out from behind clouds and for an interval of half-a-minute or so the colours burned: the sky-blue of the shutters and the dusty grape-blue of the tiles, the brilliant white of the birds, the searing pink of geraniums on a window-sill, the mellow gold stone.

It didn't remind Martin of any house he'd read about in Proust and he shook his head. 'It isn't anything,' he said. 'Not grand enough.'

He turned the car. The wheels spun in the grit and flint chips rattled under the chassis. I shut my eyes so I wouldn't forget: the house, the quiet, the startling colours as the sun shone on them.

*

The next morning I can remember, perfectly. Nibbling one of the little sponge madeleines that come with the coffee-bags and the sachets of shampoo, all part of the room-service.

In Cabourg the dawn mist curls in off the sea. From the balcony I can hear, across the sleeping town, the halyards of the yachts rattling eerily as the tide lifts them. I feel I'm waking from my hypnosis.

I'm not returning to London. I'm going back to Paris—for a bit.

I'm not 'escaping'.

I know someone who works in a bookshop. Simone—do you remember her? You can have the address, Martin, it's on the other side of this.

Blame it on who you like. 'Who*m*' you like. Do you remember, I got straight alphas in my Virginia Woolf paper? I realise you're strong on the text/life connection: I'm not. All I know is, you can have your eyes opened by what's there in a book—or, as I've discovered with Monsieur Proust, by what's not there.

I suppose it's true after all: the more you read, the less there is in this spinning world you think you can be sure about.

Let me know about the book. 'A View of Delft'. Here are *my* impressions, for what they're worth.

Believe me, it helps—getting the thoughts out of your head. Whatever happens as the consequence. It's like losing ballast, casting off: the lines drop away—and suddenly you're inching out (is this a simile or a metaphor, I forget), turning for that open sea.

The Lunch Table

Puffin is late. She's only had to come up from Richmond but she's always late. Through the custom of years, she has acquired the right to be late.

Fee is sitting at the table as she bustles into the brasserie. Their greeting is a kiss, as it has been since their teens.

Puffin throws down her carrier bags and then drops into the empty chair. 'A drink, a drink,' she says.

Fee signals to the waiter.

'What did you get in Harvey Nix?'

Puffin shows her. She's forever buying jumpers, skirts, scarves in Harvey Nix.

Fee is interested, as she's always interested, and also vaguely disapproving, as she always is. It is expected of her that she should be interested but also slightly disapproving.

'Didn't you get lilac last time?'

'I don't think so. Wasn't it jade?'

'Oh, Puffin!'

'You know what I'm like.'

'Only too well!'

The drinks arrive. They haven't given an order, but once a fortnight constitutes regularity in the restaurant and the pretty-faced waiter with the rolled-up shirt sleeves remembers. Not because the two customers are in any sense out of the ordinary—pukka London and country women in their thirties and forties are the basic stock in trade—but because he wants to make a future in the business and he takes a pride in his job.

They always discuss it.

'He's remembered.'

'I always think he'll forget. Or get us mixed up.'

'What a life it must be.'

'It's the tips that make it worthwhile.'

They choose sensible, nourishing dishes from the menu. The cost is less important than the food's health content: this is their fortnightly treat and they have no guilt left about the expense. They both like the same things, and one may share the other's mullet or fennel mornay.

They select a bottle of good red in the wine list's mid-price range and between them they consume most of a bottle of Vichy mineral water. They prefer cheese and fruit to pudding. They order two cups of decaffeinated coffee.

Neither is crankily fastidious: their behaviour only represents the state of awareness of a female generation who have reached their late thirties (as they have) and forties. They don't talk about it as a subject in itself: it's as natural to them now as the air they breathe, in Richmond and Rustington respectively—not in the cloudy lunchtime atmosphere they watch turning under the Raffles-style ventilators. The fans are unable to banish the seeping blue fumes of French cigarettes and recently the two women have begun to view the situation more critically, through narrowed eyes, but neither has yet suggested that a move to another restaurant may soon prove necessary.

Their talk is of the world, or what they glean of it through Sunday newspapers and the television and radio news reports; but, in the end, it is less about the spinning world at large than about the specific world which the two of them have shared: school in the sixties, mini skirts, Dusty Springfield, the peppermint twist and the monkey-dance, seeing John Newcombe play at Wimbledon, lazy afternoons after their schooldays in the Heaven and Hell coffee bar in the deliciously sinful bowels of Soho, dapper young men who partnered them at dances and ended up in pinstripes in the City, that hiking holiday in the Tyrol, the 'vendeuses' jobs in The Strawberry Experience boutique when psychedelic clothes were the rage.

They could discuss those memories for hours.

It's when they turn to all that came later, the time beyond, that the conversation shoots off at its accustomed tangents and loses that easy, comfortable quality.

They talk of children and dogs and holidays in rented houses and three sets of school fees apiece and the problems which they all bring in their wake, and still there is no evident strain of any kind between them. But each of them knows that this exchange of domestic chitchat is evading the vital issue of why they are sitting here sharing a lunch table every second Wednesday or Thursday.

It isn't a matter of blaming: they've both been too genteelly brought up for that. A telepathy operates between the two women after so long and they know that they don't need to speak certain thoughts aloud. Some of the thoughts aren't defined even to themselves.

Momentarily a betrayal is permitted . . .

'Philip doesn't eat anchovies. You know what he's like with seafood.'

'Jock always takes his shoes off with the laces knotted. He's just like an overgrown schoolboy sometimes.'

But the betrayals purport to be about trivia, so nothing is lost.

Every time they meet, though—it sounds like a contradiction in terms—there is something like a submerged flash point in the course of the conversation. In their eyes at that particular moment their mutual dissatisfaction registers: dissatisfaction not just with Philip and Jock but with themselves, because they won't say more. Theoretically, they could demolish this embargo of silence once and for all; the taboo on the subject could just be disregarded and one of them could begin to tell the honest truth.

Fee might admit that Philip forgot their last anniversary and the one before. Puffin might confess that, on the pretext of snores exceeding the agreed decibel limit, she and Jock spend every second or third night sleeping in adjoining bedrooms. Fee might disclose that Philip takes himself off to the golf course every Saturday and Sunday afternoon without fail, come rain or even sleet. Puffin might reveal that Jock sees what she thinks is rather too much of his Rotarian friends. Fee might let slip that she goes alone to the concerts at the children's schools, because Philip tells her he's too busy preparing his cases. Puffin might blow Jock's cover and tell Fee she's found copies of *Playboy* and *Penthouse* at the back of the garage.

They *might* say—but so far they haven't, and perhaps they never will. The subject is restricted to what is relatively inconsequential, or appears so, but the words are in the way of future depth charges . . .

'Philip's car was clamped last week. He forgot the time!'

'Jock's new secretary bakes at the weekend and brings him in biscuits. She doesn't look the "homely" type at all to me.'

'Philip does everything into a Dictaphone.'

'Sometimes I only get the answerphone when I call Jock's office.'

But perhaps even this diversion from the facts—not speaking the things they suffer in silence, in private—is only a diversion from something else: something that binds them closer to each other after all these shared years, husbands and children, Richmond and Rustington notwithstanding.

It's clear in the 'Mesdames' after lunch, it stares each of them in the face then, out of the mirrors. It has stared at them out of every mirror in every restaurant they've frequented over the years.

Puffin looks as she evens the discreet mascara she's taken to wearing, before a quick foray down to Sloane Square and then the tube. Fee looks as she applies another new shade of lipstick, before the journey home to Sussex on the train following a brisk walk up to Knightsbridge.

Very briefly, for no longer than a couple of seconds, their eyes meet. Even when they're standing at separate basins and in front of different mirrors, their eyes swivel at the exact angles and they meet.

The knowing angles cut across the exchanged snippets and civilities of the past ninety minutes and are the assertion of what is now, under the fluted glass lampshades on the walls, blatant and unavoidable: the fact that they aren't as they will be and can never be again how they once were.

Fortnightly isn't often enough to undo the damage of time, to make them not see it. They see it perfectly well, the future stretching ahead of them, but it's not an endlessly flat distance—further off it narrows and crowds in.

Matronly middle age, then drawn old age. Next year they will be one year older; in three months' time they will be three months older than they are now. 'Age' used to be synonymous with 'wisdom' when they heard people discussing it. Now neither of them—although neither says—is so sure of that old saw; any knowledge that may accrue to them is likely to be of a limited, tight-lipped kind . . . they can guess that much.

Already that knowledge is in the making, and already they seem to spend a considerable proportion of their time together echoing each other and making circles with their words, just as the old do sitting on seafront benches or chewing over their food in private hotels.

The brief look in the mirrors is the sharpest and most penetrating of the day. It does in two or three seconds what the ninety minutes fail to do. It establishes the real dependence: it examines critically, stores up an image, it confirms the condition of grace of the other, it judges the pace of a sure decline.

What lies ahead of them is growing old. Nothing more and, heaven help them, nothing less.

Then—the intensity of that moment is just as suddenly lost.

The eyes turn away, into handbags and shopping bags.

'It's eighty pence now for the tube.'

'The train costs a fortune.'

'Where's my bag?'

'I must go into Truslove. Have I time?'

'I've some wrapping paper to buy. For Claudia's birthday.'

'I've sent her a gift token.'

'How super, she'll love that.'

'I was going to get Ben some book, I wrote it down.'

'Dom's always on that wretched computer, did I say?'

'Philip loves his word processor. It's unhealthy!'

'I don't know where Dom takes it from.'

'From Jock?'

'He can't work a tin-opener.'

They walk back through the restaurant, past the lunch table with its debris of crumpled paper napkins and breadcrumbs and empty glasses smeared with lipstick, past the other couples paired along the mirrored walls. Separately each catches her image as they turn to the door.

Outside they always have the claims of 'business' to be done, in opposite directions. Puffin is heading for Sloane Square; Fee is bound for Knightsbridge. That manoeuvre, too, is achieved with the minimum of fuss and pretence after so many years' practice.

They promise to give each other a ring as they always promise: at the weekend, when Philip will be out on the golf course and Jock will be with one of his Rotarian friends—probably the one who renovates sports cars, and the two of them will have gone for a spin. They'll phone in the afternoon, they agree, when they know the children will be at their most excitable and demanding.

'Safe home, Puffin.'

'Take care, Fee.'

Recently they've introduced a new variation on their established procedure: they've begun grazing each other very lightly on the cheek with a single parting kiss. It's fleeting, and done with the best of good taste. Like the kiss of welcome before they start lunch, it's a continental custom their generation has picked up on, but the two women do it out of that strength of feeling which the years have given them. The years have given much and taken away much.

'Safe home.'

'Take care.'

And then one kiss, followed by the other. Their lips hardly touch the skin. But the gesture after the lunch's polite circumlocutions is true. Really it means 'good luck'.

For a second Fee's hand or Puffin's grasps the other's arm, then it lets go, and Knightsbridge or Sloane Square calls.

Merlewood

'When a person dies, his portraits change.
His eyes see differently and his mouth smiles different smiles.'

ANNA AKHMATOVA

Every picture tells a story. Not a 'picture' in this case, but a photograph. Preserved in the darkness of a trunk, against the odds: faded and worn from the mint black-and-white first impression, but without the damning sepia rinse.

*

We are eight.

It is a summer's day, in the mid-1960s. We are arranged on the lawn in front of Merlewood. The bay is visible in the left-hand portion of the photograph, and the single rock jutting up two or three hundred yards out, and the thin line of horizon between the sea and the vast West Coast sky.

Gregor stands in the middle of the group, rather formal for the occasion, but that is his way; he's in his late teens, and his face is already set into adult seriousness. On his left is Kirsty, sitting on the travelling rug that's been spread on the scorched grass; her left arm rests on my mother's leg. My mother occupies a low deck-chair, and is her Kelvinside self, seeming to enjoy and welcome the moment, royally receiving this person who has come to photograph us. (I can catch a trace of the lily-of-the-valley toilet water that made a haze round her movements and actions, which she sprayed on herself for a very practical purpose—to keep the Tighnabruaich midges away.) Immediately in front of Gregor, Angus lies on the rug facing forwards, supported on his elbows and with his chin cupped in his hands. Beside him, to his right, Sandy sits cross-legged on the burnt grass, twisting the bamboo pole of a shrimping net and screwing his eyes up against the sun. Behind Sandy, I stand in vague imitation of Gregor, who's on my left, but I can only reach his shoulder for height. (I still have to learn to dress like him: I'm in a t-shirt and shorts, while Gregor wears long white flannels and a Clydella checked shirt open at the neck.) On my right is Rhona, lying in a striped deck-chair and patiently holding a book open in her lap as she waits for the photographer to be done.

That's seven of us.

The eighth person is my father, on the edge of the photograph, on my mother's left. He's standing, one hand on the back of the deck-chair, his other arm hanging loosely by his side. The hand that appears to be doing nothing is, in fact—so I discovered when I looked very closely at the photograph—clenched, the fingers are curled up into the palm. He smiles, as my mother and Kirsty and I all smile, but with him it is a quiet mysterious gesture. He knows or understands something we do not, and while he is one of us he is also a man apart. The rest of us look at the camera: his eyes are focused on some point out of the picture, well out, on the sea side.

*

Cloud, sea, sand, rock.

And Merlewood.

Merlewood had been my father's father's house. It was built by one of the Clydeside ironmasters to accommodate his Victorian family —wife, children, governess, nanny, cook, chauffeur, coy servant girls brought up from the city. There were eight bedrooms and an attic of rooms, and two turrets, and a scaled-down portico à la Balmoral, and steeped corbie-stanes on the gables, and a flagpole to fly the Union Jack or the Saltire. The building had weathered very slowly, bald grey sandstone against the blue Atlantic sea-skies, the bracken hill behind, the rhododendron bushes studded with purple, pink and white heads.

We spent every summer there, and an occasional Easter or September weekend. A ritual developed.

My parents drove the hundred or so miles from Glasgow.

The day before, the rest of us would sail up from the Broomielaw on the steamer.

We would stand watching at the rails for a first glimpse of Merlewood. On overcast days the chimneys would be smoking, in sunshine the windows shone like mirrors.

Merlewood was waiting: and it was as if—I would think—I only had to see it again to become the 'other' version of myself.

As the distance to the shore grew less and less I had the sensation of sailing into last summer, and the one before, and the one before that.

We nudged against the pier; the holding ropes were thrown, and the gangways were hoisted up to the gates.

Our feet clattered over the soft, salty, echoing wood.

Trunks and cases were loaded into a Humber taxi, not the pony trap of my father's time.

Gregor and Rhona and I would start walking, as we always walked, while Kirsty and Sandy and Angus bundled themselves into the Humber.

Tighnabruaich grass was springy with moss. The sun dazzled off the sea. Wavelets slapped about the rock in the bay, standing in line with the house. The red road was always redder than I remembered. Bees as big as halfpennies stuck to garden walls. The Scoulers had this year's new model of Daimler. Rhona walked as our mother walked, with a woman's rolling hips. The steamer's hooter blew. The taxi was disappearing out of sight along the coast track, spreading a balloon of white dust behind it.

The real summer had begun.

*

My father's quiet smile.

He's not smiling as my mother and Rhona and I do, declaring ourselves to the camera.

He smiles so enigmatically because what *he* knows none of the rest of us know. He shares his knowledge with whoever watches from the future and recognises the ironies of the scene: the midsummer sloth, the carelessly splayed limbs, the props (deck-chairs, sun umbrella, shrimping net, tin spade, picnic hamper), the careless expressions and open smiles.

Even holding the photograph to the light, at first I could see no more than is there: there seemed to be no new angle of discovery, no possible plane beyond the flat one presented. Some aspect of the picture was unsettling, though, and it was only after several days of living with the image that I suspected what it might be.

*

There used to be photographs of my mother in whites, playing tennis on a court in Zanzibar. Servants stood in the background and menials watered flower beds while she lunged for low, devious shots and jumped up on supple ankles to make fiercesome returns.

She began to forget the names of the other schoolgirls and young women she'd played against in the heat, in advantaged circumstances, although once she had been able to remember and could reel them off like a litany, Dutch, Australian, Swiss, Portuguese, Venezuelan.

Her uncle was second-in-charge of His Majesty's interests in the Government Protectorate of Zanzibar. A few months after the War ended, escaping British greyness and austerity she had been shipped out to the sun and plenty of the island. The plan was that she would live with her uncle and aunt and cousins for the next three years, in their colonnaded, fan-ventilated official residence, on the pretext that her education would be broadened by 'the experience of Africa'. There were other reasons, however, less noble-sounding and rather more pressing: later I guessed at them, and the likelihood (the necessity, surely) that the removal had been effected at her uncle's expense.

By then the history of my immediate antecedents was clearer to me. After his Navy days my mother's father had embarked on his married life in the Argentine; with family funds he'd set himself up as a cattle farmer, but after seven or eight years he realised that he had no natural aptitude for the business. He took his family back to Britain and repeated the earlier mistake by buying another farm —sheep grazing and arable land this time—in Perthshire. Without a farmer's sixth sense to rely on, he fared no better than before. Each new season was worse than the one that preceded it. He was a proud man and he blamed his many failures however he could. He was also a susceptible man—or merely given to self-destructiveness in the Scottish way—and he was guilt-racked for the sake of his wife and children. He retreated into the only two enthusiasms the years had left him: painting watercolours 'en plein air' (which excused him from the house for a few hours at a stretch) and, his favourite indoors pursuit, helping himself to generous measures (ever a liberal, in stolen pleasures as in politics) from the decanters on the dining-room sideboard.

Some of the watercolours survived and hung on Merlewood's walls. I grew up with them, hardly noticing them: delicate, under-stated views of rolling Perthshire, the hills and glens, Lednock, Devon, Farg, and Strath Bran. The perspectives were always very careful and exact. By a cruel irony, my mother's father's most dependable source of inspiration and consolation was the amber spirit ('peat water' was his euphemism) by which my own father made his living and *his* father before him, and which had afforded Merlewood in the 1920s.

The affairs of the farm were constantly in a crisis state. The bursars of the children's schools (discreetly distanced in neighbouring counties) began to sound rather less gentlemanly in their letters of reminder. Repairs in the house had to be overlooked: social appearances slipped. The watercolour painting stopped when my grandfather couldn't trust his hand to hold the brush steady. All that was left to him then was the other private solace.

The parental roles were reversed after that. His wife became the provider, living on her wits, and he became the dependent. My mother, the youngest daughter, went out to East Africa and lived grandly during these three impressionable, formative years of her middle teens. Employment was found for her two brothers via 'connections', and—while my mother darted about the tennis courts of Zanzibar in cosmopolitan company—on the home front her sisters were directed towards sensible, low-risk and utterly predictable matches of another kind. Wedding bells rang in clean, scrubbed, scrupulous Dunkeld, and this or that field of grazing was sold to settle accounts on the day. On the cedar lawn the same marquee was erected three times—and a fourth time for my mother, when it was her turn—to house the celebrations. As my grandfather struggled to hold his composure till the guests would leave, his wife could remind herself that at least the token rituals of the order were being respected.

My mother's husband came from the West Coast, unlike the others. In Zanzibar she'd been introduced to a London cousin of a Glasgow family who worked in a shipping office. An invitation from the London cousin, who was visiting his relations in Glasgow, reached her a number of months after her return to depressed, grey, wanting Britain, to the far, slumbering backwaters of Perthshire. The family were called Hamilton and lived elegantly in Kelvinside (she had forgotten elegance since Zanzibar), in a stone villa with a high terrace that had views over the flatness of Glasgow, across the miles of tenement streets and smoky works to the cranes and jibs of the shipyards and the giant hulks of foundries. (For reasons best known to herself, my mother never forgot those, the spectacular views.) The Hamiltons were whisky brokers: the father (my grandfather, the purchaser of Merlewood) and a bachelor uncle were joint overseers of the firm. The one son Alasdair had come back into the family fold after his time at Cambridge; the supposition had always been that he would take his place in the business, and when my mother first met him he'd been working there, assiduously, for three years. The difference between stolid, redoubtable Alasdair Hamilton and her defeated father in Perthshire must have reassured her. She neglected the Londoner's attention in enjoying his cousin's grateful, rather sober company. 'I think I changed you,' she always claimed, and he wouldn't fail to acknowledge his debt to her for that.

In the next couple of years he came out of his shell—it could only have been my mother's doing—and he added a personable public exterior to the native temperament relied on by his father and uncle, which was diligent, industrious and (by common regard in whisky broking circles) enterprising. Maybe those were his best years: with the confidence to take financial gambles when his father and uncle had final liability, forcing an entrée with my mother on to the social scene and cutting a dash in all the right places. Much later my father would make rather complicated jokes about his youthful endeavours in those polite, fashionable circles, telling us he'd felt he was a suitor required to prove his worth, like the humble man bid to perform certain labours before he can claim his bride, who turned out in his case to have been a princess in disguise. (My father never mastered the art of telling funny stories: usually the funniness was lost, and came out sounding like the seriousness he spoke for the rest of the time.)

It was a very welcome pairing for all parties, and the announcement of the engagement was greeted with manifest approval. It may have been that Alasdair Hamilton and his fiancée were the two least able at first to believe what was happening, happening *to them*: my mother, the youngest of the four sisters, had clearly outdone the others, and perhaps my father thought he didn't fully deserve this exotic Zanzibar-bred prize for his efforts. Otherwise their feelings for each other did prove to be honest and true, and they made a notable and noticeable—if not quite complementary—partnership: my father was disciplined and hard-working, concerned at all times for the greater good of the firm, sometimes (after his father and uncle retired) over-involving himself and relying too much on the risk factor—while my mother with her superior ways and graces simply preferred the surfaces of things, and was happier attempting to influence and win others through her considerable gifts of charm, with maybe a little of that smooth-talking diplomacy she'd learned from her uncle for good measure. Somehow, as a pair, they had enough give-and-take with each other to be able to survive the mishaps and misadventures that occur in any marriage: neither had forgotten their pleasure and relief at finding the other, and that gratitude developed into a resolve to see and trust to the best in each other and to accept the 'worse', if it came, as only a temporary obverse of the positive—the riches and health of their first years together.

*

Looking again at the photograph of the eight of us, I'm prey to another suspicion: that even then Merlewood was more than a house and a garden, already our history there was passing from fact to the half-imagined.

Merlewood was becoming a myth before I was out of my adolescence, and its inhabitants—the differences time made to us seeming more marked with each successive year—were also possessed by the myth. The journey to Tighnabruaich was made every summer in search of other selves, *possibilities* of selves we'd outgrown: in our middle teens we were beginning to settle into later versions of ourselves, but somehow the illusion persisted that we could undo that confirming process of time.

In the photograph we seem too close to the images of ourselves we *should* be: the props might have been decided by a professional photographer over the telephone, the composition surveyed in advance, the gestures advised on. At first sight careless and unaffected, the group strikes me more and more as playing to the camera and humouring the expectations behind it.

But what expectations, and whose?

*

The garden was all things to us: Arizona, the Spanish Main, Swallowdale, Outer Space, the Amazon, Treasure Island.

For Gregor's twenty-first birthday party we hung it with paper lanterns, and we forgot its familiarity. The candles glowed in the trees and among the rhododendrons, and our shadows stretched ahead of us for yards, climbing hedges and walls, scaling the sides of the house. That evening we were all granted strange powers of magic and dissembling, and we hardly as much as thought about it.

Someone took photographs, but the results had nothing to do with my perceptions of the evening. We only looked dazed by the flashbulbs; the males of the company seemed rather foolish in their too generously cut dinner jackets (Gregor wore a kilt), and the females uneasy in long dresses that were at least twenty years behind the fashion. Gregor was in fine form, because Annabel Lavery's arm was linked through his: in their evening attire the pair were the very picture of middle-aged respectability. For years now their photographs have appeared in the social pages of *Scottish Tatler* and *Scottish Field*, and in *The Scotsman* at legal and Unionist functions, and their expressions and arm-in-arm poses, like the kilt and the cut of dress, have never varied from the original.

That night they could afford to look contented and just a little bland: at last Lavery Senior had the heir he required for the practice. When they were photographed dancing, it was marionettes I was reminded of: the gestures, like the smiles, were extravagant, or merely cautious, as if they were both afraid that the wires they worked on might become entangled. There were strings attached to the arrangement, of course, but they'd known that from the outset, from the moment Mr Lavery had welcomed Gregor to the first 'At Home' in Edinburgh. I could say they had no one to blame but themselves, but I know that, like the victims sacrificed in societies we consider to have been more primitive than our own, their lives were not really theirs to hold.

In the lantern-light, maybe they could have believed to the contrary.

It was Merlewood's finest evening, its supreme deceit. The Laverys had come, and the MacNaughtons, and the Todd Hutchinsons. We were eminently desirable company, and Gregor was forty years old, not twenty-one: you only had to look at him to see him in his wig and gown, or mixing drinks for a colleague in the Heriot Row office, or being lunched at a prospective client's expense in Edinburgh's own Café Royal, in the Oyster Room.

In the end it was Gregor who attended to all the legal complications when the brokers' business was compulsorily wound up, and maybe my father knew that too, seeing more in the situation as it clarified itself that evening than the rest of us could: even the ablest of our number, Gregor—ductor exercitus—wasn't to be spared.

*

But it's that earlier photograph which intrigues and mystifies me, which draws me back: ourselves on the lawn at Merlewood, one perfect summer's day in what appears to be our innocence.

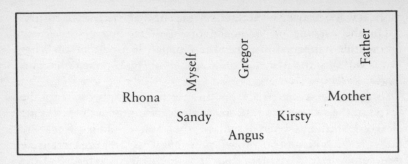

I see that these faces, intercepted at a split second one August afternoon in 1966 (the month and year have been scribbled on the back), are outside the tense in which they are living.

What it has taken me so long to perceive is this: that—at some level—we must have been conscious of the fleetingness of life and its conditions even as we were living through them. It's as if, by some most curious process of misdirection, the psychic instinct of generations past in the Western Isles has passed to us, we've picked up an echo of it in that garden: we see forward to ourselves looking back, with the equivocal aid of the Celts' third eye. Carrying the consciousness of the moment's loss and distance, we are beyond recapture.

The faces confront the lens, and that tunnel refracts the image, concentrates it into the future when these things will have passed: when the shrimping nets are lost or broken, the woollens thin and mothy, the hair of the oldest children starting to show grey, the eyes of all of us acquiring the habit of hesitation to match our sensibly non-committal manners.

The faces invite the imprints of age, they are empty vessels for the future. They are icons of the change to come.

*

The photographs of Gregor's twenty-first birthday party were mislaid, or destroyed; or maybe Gregor discreetly removed them later, either for my mother's peace of mind or his own.

All the photographs disappeared, that is, except one, which survived—for a dozen years or so, until I lost it by my own carelessness. It showed Gregor and Annabel framed by both sets of parents. What principally interested me about it was my father's face, for two reasons: because we had very few mementoes of how he looked, and (although I didn't realise it then) because the face in the photograph was doing more than presenting a public front, much more, it was betraying his certainty of the end that was coming to him.

On the evening of Gregor's coming-of-age party, something momentous happened, and we none of us paid it any attention. What it was was this: to all intents and purposes *my father wasn't with us, he was absent.*

Certainly there were six faces, and the photographer had got the better of the shadows at last, so that the features of each were quite clearly defined. But that is beside the point. I understand now that my father had left behind only the impression of his face, while really he was somewhere else: he had escaped the insolent tyranny of the camera, which boasts the authority to seize and reproduce. My father had got away, and the eyes and mouth did only the expected things, like a gingerbread man's.

With the five others in the group there was some accidental detail to note—my mother's hand caught straightening the strap of her dress, or Annabel's left foot resting on its side—while my father had too obviously been dragooned into exhibiting himself: he was on display, because this was 'An Occasion', he was affecting ease when no one else could quite manage it. His arms hung straight, his hands were positioned in line with the seams of his trousers, his shirt cuffs showed the respectable distance beneath the jacket's, his pumps were in perfect alignment. If I could examine the image again, I would see that he had disciplined his face to the point where it would reveal only what each moment required and would hazard nothing more, no possibility of a random emotion.

Even the buttoned-up Scots can let slip how they feel, but there was no danger of that with my father. Tradition—chastising and self-denying—had perfected itself in him to the 'n'-th-degree: he was its apogee. Most people might no longer subscribe to religious tenets of the 'elect' and the 'damned', but he had worked his own secular reinterpretation of them. If the damned can say to themselves, 'well, what the hell?' and do as they like—which is only what they must, after all—he preferred to put his trust in the possibility of suffering nobly: the stoic ideal, the victim-renascent as hero and martyr.

*

In the photograph where we are eight on that August afternoon, past and future cross, momentarily, in the time that was our 'present'.

The house and garden had seen their best days, and the decline was now continual, from season to season: but in the photograph Merlewood wins a reprieve, and someone who knew no better might put a more favourable reading on events already too far gone to be halted.

What seems especially untrue about the photograph is the group pose: how else, except for a camera, could eight people have been distracted from their doings to concentrate their attention so fixedly on one point? That is not how we were, never: it was impossible, except at mealtimes, to hold us, and in the dining-room we would talk over each other and listen or not listen and our simultaneity wasn't really that at all.

In the end, of course, the past caught up with us in another sense and we were shocked into the kind of stillness I see in the photograph. But by then we were seven not eight. Without our being aware, Merlewood was like a colony suddenly liberated, returned to its natural condition—wilderness.

The question only occurred to me after looking at the photograph many times, who was it who took that 'likeness' of us, finger on the shutter button or watching our reflection, squared off, upside down inside the box of the camera? Was it someone hired for the purpose? —or one of my father's visitors who came up from Glasgow to the house? Perhaps one of our neighbours wanted a record?—but there is no evidence among the props of our sharing the day with anyone else, and our visitors (especially my father's) invariably came in couples or posses.

Who was he, or she? The clues are lost. Memory has failed on that one point.

Without the memory, the history of that episode is incomplete. Not knowing, not even remembering the moments of preparing for the photograph and then having it taken, it's hard to believe that it can have happened. Yet it must have done, because here is the evidence before me.

The person is unknown: he or she was only the agent or medium, with a well-versed amateur's skill in organising a group shot. The work that resulted is a study of ghosts, of a kind: children who are already middle-aged—a woman who learned how to keep the facts at a distance just as she defeated the midges with her lily-of-the-valley toilet water, smelling of funeral flowers—and a man who's swimming through these days with one hand held behind his back, his eyes focused on some point out of the picture, well out, past the rock, where the bay becomes sea.

*

We failed to see when the driveway greened and the lawn sprouted lichen, or else it failed to matter to us.

It was a common predicament. The other houses we visited on the Cowal were also past their best.

We were caught in history's downward spiral. The steamer was taken off the Tighnabruaich route. In the late 'sixties and early 'seventies people openly mentioned money in their conversations, with hostility usually, which was not how it had been in the beginning. Cars (the only mode of transport) were required to last longer, and things that wore out weren't necessarily replaced. In the house the curtains faded in the sun and as the loose-covers frayed with too many washings the Sanderson rose garden turned thread-bare; the carpets became thinner under our feet, cracked panes in the windows were sellotaped at their weakest point, paint flaked from the sills. We carried on as if none of it mattered, as if a holiday home should have scuffs and bruises anyway: but Merlewood wasn't as it had been, not in the days when *it* seemed to have expectations of *us*. We had inherited from my father's father what he'd supposed was only our natural prerogative in life, but we found that in fact what we had taken on was the onus of living up to the standards of eighty years before, the Golden Jubilee epoch when the house was built.

It was hopeless.

*

A man in a shiny suit appeared one afternoon, driving his shiny new Vauxhall Velox up to the front door. He inspected the house and garden and covered several of the pages on his clipboard with notes, and departed. We never saw him again.

Other men came whom we *did* recognise—my father's colleagues from the offices in Glasgow—but they seemed ill-at-ease in their weekend tweeds and safari jackets, eating an afternoon tea of buttered bread with potted paste or date spread in the garden before heading back, the creases of business still on their brows. My mother presided, smiling as if the guests she was obliged to entertain were here for the view of the Sound and Goat Fell and for politeness' sake, not because they knew the worst was about to happen. All the time they were there with us, she didn't let up and played out the scene for all she was worth, with those same skills of dissimulation that always made her the winner at games of charades.

Other visitors came who didn't stay for tea—men in city suits, with briefcases—and she had no option on those days but to leave them and my father to their business in the house and occupy herself outside with a pair of secateurs. As she dead-headed, the group in the sitting-room would watch disinterestedly from the windows. They thought in their wisdom they were instructing on the fate of Merle-wood and yet it wasn't really so: they didn't know it, but unseen events were according to a darker design.

*

We 'children'—Kirsty was eleven, Sandy and Angus were already in their teens, I was seventeen, Rhona was nineteen, and Gregor was officially one of the company of adults—had gone to Kames, with a family of neighbours called the McMinns. My mother saw us off from the front door while my father was elsewhere, making a business call to Glasgow. All his life consisted of nowadays was business calls, at peak rates in the middle of the day.

I thought afterwards I must have had a premonition on the journey back: it seemed to me that the sky was very dark for four o'clock on an afternoon in early September, and peculiarly lit, with a greenish tinge to it. But dark or not, the two black police cars in front of the house were only too visible as we turned in at the gates.

My mother was upstairs, sedated, in the care of a policewoman and the locum doctor. A police sergeant took Gregor into the morning room that served as my father's office while the rest of us stood outside in the hall staring at each other.

Kirsty started to cry. Gregor reappeared, shell-shocked. He told us in a dry, patched voice that our father had been 'carried off to sea'.

We none of us knew at first what he meant: we weren't expecting a metaphor. It almost sounded like a joke.

Kirsty must have understood before any of us. Suddenly she ran off, down the hall, for the open front door. We gazed after her. Sandy set off in pursuit, then Angus.

Gregor explained to Rhona and me: he'd gone for a swim and hadn't returned.

'Gone where?' Rhona asked.

Gregor pointed to the strand of sand we always used, where the garden ended.

'Where is he, then?'

My mother had seen it: the current, she'd said, it had taken him out of his depth. I kept shaking my head, I didn't understand how: we'd swum there for years and he'd warned us so often not to 'pass beyond our limitations'. There weren't proper 'currents' anyway: the word

36

sounded as bookish as Gregor's first ones to us, that the sea had 'carried him off'.

For years afterwards, until there wasn't the need to discuss it in detail, my mother stated quite determinedly and categorically that it was 'the current'. She had *seen*, she would remind us. Her version never varied, it became an oft-repeated tale, although not told to Kirsty and the twins, who suffered a long spell of nightmares.

In the photograph the bay is placid and still, or relatively so. I see no 'current' straining beneath the glassy surface. The sea looks not unlike a length of some shiny cloth, lightly rumpled on a counter top. It is there waiting for us, and in the next few minutes—so the photograph suggests—some of us will have responded to its pull and be breasting the brine. The shrimping nets and Kirsty's tin spade and the constant horizon behind us are the clues. Whereas, so my mother's account of events would have had us believe, the sea had been a treacherous presence all along: a false friend, only reckoning on its moment, baring that stump of rock like a warning tooth.

The body was washed up on Ardlamont Point. Death was by drowning, so medical opinion would have it, not through the failure of any particular organ; the police termed the cause 'misadventure'. His blood was found on the rock in the bay, splattered on the side we looked out on to from the windows of the house. Somehow it failed to signify anything that my father had been a strong swimmer who'd taught us all and instructed us to respect the sea. My mother started shaping the story she would tell, to us, to our friends, then later to strangers, the people she met in shop restaurants, or in the dining-rooms of the hotels where she decided to live after Merlewood and the house in Clevedon Gardens were both finally sold. The death wasn't allowed to be suicide because that made the story less sympathetic: but as the notion took hold of Gregor, then Rhona, and then me, it seemed an equally plausible reading of events and no less tragic. For wholly practical reasons, it had the edge: even after the company went into liquidation, the carefully regulated funds from the life insurance policy permitted my mother to keep on the most unlikely of homes for us, Merlewood. But a willing death would have been too melodramatic a tale for her to recount to strangers, and it ventured on to foreign territory—the realm of the psychological. It would have betrayed all those family summers and turned my father from a hapless victim of the sea to someone she couldn't have contemplated having shared twenty-five years of her life with—a man alone, a knowing pragmatist who had also, with crystal clarity, recognised his own ineffectualness and failure.

*

So, of course, it couldn't be.

And while we still had the house—until my mother tired of Tighnabruaich and took it into her head that Malvern and the Mendips and Sidmouth were preferable—returning to Merlewood was supposed to reconcile us to the fate that had befallen the family.

'One thing we'll never have again,' my mother would say with relief, 'is men in safari jackets in *this* house.' Her judgments on people had recently become sharper and generally less charitable and I made the discovery from her example that no one's character is ever fixed and finally formed. At least my father had escaped any more dispassionate verdict on *his* character, or at any rate if her opinions about him changed they were never voiced aloud to us. How people *looked* seemed to count even more with her than it had, which struck me as backward thinking: but gradually I appreciated that how 'we', the family, had all appeared, meeting and engaging with the world, had been of the essence all along.

Studying whatever photographs I could find, I realised that they had always composed themselves around *her*, and it was she who had determined both the shape of the groups and our mood. We would take our cue from her, even my father, and in this one last surviving tableau of the family—ranged as we would be for another four or five years against the slowly declining grandeur of Merlewood—we could show whoever would chance to glance at us that it was *we* who were the fortunate ones, living our charmed lives.

*

Guilt afflicted Gregor later that, if he'd gone into the company as our father had been obliged to after his, the situation might have been otherwise: they could have chosen a moment to sell, even undersell, rather than have had the money slowly and systematically and humiliatingly bled from them.

I remembered mornings or afternoons I'd spent on the premises, being shown this or that process of the business: my father's colleagues smiling, my remarks given attention and answered with a serious nod or a smile. Mr Letham explained the broking business to me on three or four occasions—the ledgers were produced and a nicotine-stained index finger ran down the columns of figures. I was shown round a distillery at Killearn. A friend of my father's took me into the Glasgow Stock Exchange and then bought us both lunch at the Malmaison. Undeclared expectations seemed to accompany me on my visits to the offices, like a shadow falling behind me which I could never catch. But I had no taste for the whisky I was permitted in very small measures, and I didn't care for my father's over-heated room with its outlook of rooftops and chimney pots, although I pretended to be at home there.

I wonder now if I didn't pretend too hard, and only gave him false grounds for hope.

But those hopes failed in the end to count for much, and that guilt at what seemed to be my own fecklessness and duplicity has taken me years to get the better of. There was nothing to be done, though —nothing I could have done—and I knew it then, in my bones, in my blood.

After my father's death I used to puzzle why we had persevered with that charade, making a unity of eight for the photographs, when—at that time of my life, smiles and metaphors abounding —the strings and links between us hadn't been strong enough for the work of lifelines.

*

Merlewood became someone else's (a hairdresser with a chain of salons bought it: my mother specifically asked us not to tell her who the new owner was, and what 'sort of person'), then it was re-sold in inflation days and the house divided and the property put on the market as time-sharing accommodation.

The steamers only ran to Tighnabruaich on nostalgia cruises. I went on one once, with Rhona. It lashed with rain that day, but as we sailed up the Kyles of Bute we doggedly stood at the rails for a first sight of Blair's Ferry, then Kames, then Tighnabruaich. We mistook another house for Merlewood, and then we saw it. The garden was missing the evergreens and most of the rhododendron bushes; it looked naked, and functional and very modern. Someone in a yellow kagoul and sou'wester was walking a dog. The rock in the bay hadn't been claimed yet, as we'd always told ourselves we were going to do: we would row out and christen it with one of our father's bottles and an Arthur Ransome name, and fly the Saltire. The thought of the blood-smears must have been in both our minds.

The upstairs tea-room had gone from the pier, the room was empty. The slippery boards under our feet were very worn and in the gaps the sea sternly churned beneath us. We bought a postcard and sent it to our mother, now resident in a private hotel in Budleigh Salterton. We searched for a post box and eventually found one, in a mossy wall.

The red road with its pot-holes and puddles of rain water was redder than I remembered. It was raining too hard for us to spot any droning bees. Under a golf umbrella we walked along as far as the boatyard, which seemed—oddly, in these doldrum days—to be doing good business.

We imagined how the postcard would be received; my mother's favourite time of the day was the topping-up hour before dinner, and we saw her handing it to favoured fellow-guests over a snifter. In Zanzibar she'd shown her svelte international friends her family's postcards from Scotland and (so she would tell us) they had envied her. Life goes round in a circle, I said to Rhona, and she agreed with me, in a slightly strained voice she'd had all day.

We looked in at Merlewood from the gates. The creeper on the south wall of the house had been taken down—by the builders or on the hairdresser's instructions—and double-glazing fitted to the windows.

We only had an hour between landing and setting sail again. Rhona said she thought we'd done something 'useful' with our day, but I couldn't think quite what.

I felt we'd travelled to a place which had any number of realities, as many as there had been people to live there and days to be lived. But more than that, though, reality blurs—and imagination does a magician's trick on events that may have happened or not happened.

'The past is like a prism,' I said. 'All those reflecting surfaces.'

Rhona looked backwards over the rails, to what was being left behind in the rain.

'But it's *not* empty, a prism, is it?' she said, thinking matters out *her* way. 'It's solid. A thing, it exists.'

I couldn't think how I should reply, if there really was an answer —or a question.

*

In the photograph it seems that no question could be grave enough to bother or perplex us. The mysteries belong to our future selves.

Meanwhile the sun is too high in the sky to trouble us with shadows.

After noon the shadows will lengthen and obtrude, but we put a family face on what we can do nothing about. The third eye *sees*, but it can't turn time and tide.

Although there is nothing to be done, will-power and light-magic confer a modest substitute for grace. History was raging all about us and at last we were caught in the vortex: but the day blazes out splendent and undimmed, and, with a smile she learned in Zanzibar in the lucky peace after the War, my mother confidently claims the victory—for my father, for Merlewood—against all comers.

The Blue Jug

I wonder if there has been a more perfect summer. I watch it all day, until the light goes and the sky fills with stars.

He always said the glory of France was its night skies: as if the stars had been thrown up in handfuls.

He knew this was where our lives would be happiest. Just ourselves, here, and sometimes our little forays, together and separately.

He taught me that two lives require their truces, their concessions —a gentle understanding.

*

Students still come to the house. They've come for years. I don't mind. I tell them the doors aren't locked. They wander up and down stairs, clattering on the bare floorboards.

They bring me flowers. Slow, sad Celeste makes them tea. Black cherry tea.

He discovered the tea in Paris, in Fauchon, after the War. In those days we could both live here on four pounds a week, without a thought of a maid. Four pounds bought us our food, wine, cigarettes. The exotic tea from the Place de la Madeleine was our one extravagance. And the Japanese paper he liked: from a queer little shop on the Avenue de l'Opéra.

*

I wake up thinking the jacaranda tree is on fire.

The flowers at the window are larger, redder, waxier than I've ever seen them. As if they meant this summer to be one never to forget.

The students won't forget. It will become '*that*' summer. *She let us wander about the house, up and down stairs. She didn't mind. We drank black cherry tea with her. She told us, look at the jacaranda tree.*

He only painted it once, I think, the tree with its scarlet flowers. '*The Burning Bush*'. He said the richness of red eluded him, the 'reverberations'.

I thought it was glorious, whatever he said: it burst out of the frame. But it was nothing like this.

The students photograph the garden, they inspect all its angles. They ask to photograph *me*. I say 'no', politely. I tell them 'Take one of the jacaranda'. The burning bush.

Its beauty grows with every year.

*

And they *bring* me flowers, when there's a garden nearly strangled with them!

They bring me other things too, according to their pockets. Truffles, greengages, *cèpes*—and briny oysters, tasting of the wild Brittany sea. I'm reminded of this painting or that: a basket of mushrooms, a scatter of truffles or dusty greengages on a table top. I remember the famous plate of oysters, and my hand splitting them with a knife. That was longest ago of all. We were in Paris, before the War, we were so poor he had to sketch them at a stall in Les Halles, at five o'clock in the morning before they were sold, while the oyster-men stood opening them a dozen a minute—then he added my hands another day, slicing into, not a crinkly oyster-shell, but a wizened dried-up apple.

The trees are heavy with apples this year, sagging with them, the boughs are almost touching the ground. There can't be enough baskets to hold them all, the good unbruised russet-flush ones *and* the windfall. Like that other year it happened, the cows will nose their way into the orchard and gorge themselves on the glut and the milk in their udders will ferment to cider again. That was the year we got tipsy on milk.

*

For something to say, I ask them 'Which is the best picture here? Tell me honestly.'

They all give me a different answer. They're all so earnest, they explain to me why: composition, perspective, colouring. I nod knowledgeably.

And which is *my* favourite, they ask me. (Not, I think, that it's the same—a favourite needn't be the best.)

I tell them, that one in the corner—do you see?—'The Bather'.

I don't say, I always used to keep it back when the dealers came, in their shiny Facel sports cars and bearing me gifts, little pots of Beluga

43

caviar or fancy boxes of chocolates or marrons glacés from Lenôtre or Dalloyau.

The summer he painted it we were staying at a boarding-house called 'La Baigneuse': one of those crazy, top-heavy Normandy houses, so fussy and solemn for a little beach town.

I don't know why 'The Bather' is my favourite.

I'm asked 'Who is the woman?' He's only suggested me with a few strokes, but there I am, Venus Ascendant, not in the nude that day but in my yellow swimsuit.

We'd had a rough year, sometimes we just couldn't hold each other. In the end he came back to me and I came back to him and we went to Normandy and we didn't speak any more about it. There he painted his slightest image of me and also his most beautiful, and he caught me in that moment at my best.

When I saw it finished, I knew I would never be quite like that again: and I knew our life together would be different too, it was taking on a certain form, a pattern: his regular trips every few weeks to collect his Japanese paper from the fusty little material shop in the Avenue de l'Opéra, and the black cherry tea bought for me as if he was a solicitous husband and I really was his neat, meek little wife waiting patiently at home.

He knew I wasn't like that. *I* knew he once didn't go to Paris but he trailed me to Bergerac instead. I can't remember all their names now, the men I spent my racy afternoons with and tried to hide my guilt from: I couldn't remember names now, even to save my life.

*

Or 'The Blue Jug'. It's either that or 'The Bather' I like the most.

I'm sitting with my arm on the kitchen table, the blue jug's beside me. I'm older, I've grown a little portly. Before he started on it I told him 'Show me honestly. Please.'

He did. In the picture there is *affectionate* honesty. There is the truth of our lives.

What's the expression on my face? Not submission or resignation: rather it's—I must be careful—a mellow, considered acceptance. (Even—contentment?) Every element adds to the mood of unexceptional stillness, peace: the solid workaday table, sunlight falling through the doorway, a cat asleep on its side, my bared arm crooked round the slender, curvaceous blue jug.

Like the picture, like me, the jug has survived all the years. Close to it's pocked and raw, here and there you can see the terracotta red under the glaze. But the blue on top is the summer blue of cornflowers, as fresh as the day we bought it for a few francs in a tiny shop in the back streets of Périgueux.

I've imagined its genesis so many times. The gruff, stubble-headed potter throws the mixture anyhow on to his wheel. He means to shape a flat dish out of the red clay. But for some reason his hands that particular morning or afternoon have a magic touch. He cradles the wet clay and he's remembering a lifetime he's spent tracing the ripe lines of women's bodies with his fingers. It's then he realises what his inspiration is going to be: it passes from his fingers to the clay and the jug begins to take on a life of its own.

Later it was glazed: we chanced to be in Périgueux and we saw it, and we bought it, and from then on it had a place on the table at all our meals. It was as familiar to us as another person would have been: someone we'd known for years but who hadn't changed, who'd outwitted fate. That sensual outline the potter gave it still hasn't altered, it belongs to the same bold young woman who's understood: she won't look better than this, she won't be improved on—now she's at her best.

The jug came with us on our picnics too: we filled it with wine and let it stand in a stream to keep the drink chilled, and we tied a length of string to its handle just in case. Its curves held a lot. Liquid poured well from the full, thrusting lip like a pout. We collected milk in it for a while, the milk that will taste of cider this year. It's held paint-brushes. Witch-hazel. Christmas holly. The first catkins of spring.

Someone put some of the funeral flowers in it. And when it hasn't had some job of work to do, it has stood proudly, assuredly alone, somehow complete in itself.

*

Seen from this angle—on the day-bed, with cushions piled under my back—all the objects in the room have an authority, a dignity. Their shapes are exactly right for their functions.

I fulfilled a function in the life of this house. His pictures tell that. Moments of time frozen for all time.

Now in the silent house the things triumph. The pictures: and the wooden bowls, the spoons and ladles, the copper pans, the old paint-brushes worn to stumps.

I am—I have always been—the servant of the *thing*. With my matronly arm crooked protectively around the alluring, sinuous, youthful curves of the blue jug.

Whatever their chances seemed like in the beginning, the things are to outlive me. I couldn't have guessed the blue jug will be standing there on the window sill the morning I don't wake to see it.

*

The same day, or the day after—it will come—someone will brightly suggest the scarlet jacaranda flowers would look good in it. Before they fade. It'll cheer the place up, after . . .

Celeste is out in the rain picking apples in the orchard, like a mad woman: she's too old to cry for me.

In the house the brisk, stranger's voice says 'Open the windows, there's a musty smell in here. Careful with the jug—oh, it doesn't matter, it's only a jug. But, *mon Dieu*, what's to be done with the *paintings*? All those people who used to come, *they*'ll know. Is there a telephone number to call?'

The Camelhair Jacket

'It isn't a proper story at all,' the man began. 'Nothing very much happens.' He shrugged. 'Still, for what it's worth.'

The event took place one afternoon when the man—another man, not the one telling me the story—was in the house and his wife was returning in the car with the three children, from school. The husband worked at home; he was an architect.

'As I said, nothing "happens" really. Although possibly it just *might* have. It begins with the car pulling into the road and the children getting out, then the man's wife . . .'

It was the husband's claim that he was sitting at the desk upstairs, that he heard the car draw up and the doors slamming and the children's voices as they chased each other up the garden path, followed by the clacking of his wife's heels. He heard the front door open and the children come running into the hall, and the front door bang shut. He called out something, and then concentrated again on what he was doing.

Another ritual of sounds began—piano scales, the bath taps gushing, feet jumping up and down on the spot—and everything was just as it normally was. As normally happened too, the man's wife came upstairs about ten minutes later with a tray of tea things for him. He smiled over his shoulder as the door opened, then he got up and walked across to take the tray from her.

'Oh,' she said, 'you've changed.'

'Have I?' he asked her, sounding surprised.

'You must have done,' she told him.

'I believe,' he said, meaning to be jocular about it, 'I am the man I was when you left.'

'No,' his wife told him. 'That's not what I meant.'

'No?' he repeated.

'You were wearing your camelhair jacket.'

'Was I?' he said, not concealing his surprise. 'When?'

'Earlier.'

'Not when you left?'

'No,' she said. 'Not when I left.'

'Well, when?' he asked.

'Just now.'

'No, I wasn't,' he said.

'Ten minutes ago.'

'No,' he repeated, and laughed. 'No, I wasn't.'

There was no possibility of confusion about the jacket they were discussing: it had been a recent purchase, an expensive one, worn on 'special' occasions.

'Of course you were wearing it,' the man's wife said. 'I saw you from the car.'

The husband, dressed in a navy blue guernsey jumper, crossed his arms.

'It wasn't me,' he told her, 'whoever it was you think you saw.'

'You were standing at the window,' she said.

'But I haven't been away from this desk,' he told her.

'Weren't you?' she asked, and sounded and looked disbelieving.

'No,' he said, and said it—he wasn't sure why—quite firmly.

'*Weren't* you?'

'Of course not.' He uncrossed his arms and dug his hands into his trouser pockets. 'And I didn't put on the camelhair jacket either. Why on earth should I have done that?'

His wife shrugged. 'I didn't make it up.'

'But why should I say I haven't worn it if I really did have it on,' he said. 'That doesn't make sense.'

His wife looked lost for an answer. The pair of them stared at each other for several seconds.

'You were mistaken,' he told her.

She shrugged again. 'I don't think so. I don't see how.'

'You must have been,' he said. 'Mistaken.'

'Not if it's what I saw.'

'*If* it was . . .'

'If it's "if" for me,' she said, 'then it should be "if" for you too. Surely.'

'But it didn't happen like that. None of it happened.'

'I'd tell you I was mistaken if I really felt like that, that I *was*,' his wife said, her voice unsteady.

'Well, you were.'

'But—to my eyes—I did see you. You were—over there, standing at the window—you were wearing the camel jacket.'

'There's only *one* camel jacket. I've nothing else like it.'

'Yes, I know that.'

'I always wear a jumper to work in.'

'I know that too.'

'And there aren't *two* of me,' he said. 'Are there?'

His wife seemed disturbed. She shook her head.

'I can't explain it,' she said.

'Of course not,' her husband told her. He considered himself a man of rational and sound reasoning. 'For the very good reason that I was in here all the time. At the desk, not at the window. And I wasn't wearing the camelhair jacket.'

'There must be *some* reason,' the wife said. She certainly didn't consider herself an *ir*rational person.

'Some reason why you *think* you saw me in the jacket?'

'My eyes are better than yours. You're always telling me.'

'I know,' he said.

'Well, then?'

' "Well, then" what?'

'You probably want this tea anyway,' his wife said. 'I think you'll find *it*'s real enough.'

And then, without another word, she made for the door and left the room.

They referred to the matter later, but only once more, in the evening, before they ate. The husband asked his wife if she'd thought of an explanation. No, she replied, *she* hadn't, not at all, the situation seemed exactly the same to her. Then, the husband said, she must have *imagined* she'd seen him, mustn't she?

'Oh no,' she answered. 'Not at all. I didn't *imagine* it.'

'What other explanation *is* there, then?' the man asked her.

'It's you who's telling me there *has* to be an "explanation",' the wife said.

'It's *your* word, *you* used it. Upstairs. But it's because you don't really believe me,' the man said. 'You don't, do you?'

They tacitly agreed not to talk about it. Supper was eaten in silence, except for the din of the children of course; or rather, beneath their noise the two of them ate without speaking, without communicating, while the voices and clatter of cutlery was like a rising tide of sounds.

'Either nothing happened,' the man telling me the story said, 'or perhaps something of great significance in the circumstances did. In future, you see, the man never wore the camelhair jacket again.' He repeated that it had been an expensive purchase, one the couple had discussed for at least three or four weeks beforehand. Now the husband chose to leave it hanging in the wardrobe, and his wife said nothing when she saw that he wasn't wearing it, even on those occasions when they'd planned he would wear it. After six months or so he still couldn't bear the thought of putting it on. It was as if some harm belonged to the jacket and existed in the cloth: something contrary. Moreover, ever since the incident he and his wife had separately been conscious of a remoteness gathering. It hadn't been there before, or rather not to the same degree: but when they did look back, separately (they both told their own version of the story, and seemed equally sure of what they said), each of them understood that there had been lurking dangers, that they'd already sensed cross-currents and undertows pulling beneath the supposedly harmonious and settled waters of marital life. It caused both of them to consider the question, just how much one person ever completely knows of another: and a second question quite naturally followed out of that one—to what extent do we create our own versions of other people?

It set the husband wondering how his wife saw him, in her mind's eye, or how she wished to see him, how she wanted him to be—since it was she who'd been responsible for at last insisting on the indulgence of the expertly-tailored camelhair jacket. And *she* wondered if it wasn't now the case that she relied on distinguishing between the two images in her head, and that on that particular afternoon she'd been depending on seeing the 'other' man at the window—the husband he claimed he wasn't.

'Perhaps someone would tell you that domesticity frightened her, it frightened them both,' the man said to me, 'someone who's got the right words and theories, that is. I don't really know myself all that happened afterwards—if the wife and her husband continued faithful to each other, or even if they *had* been all the time before. I only know that he never wore the jacket again, and that eventually it disappeared from the wardrobe. They both admitted as much to *me*, a stranger, but they didn't discuss the matter with each other, not at all. I suppose it had to do with an absence of some kind,' the man said, finishing his story that he'd told me wasn't going to be a 'proper' story, 'it had to do with some lack they never confessed to, which they never even referred to together. If you like, call it a wanting.'

Incident in Le Lavandou

The view was not as Miss Simm remembered it. The plane trees must have been the same ones—their tops were just visible—but white buildings pressed in on the old streets from all sides and she could see no plan to the town. There must be one—she might find it down at street level—but the longer she looked the more confused she felt she was becoming.

She finished dressing in front of the wardrobe mirror, with the open balcony doors and the blue Riviera sky behind her. She thought, perhaps if I'd lived here I should scarcely have been conscious of all the changes in half a century?

She stood straightening her skirt, pulling at the cuffs of her blouse, telling herself how different it was from Largs. *I'm here, I managed the journey after all, there's life in the old girl yet.*

But when the wardrobe door and the mirror swung back on creaking hinges the view and the confidence disappeared, and she felt elderly and rather foolish and terribly Scottish in her tweeds as she looked about her to find the canvas shoes she'd brought with her as a concession to the town's hot streets.

*

Madame Lépront stood drinking her coffee at the little filigreed balcony, watching the patterns of life on the streets far beneath her. It had been her idea that the junk-filled attic of the villa could be turned into a commodious, sunny apartment, and the result justified all the hard graft of long ago: a quiet, forgotten spot high above people's heads, easily kept in order, cool in summer when the shutters were closed and, with its low ceilings and because the rooms underneath were always occupied by tenants, not too expensive to heat in winter. Bright and airy, it suited widowhood. Few people suspected that anyone lived up here among the rafters, which even the pigeons had abandoned by the time they got down to the conversion work.

She took mouthfuls of the hot milky coffee. She swallowed it noisily, in gulps, and heard herself. Her manners had suffered a bit since Guy's death. When she'd married she'd had to get used to the

French way of attacking food with such relish, and now nearly fifty years later she couldn't undo herself of the habit. She might have passed for 'Made in France'.

Madame Lépront always enjoyed the early heat of the day and she liked to feel it warming the stone of the balcony under her bare feet and the roof tiles she leaned her back against. Later on in the day she wasn't so comfortable with it. She stayed indoors, or she would make her forays in the car; if it happened she was meeting someone and she had no choice about being out, she kept as much as possible to the shade. About six o'clock the sun lost its spite and she reappeared on the balcony to have a drink, whatever there was on the sideboard. A couple of hours later the sun turned to the colour of a blood-orange as it sank slowly behind Africa. The sky would have a mysterious greenish tinge some nights; on others it would suddenly catch fire from the sun, flaming to crimson, and she would watch as other colours composed themselves around the red-hot core, vermilion, couleur de rose, then lighter fleshier pinks, cooling to topaz and Indian yellow and lemon on the extremities.

*

The heat, thought Miss Simm, the heat: that would have been the worst of it, I should never have adjusted.

But the skies, *they* would have been something to see, evening after evening. Maybe I would have taken up sketching, water-colours, pastels, gouache: maybe even proved myself quite adept.

Maybe.

*

Indoors again—the coffee doing its work and pepping her up after her night's deep sleep—Madame Lépront dressed.

Summer-wear was straightforward: a pale cotton shift and es-padrilles, it couldn't have been easier.

She combed her hair back over her ears, and applied a very little, very discreet liner to her eyelids.

She looked hard at herself. Her face had become thinner with the years, and longer if that was possible: or perhaps it was because she only saw French faces that she viewed her own differently now. Decades of sun had bleached her hair, so that she was scarcely able to recognise the dark-fringed young woman in photographs, posed with her mother and father and her sister and two brothers. The sun had also toughened her skin and lined it, and sometimes she smiled rather sadly when she told people about her foreign youth and her 'peaches-and-cream' complexion, as the term used to be.

This morning, though—thinking positively—she felt that her appearance had an *authenticity* about it which it never used to have. She was wholly herself, she didn't need to satisfy other people's expectations of how she should look. The longer she lived, the simpler the presentation and final version of herself became. For that she thanked her years in France, now—unbelievably—two-thirds of her life.

*

'*Une tasse de thé, s'il vous plaît. Comment? Un thé? Très bien. Pour moi seule. Thé de chine. Merci.*'

Miss Simm had never felt comfortable with such an extrovert language. Passing the simplest remark involved contorting your face to pronounce some absurd, indecently sensuous-sounding hotchpotch of syllables.

At least the waiter nodded his head: but curtly, Miss Simm thought. Frumpy British types obviously weren't worth humouring. No tip for *you*, she decided, and the little revenge in prospect reassured her.

Miss Simm placed her day-old *Telegraph* on top of the table, and she laid her room key on top of it.

What would her friends be doing at home, she wondered. Probably wondering what *she* was doing with herself and why on earth should she want to hire herself off to the South of France at *her* age. They'd be puzzling about that, and about the other matters that preoccupied them, which filled their days and hers because there was no getting away from them: annuities, the sloth and miserliness of the faceless dispensers of company pensions, the tardiness of lawyers dealing with a cousin's will, a shares statement, the red print demand on an electricity bill which had already been paid, the new rates estimate, an accountant's fee for offices rendered, the state of the roses in the landscaped gardens of the block where they lived.

How odd that she was suddenly feeling so disengaged about it. But, she thought, maybe in another couple of days' time I shall have reverted again?

Normally she didn't go on holiday alone, she went with one of her neighbours, or with someone she'd worked with in the manufacturers' agent's business her brother had built up and which he had 'invited' her to lend her services to—and the conversation wherever their travels took them would inevitably return to home, and to the past. This time the past that concerned her was known only to herself and to her twin cousins in Strathpeffer, the three of them being the sole survivors of that family group who'd come south in 1936. And perhaps—just perhaps—it was still known to *him*: the Frenchman she'd never been able to forget even though she couldn't have described his face to save her life and whose own life had been more or less a mystery to her, then and ever since.

*

Madame Lépront enjoyed her privacy and independence. No one here saw her comings and goings, even though the rest of the building was occupied. The villa was hers now—it had come to Guy through the will of an aunt—and perhaps she was allowed her privacy out of respect, she couldn't be sure. 'La Châtelaine' and all that.

She drew an income from the tenants, here and in several other properties which Guy—with his professional land agent's eye and sixth sense—had had the good sense to buy. Nowadays she was a bona fide businesswoman: at this comparatively late juncture in her life she had the self-assurance and the financial say-so—and, still, the mental and physical stamina—to be able to badger lawyers and accountants, and she made it a point of honour not to be brow-beaten or fobbed off by any of them. She could be quite charming when she chose to be, but that never obscured the fact that her husband's death had turned her into a very determined and very knowing woman where the practicalities of commerce were concerned. People could tell by the authority of her body walking into a room, the set of her face, the shine in her eyes. She'd had to work at it, but now she wouldn't have wanted to be any other way than she was.

She closed her front door behind her, heard the lock turn, then she hurried down the three flights of stairs with a swiftness of foot that she knew belied her years.

*

Well, at seventy-two one presumes there just isn't the energy—the vim—left, thought Miss Simm. Not for gallivanting off to foreign parts. Even if this isn't exactly gallivanting, not quite. And of course these aren't just *any* run-of-the-mill foreign parts . . .

She crumpled the paper napkin and, after hesitating, let it drop on to her plate of croissant crumbs.

She couldn't have taken to French breakfasts, she was quite

54

positive about that. Too much fuss for nothing. And why did croissants always *have* to have that greasy feel to them?

Better off with her Bran Buds, and one slice of wholemeal toast, and the Frank Cooper's, and Algie's no-nonsense Ceylon tea.

'Better off as I am.' The words were on the tip of her tongue to say, but she realised there was no one to hear if she were to open her mouth and say them, and she also wondered if she was really the person best qualified to judge.

The words lacked, somehow, *conviction*.

*

No one in Le Lavandou was certain how old Madame Lépront was, but it was general knowledge that she'd first come to the town in the 1930s, when she was someone else, the younger daughter of a foreigner and his wife on holiday here—a businessman, a 'tea merchant' hadn't she said, *un marchand de thé*: when she had been a pale and fragile young woman, shy beneath her fringe of dark hair.

The most precise of her neighbours guessed that now she must be seventy or thereabouts: 'guessed', Madame Lépront was perfectly aware. (In warmer climes, she knew, it's often easier to make a riddle of numerals—sixty-five, seventy, seventy-five—among faces prematurely wrinkled and veined and stoically smiling under their uniform tans. In sunshine you can dress to virtually any age you choose: other people are more charitable about any sartorial miscalculations and errors of taste, it's merely amusing—for a brief time—then assimilated into the everyday way of things. Madame Lépront realised that public opinion was decided that on the whole she dressed with sense but also with some 'chic', in styles that would have looked just as well worn by a woman half her age. It was a verdict that gave her much secret satisfaction.)

Guy Lépront's widow stood in the downstairs hallway opening her morning's mail. Sunlight flooded through the open double-doors and washed over the checkerboard of black and white tiles. Vaguely, as she read, she was conscious of the heady brew of the garden's perfumes: pine, floribunda roses, rosemary, orange blossom, the inevitable lavender that the town was named after. The fragrance and the heat lapping round her always made her feel well-disposed even when her correspondence was about financial business and she was required to make some brisk mental calculations there and then. The men she dealt with in the business line were there for a purpose, they had specific duties which she was paying them to perform and she refused to be intimidated or confused by their manner: when they wrote to her they were required to express themselves, please, with particular clarity. '*Élucidez, s'il vous plaît. Avec concision.*'

Madame Lépront bundled the assortment of letters and postcards into her bag, shut the clasp, and dropped the bag into her basket. Walking down the front steps and across the gravel, out of the villa's shadow, she felt buoyant and prepared for whatever the day might be bringing her.

*

Back upstairs in her bedroom, Miss Simm debated whether or not she should take her plastic mackintosh and rain-mate with her. Yes, she decided, yes, I *shall* take them.

It always paid to be on the safe side. Better safe than sorry. And who knew more about the safe and sensible and least hazardous way of living this life than herself?

*

On cloudless mornings when she felt like walking on the balls of her feet, Madame Lépront could believe she'd taken full and proper advantage of all the opportunities that had come her way in this life. She'd allowed life to take her, not always where she'd been expecting to go, but where it seemed to have determined that she should be taken. Life's plans for her hadn't been the same as her family's, and she'd had to persist in the face of their opposition. She could have heeded the puritan designs of her father and mother and the clamouring maiden aunts and made of herself whatever they would have decided according to the models of their class and country: a stainless wife-to-be for a redoubtable fiancé, or a meek and modest stay-at-home daughter, or—had they been willing to allow her a little more independence, plus an allowance—she might have become an untested, prim-mouthed young woman settling prematurely into spinsterhood in a decent community of like souls.

Instead she lived on the Côte d'Azur and in sunshine: and if there must be shadows, they were no threat to her, not now after fifty years. When her children and grandchildren quizzed her gently about her past, she let them see that it was neither here nor there to her—concealing nothing that they wanted to know—but that really she preferred to think of the life she had shared with *them* as her true history. She had given much thought to the past, however, in a more abstract sense. She'd often wondered if people's lives don't all contain some emotional apogee, some heightened and climactic omega of experience, its highwater mark, which might occur at any point—early or late—and turns into an epiphany, a moment of revelation. One of two consequences ensues from the event: either everything else that follows proves a falling-off and tailing-away and nothing is ever felt so intensely again—or the opposite happens, the incident becomes a pointer to possibilities that previously hadn't occurred to you and you turn towards them, freshly confident and cast in a new frame of mind.

Confident, but with the uncomfortable consciousness of betrayal. For hadn't she committed the one heinous and finally unpardonable crime: she'd left the country where she'd grown up and its northern climes, she'd abandoned its morality and the bracing winds and grey days of soft Atlantic drizzle for marriage and the white Mediterranean light and empty Latin noons and green African twilights of this lavender town, Le Lavandou?

*

After breakfast Miss Simm stood in the hallway of the hotel consulting a map on the wall. Unconcerned voices passed up and down the corridor behind her as she cocked her head this way and that to get a better perspective on things.

She tried to spot where it had happened. With her index finger she jabbed at various points on the map, intersections where streets crossed. Perhaps she would recognise the place when she came upon it.

In those days, ironically, there had been so much less motor-driven traffic to have to be careful about. What had got into her she had never been able to understand. Was it like vertigo, which (she'd read somewhere) is supposed to mask an unconscious wish to step off a high point and experience the elation and oblivion of plunging downward: or, like insomnia, which (she'd read somewhere else) is really the fear of falling asleep and discovering what thoroughly nasty and sordid imaginings you might conjure up in your dreams.

She'd walked off the edge of the pavement on to the road and in front of the car because . . . Because . . . Not because she'd guessed the man, *that* man, would reach out his arm and grab her and haul her back: she only knew him as a face—a handsome face—from the hotel, and it was only by chance that she'd turned and looked behind her a few seconds before the incident occurred and seen that he was there. Maybe it was because she'd disorientated herself slightly, turning her head on her shoulders to look round, that the episode had happened? Or could there have been deeper causes why she'd stepped on to the road at the very instant the car was rounding the corner?—the memory of Ranald Forbes waiting at home, in douce, sooty Glasgow, and the prospect of, first, the inevitable return to Scotland after their visit to Aunt Bessy in Menton and, then, the decision she would have to make before she saw Mrs Forbes and her elder son again. Perhaps her backward glance at the man—someone she'd noticed no more than half-a-dozen times and whom she knew nothing about—had disturbed her morning peace, it had prompted the thought of Ranald Forbes (never very far from her mind, but less insistent when she was walking in the sunshine): and the incident that followed had been set in motion by her subconscious acting?

Or the quality of light, could it have been? Had the sun been in her eyes on the crossing, and that was why she hadn't been able to see the car's hushed approach?

She'd been dazed for several seconds afterwards. Faces swam in front of hers, buildings teetered, the trees jigged. Then she'd focused, and it was the man she'd found she was looking at.

How solicitous he'd proved himself, how concerned everyone else—her family and their friends—had been for her. Concerned and also, she'd guessed, anxious and uneasy to know how it could have happened: as if suspecting that so terrible a thing couldn't have happened merely by chance, because how perilous then must every action in our lives become?

*

Madame Lépront ran her eyes down her shopping list. One person required almost as much as two, that was the strange thing. Two people *could* live as cheaply as one, not that economy had ever been a consideration with them both.

Buying for one sometimes seemed a futile occupation. But she had her family to owe an obligation to, and she was Guy's widow, with all its responsibilities to his memory. There had been so much—there was still so much—which she should feel grateful to her late husband for having given her: even this very air to breathe.

*

Without the incident happening, Miss Simm knew—the car turning the corner—the man wouldn't have had the excuse to see her as he was given permission to do afterwards. Otherwise her mother wouldn't have welcomed him to their table in the hotel dining-room of an evening, she wouldn't have allowed him to show them the lie of the coast and the rocky inland terrain as he did on half-a-dozen picnic expeditions. Frenchmen had always been untrustworthy on principle, but *he* was unconditionally exonerated of the faults of his race and granted a free pardon. If he hadn't had such excellent reflexes that he'd been able to shoot out his arm and tip her out of the car's path that day, she would most certainly not have found herself dining alone with a gallant foreign gentleman on a restaurant terrace strung with vines above a wild sea crashing on to boulders. In all probability she would have been maimed, or dead.

By the time she was meeting him alone, unchaperoned, her life seemed to have gone off at an improbable tangent, she was suddenly walking on an unlikely track, further and further from the landmarks she recognised. At twenty-two years old she wasn't quite prepared for it, nor for her second offer of marriage in a troubled season. In another year's time—who was to say?—perhaps she might have been.

Perhaps the car had turned the corner a year too soon?

*

Madame Lépront glided silkily through the network of lanes that webbed the town. She felt cool in her washed-pink cotton shift. It billowed out behind her, in the fashionable style. She had good enough legs still to be able to go about with them bare. The espadrilles couldn't have been a better fit for her feet, and they might—in her current mid-morning frame of mind—have had wings.

Through her dark lenses she was aware that people were looking at her. She hoped they weren't playing the guessing-game about age: not that she was ashamed, but you *are*—the hoariest cliché in the book—as old or as young as you feel. Sometimes she felt rather less in command of herself, when the weather changed and the salt wind blowing inland over the rooftops seeped through the rubber seals on the windows and made twinges in her arms and shoulders and back. But that was only occasionally, and no one escapes scot-free.

A few people were in the habit of exchanging 'good day' with her and she would drop a reply over her shoulder. She now passed as a native—and anyone would have been hard put to conclude that she was not. The language hadn't come easily to her, not until her first child was born, and then all the bits and pieces had seemed to fit into place. '*Écossaise*' she would reply if anyone did ever ask her where she was from originally, that rather than '*Anglaise*': it left people much less certain about what to expect of her, and she preferred that her past should belong somewhere on the misty perimeter edge of their imagination. She chose to believe that every departure and new beginning in life is like a skin being shed: a character is compounding itself, and while the past is inevitably a part of it, it shouldn't be allowed to make falsely demanding claims. It doesn't—or shouldn't —ever *own* anyone.

*

Miss Simm thought she had found the spot: then she wasn't so sure.

She couldn't quite get her directions. The names of the streets on the signposts meant nothing to her. Payot, Péri, Cazin. After fifty years the country had a different set of heroes and liberators to commemorate. Avenue des Martyrs-de-la-Résistance, Avenue du Général de Gaulle, Boulevard Winston Churchill, Avenue des Commandos d'Afrique. She asked herself if they *could* possibly be the same plane trees in the square, if they weren't too sprightly to be the ones she'd walked under in 1936.

In those days the coast had also been a working one, and among the sights had been the schools of fishing boats chugging for the jetties after a day or night at sea. There were far fewer of the smacks now, only a handful. Of course there had been a *plage* then too, and flashy cars with running boards and white tyres, family groups like her own eating from picnic hampers, but the two ways of life—the indigenous and the elegantly fanciful—seemed to coexist in her mind. Now most of the town's business had to do with the wholesale pursuit of pleasure—and frankly she was disappointed. Shops were like stalls, their wares spilling on to the pavement so that it took all her concentration to keep herself from being directed by the pressure of bodies towards the kerb. People ate and drank as they walked about, just as they did at home. One or two of the cafés, with their customers fenced in from the drifting crowds, had something of the charm and style of those in Aix or Avignon. She could remember a restaurant along the coast—remember it just, the details—with a trellis or pergola and a vine overhead, and candles under glasses on the tables, and a trio walking between the tables playing she'd forgotten what on their violins, and a man talking to her: the words turning to ether as soon as he spoke them, his face only a couple of feet from hers but crossed with those shifting blue shadows.

*

The past didn't *own* her, Madame Lépront knew. Nor was it an anchor. But her mind would play with it, turning it over as she turned over the curious debris of shells and sea life she found washed up by the tide on her beachcombing walks.

Thinking how, if she hadn't had an opportunity to meet Guy in the way she had, none of the rest would have happened. But how she might have had an opportunity to meet him at another time and place—and so the rest would still have happened, wouldn't it?

She was an optimist in these matters. If something is meant to occur, you may be given more than one chance, if you bungle the first. But it's up to you not to let it go a second time: fate has limited reserves of patience and doesn't tolerate fools, those who won't learn.

'My Robert the Bruce principle', she sometimes joked to those who would understand the parable of the spider and the watching king. Without it the Scots wouldn't have been the enterprising, persevering race she knew they were, and which she had proved by her own example.

*

Conveniently, Miss Simm thought, I have presumed he must be dead—but what if he isn't?

She calculated. How old would he have been then, in 1936? Twenty-five or twenty-six, at least. Thirty at the outside. Add fifty to that.

It was perfectly possible that he *was* living: he was alive and well, walking along a promenade somewhere in white summer clothes, tanned and spry: his years of travelling here and there in the land business were behind him, but they'd left him handsomely provided for.

A bachelor? She'd stopped allowing for that possibility long ago, about the time she decided to call off her engagement to Ranald Forbes and watched Elspeth Colquhoun take her place. She had realised from people's shocked reactions in the two cities, Glasgow and Edinburgh (and also in such respectable havens as genteel Helensburgh and decorous Kilmacolm), that it was only the few hard-bitten cases who resisted the mating call, and that she'd chosen to do something quite unnatural.

He wouldn't have given up so easily, her Frenchman. On another evening in the same restaurant above the sea, the same scene would have repeated itself. She had imagined it so often. The girl who sits at the table listens to him and considers well as the trio coax such sweet music from their violins. The vine trellis maps an exactly similar grid of shadows, and this time the scene plays to its intended conclusion. The man smiles, so does the girl. His face and hands reach forward out of the blue shadows. The sea tumbles on the rocks far beneath them, its roar muted to polite, whispered sibilants. His companion smells lavender, a fragrance carried off the hills on the warm breath of the wind, and she dares to hope that all her life with the man will echo the happiness of these perfect moments.

*

Madame Lépront walked downhill with long, confident strides. She wore dark glasses against the sun's glare.

The town spread beneath her, and beyond were the wooded slopes of Cap Bénat. She glanced at the promenade and the leafy square: gardeners were laying the dust, and the cafés had set out their wicker chairs and tables to lure customers.

The narrow back streets were the quickest way down and she was familiar with all the short cuts. Even after all her years in other cities she knew her way about like a local-born. Curiously, though, something about the place eluded her—a spirit—which she imagined she might have felt if she'd been living in, say, Antibes or St Jean-de-Luz. Maybe she hadn't been here long enough since her return to discover that sense of place, or was the town not quite big enough or old enough? The 'spirit' had escaped her fifty years ago when she'd first arrived, when her eyes had been blinded by the sea light and she'd lived in a dizzy muddle: morning excursions in the car to what was judged worth seeing, evenings at the hotel enduring unending meals, lazy beach afternoons under sun umbrellas, expeditions across the sand-strewn streets to dark, cool shops and a café with a yellow awning that served green drinks and where a grinning man played an accordion accompaniment while a woman in a long nasturtium-coloured dress like a kimono sang slow, dirge-like songs that never seemed to have a melody.

*

Now there were so many cafés and none of them had a yellow awning. Miss Simm searched but couldn't find it. Pop music seeped out of passing cars and floated down from upstairs rooms and wafted up from basements and she couldn't hear those tuneless songs any more that she used to listen to. The woman who sang them had had a painted face and most of the songs had been to do with Montparnasse and the *quartier* Saint-Germain. She used to wonder, why doesn't she go back to Paris if she's so homesick and spare us all? But the songs, their words and melodies forgotten now, had been woven into the woof of those oddly static, becalmed afternoons when she'd sat with her sister or brothers or cousins, sipping tea, watching the few cars pass, seeming—it occurred to her now—to be only waiting for something to happen to her.

*

They'd lived in half-a-dozen places, and she'd come back to Le Lavandou. She wasn't sure why. It wasn't what it had been. Along the coast road there were still quieter spots, coves hidden by rocks and pines, and a couple of superior restaurants she sometimes went to, with terraces above the sea. Friends wrote or rang or visited from Paris and Geneva, and there was no risk of losing touch. (From longer ago there were still two cousins alive, ensconced in a Scottish spa town, but that was as much as she knew about them.) Children and grandchildren existed on the fringes of that mental map which composed her knowable world, in Switzerland and Belgium and America, and she believed herself distantly indispensable to them and never an intruder on privacy or a burden to conscience. At the centre of so much attention, she lived contentedly alone.

Maybe she'd meant coming back to Le Lavandou to be a drawing-in of all the threads? Here it had begun for her, one summer before the War, when she was another person: a silly accident-that-almost-was, stepping on to the road without looking first for traffic, and a hand—*his* hand, Guy's hand—reaching out for her. Now she was only paying her own homage of sorts to that fleeting incident which had made her busy, practical, necessary life possible in the first place.

*

Miss Simm wondered why she wasn't getting the 'feel' of the streets. She had imagined that, somehow, instinct would guide her.

She was aware that people were looking at her, smiling in her face, but not for simple civility's sake.

She felt her tweeds were hanging heavily from her; the inside of her waist band was sodden with perspiration; her canvas shoes pinched.

She walked along the pavement however she could, jostled by arms and shoulders and hips. In *her* day there had been nothing like

63

this: the people who'd come then, the cognoscenti, had behaved with tact.

The proximity of so much unclothed flesh was alarming her. She smelt the sun oil: a brash, impertinent chemical odour that seemed first to fill her head, then to be weighing it like a stone.

Suddenly she thought she couldn't trust her knees to hold her up any longer. She looked anxiously to either side of her before reaching out for the trunk of a plane tree to steady herself.

Her head was spinning. She blinked her eyes several times. With the tips of her fingers she stroked the silvery smooth bark. That at least was real, and confirmable, whether it was a tree from *then* —that long ago—or later.

It worried her that 'then' could vanish with so little trace left behind: or, just as bad, that it could play these confusing tricks of identity, hiding up side streets where it knew she had no hope of finding it, changing its name and purpose and disguising itself behind smart, modern frontages and the swarms of smart, modern people.

Mystified, Miss Simm shook her head. Then, gingerly, she let go her fastness, the plane tree's trunk.

Screwing up her courage, she rejoined the tide of holiday-makers, and allowed herself to be carried along on the drift.

They moved more quickly than she or any of her friends were used to moving. Somehow, at a certain point in your life, you felt you should be spared the urgency to reach anywhere: what was coming to you would come, and whether you rushed there or not didn't make an iota of difference. But who would have understood that here, even if she'd been able to speak in their language?

The pavement burned through her shoes' thin soles. Her legs seemed to have hardly any strength left in them. If she'd heaped pebbles into her pockets—like Virginia Woolf in the biography from the library she'd once read—she couldn't have felt any more lethargic or doomed.

She stopped looking to her left or her right and gazed, blinkered, over the heads of those in front of her. She was still being stared at, she knew, by incredulous people trying to guess what had brought her here. Her Scottishness must be written all over her, her age must be a joke.

*

Madame Lépront was remembering something else for her shopping list.

64

What was important was always to have an active mind. You couldn't keep age at bay, so why not accept it in a spirit of good grace, with a modicum of enthusiasm even? She'd known people who'd been middle-aged in their twenties, and people in their forties who'd seemed older than their parents.

It was all a matter of the mind's willingness, she was quite certain: a successful life answered to a positive, assertive attitude.

Attitude. Acknowledging the unlikeliness of failure was the best means of ensuring that failure was avoided.

Madame Lépront kept the spectres where they belonged, in the shadows. Far from Helensburgh and Kilmacolm, a thousand miles away, she walked in sunshine, in the widening, brightening glare of day.

*

On the Place Reyer Miss Simm was thinking of Largs.

At home in the block of flats most of her neighbours were contemporaries: slow, creaking, stooped in their varying degrees. She and her friends took their daily constitutionals on the sea front where the wind blew briskly; they'd sold their real homes, their families had scattered far and wide, and what they had left was Largs, and each other, and the view across Gogo Water to Cumbrae and Bute and the peak of Goat Fell, and that other, much more intriguing prospect—the past.

As they walked to the Pencil at Bower Craig or to Barrfields or along the residential avenues, her group would watch with impatience their less able acquaintances shuffling and halting; one woman was always speeded past them in a wheelchair, as absurdly bright-cheeked as a baby in a pram.

They must be here in Le Lavandou too, Miss Simm thought, deposited in blocks of flats like filing cabinets—human retrieval systems—but discreetly removed from the biz, in some other part of the town.

As she walked on, willing one foot in front of the other, she felt she had escaped from elsewhere—that she was treading where she shouldn't, out of bounds now, that the middle-aged in their holiday undress were looking at her with the unkindest stares of all, as if she was a bearer of bad news.

Ridiculous, she told herself, I'm hallucinating: it's the heat's doing, and because I've found out there's nothing whatsoever to discover. I should never have left Largs. I'm a stay-at-home, I always was, Le

Lavandou can't tell me anything I don't know already. That all was really for the best: that I decided according to the person I was, the one heredity made of me, because I was born to certain parents in a certain place far to the north of here at a certain point in the history of human affairs when a properly-reared young Scotswoman did not —most emphatically did *not*—lose her heart to an olive-skinned, dark-eyed Frenchman, however impeccably upright and principled and chivalrous she afterwards discovered his reputation to be.

*

They'd lived well, she and Guy, to the full. The days had never been long enough for them, no sooner here than they were done. Like paper days being stripped off a calendar in films she'd seen. Their years together had flitted past, the allotted thirty-nine had been used up and she was left confused afterwards, unsure how she could have lived through so long a span and been so little conscious of its passing.

They'd balanced each other, she'd always felt. (Or did she mean 'complemented'?) Guy had been resolute, unpersuadable once he was decided on something; but also fair, willing to understand a weakness in another and why it occurred; he'd had a tender and romantic side to his nature too, being so absurdly protective of her. Since Guy's death, she'd assumed those qualities to herself: the romantic impulse least successfully of all perhaps, because she'd been born a Scot but the kind who turns with age, not maudlin, but eminently practical and matter-of-fact.

Married to Guy, she'd felt she was one half of a whole: now she felt she was more than herself, she was one-and-a-half people, herself plus as much of Guy as she had managed to save.

He was with her, because so long as one of them was left, the other must be too, since they had been so close. She had no dealings with the widows—the handless kind or the guilty ones—who depended on their faith in mediums. A marriage was between two persons, and if mutual trust and confidence weren't there as a bond in the beginning they most definitely couldn't be learned in the hereafter.

*

It was the tramping and slithering of feet Miss Simm heard on all sides of her, then—further off, so she imagined, but really only yards away and separating her from the palms and the promenade wall —the groaning and screeching of traffic, engines straining, brakes squealing, horns blaring. There was a smell of burning rubber, and she wondered how the trees survived so bravely and shiny-leafed after years in the suffocating, choking atmosphere of fumes.

She looked forward, over the heads in front of her, blinkered against the watching faces to left and right of her. She could ask, try to ask, but she didn't know what exactly it was she was looking to find. It was her feelings she was relying on to tell her, her instincts. Relying on, but she couldn't be sure . . .

Then, just seconds later, it seemed she had no doubts at all. She suddenly stopped in her tracks. She'd reached the end of the block. Turning her back to the shore and the sea, she looked up at the front of the building nearest her and saw with a start the word 'Hotel' in old-fashioned script, shining through the paintwork from another era.

People jostled around her, oiled limbs passed brazenly by, and she continued to look up. What had its name been? The Hotel What?

She closed her eyes, trying to remember, trying to call it up, abracadabra it out of the past. A girl's name, wasn't it?

She opened her eyes slowly. She realised she was swaying on her feet. An arm reached out to steady her. Someone said something, in anxious-sounding French. She couldn't reply, not in kind, and she smiled as best she could.

'I think—I can manage, thank you,' she said in a croaky voice, meaning to sound game, plucky.

She turned round. Ahead of her the building on the other side of the street was modern, it had too much glass. Or—her eyes widened —perhaps the glazed terraces on the ground and first floors were only recent additions, to what was much older?

She tilted her head further back to take in the rest of the building. One second it seemed as close as could be, the next it was as distant as what had happened years ago, or had not happened.

She tried to focus, to concentrate, but her eyelids wouldn't stay open. Her legs continued walking, but without any instruction from her that they should, no command at all. It was as if her limbs were another person's, or it was as if she was living in a stranger's body, she had been for years and only now did the ruse declare itself, at the very last moment.

Her legs carried her forward and there was no stopping them, nothing she could do even if she'd had the will. The traffic pulled and sucked like the tides, the people on all sides of her fixed her on her course, the pavement was like a channel running under her.

But just ahead the pavement shelved and as she felt her legs start to give way beneath her she waited in that split second for a saving hand to reach out and grab her.

It didn't come.

Instead one side of her seemed to be blasted away with the impact, her right hand scorched on the metal.

Someone screamed. She heard, somewhere on the periphery of the moment, shouts.

Then she had the illusion of flying as Le Lavandou bore on her from every angle.

She was inside a kaleidoscope, she found, she was rattling round and round with the pieces, far from the sounds. Topsy-turvy, head-over-heels, round and round and round and round . . .

*

In another part of the town Madame Lépront continued on her way, sublimely unaware of any mishap anywhere else.

Her shift blew behind her, her feet hardly touched the cobbles or paving stones in their haste to reach wherever it was they were taking her. She felt—even for her—unusually light and weightless.

She listened to the muffled roar of traffic beneath her in the crowded streets: revving cars, spluttering motorcycles, air brakes sighing on lorries, the tourist coaches sitting with their engines rumbling to keep the air-conditioning turning over.

Le Lavandou wasn't what it had been, but nowhere was: and it wasn't as it would be in another fifty years, nothing like.

She slowed as she walked downhill, towards the sea that gave the town its raison d'être. She removed her dark glasses and dropped them into her basket. Her eyes filled with bright crystalline light: it poured inside her head.

A breeze blowing uphill ruffled the folds of her fashionably pale pink shift around her knees.

A siren separated itself from the traffic noises and the squawking of seabirds overhead. She noticed an ambulance passing at the bottom of the street, with blue beacons flashing.

Momentarily her brow furrowed, but only for a moment—then the skin became smooth again and her expression cleared.

She carried on walking. Her shift blew out behind her. To anyone who might have seen, the breeze would have seemed to cut clean through her, just like a spirit.

Feather-light, as light as air, she passed on, unhurried and uncomplicated, like someone with only the livelong day to fill and not a thought in her head to hold her back.

*

Then finally—in blissful, relieved slow motion and beyond pain—Miss Simm was diving
                    diving
                    diving
In her mind's eye she caught a last backwards glimpse of herself, reduced to just a speck, a particle.

Deeper and deeper, she was fathoms down in the silence, diving for oblivion and fade-out; disappearing into the cool blue wastes of all that annihilating summer sky.

Fandango

After Robbe-Grillet

All the newspapers carried the story, the Mexican ones and the American *News*. It was a story for that day; then it became a campus tragedy, and a source of endless speculation; and then, no doubt, it started to fade from people's consciousness till, by now, it may only be a memory, an almost forgotten myth like so many of Mexico's others.

Not that the protagonists have anything very much to do with their romantic backdrop, except tangentially, contingently. We were players of parts, and maybe the setting was arbitrary, like a film lot we'd strayed on to, by accident rather than by design. Of course I had a lesser part than he did, significantly so: indeed I may appear to have almost no significance to offer, no real claim on the story.

It was a Friday evening, there hadn't been any teaching for me that afternoon. I chanced to buy a newspaper and then and there, standing near the ring road—in the fumes of the hotdog carts and taco booths (what else?)—then and there it was I first read about the business. I grabbed another newspaper from the stand, and took them into the nearest bar. 'British Lecturer Killed', 'Englishman's Body Discovered in Pedregal', 'Mystery Death Riddle'. I listened to the news bulletins on the television and radio sets behind the bar counter, through the music and soap dramas. Evidently some act of violence had occurred: a car accident, it was presumed, a hit-and-run driver. The owner of the car was out-of-town, no one knew where.

I stood at the counter, drinking: gins (*ginebras*) probably, maybe those lethal cactus Mezcals I developed a perverse taste for latterly. It should have muddled me, addled my thoughts. But alcohol preserves and it was the past that came to me, briefly. And then, more vitally, the future. I saw the danger to myself, as a Britisher (the only other in the humanities faculties) and as someone who was not only a colleague but an acquaintance. The general consensus of opinion had always been that Egerton was 'his own man', but I was the one, his countryman (they presumed 'Scottish' to mean 'English'), who —reputation had it—knew him best. I'd always suspected that I knew him very little in fact. Nonetheless the questions would begin with me.

Already I could hear the police voices inside my head: they were pitched low, I was sitting down and the words were being directed to me at head height, on the level of my ears.

Describe Señor Egerton to us.

What were your feelings for him?

As a professional colleague, señor—

—and as a man . . .

Disinterest?

—surely never!

Interest, then?

Jealousy, maybe?

Some sort of fascination?

It is rumoured, señor, that you borrowed money from the deceased. For your modest schoolboy marijuana habits, which we shall say nothing about until another time. But borrowing may become a habit, an addiction too, not causing your life to be any better but—as is the way of addictions—making you dependent on it beyond thought and conscience. Dulling the senses, señor.

But not dulling them to the point that I couldn't understand what I was likely to lose: the job, the relative security I had, my freedom —or what I'd imagined was my liberty to come and go and do just as I chose. I feared being found out for the person I was, in a bare white-lit room at police headquarters; it was on my *own* account that I was afraid to acknowledge the discoveries about myself I still had to make.

I had to rewrite the scenario, I had to knock events out of sync—and get away. Anywhere would do, so long as it wasn't Mexico, or worse. The vacation season hadn't yet arrived and there should be no difficulty about getting on a flight. I knew without looking in my wallet that I hadn't enough, not even for a taxi ride half-way across the city to do what I always did when I needed money quickly. It *was* a habit, an unthinking custom, and conscience didn't come into it. This time of course it would be different: I'd be doing the deed for sentimental reasons, as it were. The very last time wasn't the occasion to become saddled with guilt.

*

I borrowed a car—Hart's Mercury (he was out of town)—and drove out on Insurgentes Sur to Pedregal.

I should explain: our addresses represented the essential difference between us. I lived in an apartment block which had long outlived its glory days, ninety-five dollars a month, behind the end of Main Street, near the Las Americas cinema. Egerton was installed in a smoked glass and pink marble complex of maisonettes and it was a mystery to some how he could afford the accommodation on a lowly lecturer's salary. (The hypotheses were elaborate—a financier's wife for a mistress? pay-offs on drugs deals?) For his part he seemed to enjoy the idea that four thousand years ago the whole of haut bourgeois Pedregal had been a bed of boiling lava, spurting out of a volcano at white heat. Now it was very smart and very modern, futuristic, and also—I thought—more than a little anaemic. Maybe I preferred Main Street, my end, before it became fancy-chic Insurgentes boulevard, the Emerald Zone, or maybe I just pretended to prefer it: at this distance it gets harder to remember.

On that evening—of the 24th of May—I drove out, past the bullring at San Antonio, past Felix Cuevas, San Angel's tourist board shutters and verandas up on the hills, Obregon Park: names to me now. At the first sign to Cuicuilco, where they'd started digging in the lava, I turned off.

A few blocks on, on San Jeronimo, I passed a couple of restaurants he'd taken me to à deux, his 'locals', ritzy evenings which had cost him as much as my month's rent—to 'Les Mémoires d'Outre Tombe' once for French steaks and Mozart à la Waldo de los Rios, and another time to the 'Si-kiang' for Cantonese, where we'd sat watching bored pink flamingos wading in the atrium pool and bored jowled wives in Halston and Saint Laurent watching the starlets and gold-diggers performing on current—and I puzzled again (I seem to see myself puzzling again, sitting there in Hart's Mercury) how it was these godawful places could possibly have contented him. Unless of course he'd been doing it all for my sake?—because he'd thought it was likely to impress me, or else to disorientate me?

The block of apartments was at the front of the complex, on the road side. I drove the car down into the underground parking lot. For some reason, stepping out into the neon-strip lighting and hearing the hum of the air-conditioning motors, I forgot about Egerton's death and felt a bleak rage at the life I'd given myself for the past five years. (Here follow one or two details of autobiography I am obliged to supply . . .) I had drifted into the academic way of things, and been lured to Mexico to escape another Edinburgh winter—and at the other end of the world, in the El Dorado, I found myself defeated by so much noise and squalor and luxury and heat and inescapable *life*, and by the mimicking of other people's lives, and by the fury of colour on those murals painted on every public wall, and by the hidden significance of each Aztec and Toltec and Olmec symbol which must be the key to understanding them, living with them. All to reach where I had, the fluorescent-lit harsh-shadowed basement of Egerton's salubrious condominium block.

Overhead, pipes formed a latticework of correspondences that also—in the frame of mind I was in—seemed determined to defeat me. Not that the web of functions could matter to me, except as a concept of what it was possible to know and what not. I realised I should have stopped and had another drink: a beer, a mind-numbing Moctezuma or Nochebuena.

I wondered (conceivably I wondered) what Egerton found to keep him there. With the means, of course, a lot can be overlooked. But Egerton lived so privately, he could have done it with far less discomfort—no glassy rooms such as the ones we had to teach in, facing into the sun, no fetid staircases swarming with un-deodorised students at change-over times—he might just as easily have chosen a North American climate instead. Nothing about him seemed inclined to the Latin: he spoke Spanish easily and effortlessly but he had no enthusiasm for it, he preferred French novels to the vogue-ish South American ones, he kept well out of the sun's fire and the pressure-cooker heat slamming down. I had accompanied him on one or two obligatory sight-seeing trips, but only as far as the Fodor tourist-haunts, Tlaxcala for the murals, the Cholula labyrinths, the broken windy temples at Tula, the park of Popocatépetl, the warrior prince. A few times I'd heard people say they'd seen him 'about', sitting in bars: the discreetly lit sort with English wood panelling, men-only drinking holes, the refuges from *esposas* and home and mistresses who demand too much. In what were to prove his last days, some of the women in the literature faculties—I could tell from their expressions—were starting to take pity on him.

I had an open invitation to visit whenever I liked: presuming he was there to answer the intercom. On the evening in question—the 24th of May (I must be particular)—I found him upstairs sitting at his desk working on a lecture.* The desk was the leather-topped

* His latest 'cause' was the work of Alain Robbe-Grillet. This is an important point, deserving more than a mention in a footnote: the relevance of the fact—that Egerton happened to be studying the 'nouveaux romans' of *that* writer—is more than circumstantial, since it is already intrinsic to the shaping and content of this narrative re-telling of events.

mahogany kneehole variety; each time it would remind me (I didn't know why) of what a respectable lawyer would have done his business at in a fusty office in a dim and dusty, pre-War, backwater English town. It had always seemed to me a triply inappropriate item of furniture: suiting neither our location nor the little I'd gleaned of Egerton's history and background, nor indeed according in any wise to his current field of interest, the modern French novel. Standing in the doorway, on the early evening of the 24th of May, I experienced as a blur of memories those nights—maybe five or six over the months I'd known him—when we'd sat up talking, drinking, picking at the meals the maid had prepared for us, talking on and drinking more. Happy times, of course. Also—I remembered as I watched him—fraught in some unspecified way, in that English room in the Pedregal, a superior apartment's public room which he'd furnished with leather tub club-chairs, and pale and tasteful English watercolours, and understated Chinese vase lamps with box silk shades in neutral hues. Seven storeys beneath, Mexico City's traffic barked and snarled and Egerton, apparently unminding, might have been practising those flawlessly, immaculately Anglo-Saxon gestures in a faded room—the den of the favourite (doomed) son—in some ancestral country manor house in a by-passed corner of England's damply green and pleasant land.

As for the business in hand, I had never hesitated in the past about asking him for loans. Time wasn't yet quite 'past'. I knew a firm of accountants despatched a monthly money order from London, and his (doubtless doting) mother frequently sent her youngest son Coutts cheques from the far remove of her fastness in the shires. (Herefordshire, he told me: an area I hadn't had an occasion to visit but which I would nostalgically imagine for myself.)

On the vital matter he never refused, nor even showed any reluctance. 'Roughly how much?' he would ask, for words to say, and would offer me twice the sum that I needed. 'That's too much,' I would (routinely) counter. 'Take it anyway,' he would tell me. I always repaid him, I plead in my own defence. In the absence of an English mantelpiece I would leave the money in a sealed envelope on the scagliola marble top of the gesso table.

This time my request was to be for more. As I stood watching him, I thought he looked pallid and wan: maybe not unhealthily so, certainly not deathly so, but quite enough for me—and presumably anyone else—to notice.

'I've got to fly somewhere,' I said.

'A holiday?'

'No. No, not a holiday.'

New York, I told him.

'You're not getting out? Leaving me?'

Did it matter to him that I was, I wondered. Yes, maybe it did, I thought, seeing the expression of concern troubling the features of his face: fine features, befitting his highly bred, rarefied pedigree-stock.

'I just thought I'd go up,' I said, trying not to betray myself by my voice.

'Is there something wrong?'

'"Wrong"?' I repeated. 'What d'you mean?'

I caught sight of myself in the gilt framed pier-glass behind him, set in panels decorated with painted views of a watery Venice. I looked as pallid as he did, lunar, as white as an egg.

'How long for?'

For a moment I thought he wasn't going to say 'yes', that he was going to refuse. Is it my memory of the occasion or a reconstruction I've effected from it that has me standing staring at the pendulum clock under its glass dome, seeming to imagine how I might hold its weight and bulk, already balancing it in my hands.

He smiled, hesitantly. He took his wallet out of his jacket pocket.

'I was going to say—' He passed his hand across his brow. (Or if he didn't he ought to have done so: it seems the apt, the true gesture.) 'We should go away somewhere.'

'What's that?' I said, meaning I wasn't listening, I hadn't heard.

'To the coast. Zihuatanejo. Ixtapa. I could do with a rest. It's only what you're going to tell me, isn't it?'

'Is it?'

'How tired I look. Tired to death.'

'I hadn't noticed,' I said.

He smiled.

'Some weekend we can,' he said. 'Make a long weekend of it.'

I nodded.

Standing there I had the curious sense I was speaking dialogue it was intended I should speak. I already felt involved, implicated, embroiled. I had a split second's recollection of the fretwork of pipes on the basement roof, the interior complexity of this seven-storey shell, an aloof confection of smoked glass and pink marble.

His eyes were watching me with diligent, microscopic attention.

'When you get back,' he said.

But you'll be dead, I remembered, it'll be too late then.

'What would you do?' I asked him.

The eyes narrowed. His fingers found the knot of his tie. A school or college tie, bright magenta stripes on a black ground.

'I'm sorry?' he said.

'On this outing you seem to have planned for us.'

'I thought—well, I don't know. We could—look at history. I suppose it's just beneath the surface. All around. The air we breathe.'

(And waiting for us in the future, I could have added.)

He was reading Robbe-Grillet's *La Maison de Rendez-vous*: it lay open on his desk, cover upwards. (That's another detail which seems to have registered, or maybe it's too fortuitous to be strictly credible.) There was an open notebook beside it, and he'd written down a column of brief remarks in his small, exact academic's script.

'You can let me know what you think,' he said, his smile back in place. His fingers reached inside the crocodile wallet. 'Would this be all right?'

Money was his proper element, like air to breathe. Officially he was on a higher salary scale than I was, but it had suffered with continual, remorseless inflation and by rights he should have been struggling to make ends meet. He did anything but.

He held out several five hundred peso bills. I remembered what their function was, to get me as far from Mexico City as was expedient. Egerton didn't have more than half-an-hour to live, at the most generous calculation (the flamingo-pink twilight was already visible through the grey-tinted windows), and I had to be out on the first plane I could get a seat on: north, to wherever, Los Angeles or El Paso or the seaboard.

We'd perfected a very English ceremony of tact on those occasions: we didn't discuss the transaction, decorously and fastidiously we averted the topic. He returned the wallet to his pocket.

'If it's—' He paused. A precept was about to be breached. 'If it's a question of money—'

I contrived to look surprised.

'For going to the coast,' he said. 'I mean, it's all right.'

I nodded, hurriedly.

'It doesn't matter,' he said.

I nodded again, finding myself wordless—as shocked as a spinster —by his off-limits indiscretion.

There was a pause, an interlude, a vacuum of several seconds when nothing was happening. The gap felt unscripted, but maybe even that had been meant to happen?

'Sure,' I said. I was lying. 'Sure.'

Perhaps he understood as much, that all it was was a dodge, and a flagrant untruth. He fingered his tie again: always his most eloquent form of silence when he performed it.

He didn't ask how long I would be away, why I was going, if it was for a reason, for the sake of some*one*. Christ-like he said nothing, and only stood there, directly in front of me, suffering. Suffering in his Mexican recreation of genteel English respectability.

Then I really *could* have struck him, with the clock under its glass dome. Felled him, brought him to the ground, there and then. A crime of the moment: a crime of despair, not of passion. But, in every sense, there was only minutes in it.

I took my leave, no more awkwardly than I had four or five times before. A little drily today, naturally, knowing what the import of this particular occasion was.

I took a final look round the room, at everything so apparently above-board, and at Egerton, so angular and fair-haired and blue-eyed to the last.

At the doorway I felt a restraint and looked down and saw his hand on my arm.

'I'm not sure I can go on like this,' he said, in a dull broken voice.

I suppose what also matters is that I didn't ask him what he meant, why he was speaking these words that were the creation of a romantic novelist.

His hand moved up my arm, to my shoulder. His fingers clung.

I felt myself starting to tremble. I stepped back, took several steps back; he lost his hold and his face fell. I kept moving backwards, then I turned round and walked off, jerkily, across the room. I got into my stride, I reached the door, and I didn't look back.

The basement when I walked/ran out of the elevator was cool. At first the neon light had a greenish, underwater tone to it.

I sat in the car—*that* car, the Texan-registered midnight blue Mercury compact Hart had bought in Houston and driven south —and I tried to concentrate on what had just happened.

I don't doubt there is a clinical explanation. That I wasn't 'affronted', not—God knows—in this day and age: rather, that I was distressed to find the episode answering to some suspected truth about myself inside myself. The clinical can elucidate and evaluate so much, and yet . . .

There was a hiccup—a planned interruption, a regular irregularity—in the mechanism of the air-conditioning generator and I jumped. (I could say 'out of my skin', but that doesn't abnegate *responsibility*, such an endearingly old-fashioned word.)

A couple of seconds later the basement settled back into its normalcy of mechanical angst. I just sat gripping the rim of the wheel, in a strip-lit imitation of how many scenes in how many films. Seen in the driving-mirror, in that stark, ungrateful neon glare, my face must have seemed unearthly—distracted—possessed— evilly disposed—bent on a dastardly revenge. (Take your pick: select the identikit rogue.)

I turned on the radio, and the receiver crackled. A Mexican band played brassy music, but far enough away to sound as if they were entertaining on the moon. A lunar fandango.

Maybe it was to drown it I started the engine. My foot played on the clutch pedal. A straggle of conversation from one of our late evenings came into my head. We'd begun by talking about Robbe-Grillet, and been led on from that. Egerton said, didn't I think certain people volunteer themselves for murder, they wish themselves to be victims? There was another theory, I said, which maybe had its source in that: doing the deed, murderers make offerings not of their prey but of themselves. Had I heard, he then asked, what they say in Mexico, that you have to kill a man to be able to believe in him? On and on, around and around, and the sentences unwound like ribbons.

I jammed my foot down on the accelerator and snatched at the handbrake.

The light pressed two thumbs into my eyes.

The engine roared as the car shot across the lot. I tugged on the wheel, too hard, and the car turned sharply on two squealing tyres.

I noticed Egerton's black VW Rabbit tucked neatly against the side wall. It had been spotted in town parked outside various dives, and with commendable self-control the witnesses had refrained from questioning him on the subject.

I steered in a straight line, making for the ramp. Next to it was the elevator shaft. According to the newspaper reports, he'd probably just stepped out of the doors when he was hit.

It might have been accidental or deliberate, who is to say: and if deliberate, on whose part—his or the driver's? A woman standing on a balcony noticed the dark blue car with American plates come 'raging like a lion' (apparently her own words) out of the basement car park and then swerve, tyres screeching and burning rubber marks, out on to the road, just like cars on television cop shows. She'd just been saying to her husband, you'll think I'm a little bit loopy but I know tonight there's a bad feeling in the air, a kind of *pava*, danger for someone we know but do *not* know.

An hour later all the dark blue cars in Mexico City with American registration plates were being traced. The first version of the story had speedily been written up; inky presses rolled in newspaper print rooms. The theme awaited its variations.

Meanwhile an Aeromexico flight to Miami/Tampa had just taken off and the runway lights were dropping behind it. Over-orchestrated Mexican music rattled through the tannoy, to put us at our ease. Three rows in front of me sat a man who bore an uncanny resemblance to Egerton, but the resemblance only lasted three or four seconds: something to do with the finely striped Oxford cotton shirt, perhaps. I felt resemblances would exist in other places too, at other times—when I least expected to find them—but, like these orchestral permutations of the dance rhythms, they would only be the author's playful diversions: as it were, momentary asides from the text.

Prelude and Fugue

'Who has written the novel . . . ? I, who have told you the story?
You, who someday will tell what I have told you? Or someone else,
someone unknown? Here is another possibility: the novel was
already written. It is an unpublished ghost story; it lies in a coffer
buried under a garden urn, or under loose bricks at the bottom of a
dumbwaiter shaft.'

CARLOS FUENTES, *Distant Relations*

'Words bearing offerings, riches brought back from the four corners
of the earth and laid on the altar before a god of death seated in the
farthermost recess of the temple, in the secret chamber, the last
chamber . . .'

NATHALIE SARRAUTE, *The Use of Speech*

Avant-Propos

Once, when she was seven or eight years old and the memory of her mother was already starting to fade, her father had taken her with him to visit one of his friends. She had always remembered *that*, her afternoon: because of the absence of her mother, of course, and no less because of the fiery summer heat—the fields shimmering, Kent pale and the colours washed out of it, the sky no colour at all.

She'd left the two men in the garden, drinking tea and discussing the academic matters that were the staple diet of conversation whenever they met. High above them the rooks chattered in their perilously angled ships' nests.

She'd let herself out by the latch gate in the holly hedge, and set off with no destination in mind, following the line of the ditch that marked the boundary between the house and the fields. After a few minutes she came to a copse, and—with no other plan of what she might do—she began trampling through the knee-high bracken, making for the shade of the trees.

At some indeterminable point the copse became a wood, but she walked on without realising, without attending to particulars, this sapling or that fallen trunk, which might have served her as markers. Passing beneath the trees, all she was conscious of was how warm or how cool the filtered sunlight and shadows felt on her face, her arms, her legs. The words in the garden were forgotten, and the obligation of not letting her manners drop in the public rooms of the quirkily named 'Dolphin House', which her father had told her would be described in great and loving detail by art historians in years to come, when she would be grown up. ('You will see that you have been a little part of history, Helen.')

Birds sang—she heard them—and the bracken crackled as creatures scurried and scratched for cover, but it was all in the moment and she hadn't time to be alarmed or cautious. She held out her arms and flexed her fingers and watched the effects of light and shadow as they ribbed her skin in sequence. Sounds like drips reached her, and she might have been in a cave, or even lost beneath the surface of the sea, walking on the ocean floor. Every so often she craned her neck and looked up, through miles of branches, to the dizzying source of the light.

Maybe that was how, in the end, she lost her direction.

She stopped between steps. She stood quite still, looking forward and behind. Something disturbed her—the beating of wings like the pumping of dragon's breath—and her eyes travelled through the distance of subterranean green. She felt she'd fallen between the pages of a book, the dog-eared one Nanny Brechin and then Nanny Hine used to read to her, and she'd woken up in the dark forest every fairy-tale had at its centre. A witch might appear, or a prince might ride through on a white horse—but would he see her in time to be able to reach her and save her?

She turned round. Looking on all sides of her she began to panic. Her breath choked up into her throat. She forgot where she'd started to look, and which direction she'd come from.

Then by some chance she noticed, further off, a path trodden through the undergrowth. An escape, perhaps.

She didn't waste any more time, and started running towards it.

She followed with her head bent, eyes down. Gradually the path broadened out, to a track; the ground under her feet became firmer, and her heart hurt less in her chest. The prints of horseshoes appeared, and she thought again of the prince riding through on his white stallion, bid to go fetch this or that and to prove himself in some spot far from the court of the castle, otherwise he would never win the right to claim his bride.

Later the true conundrum of this day presented itself.

The track ceased to be a track.

It forked: it divided and became two tracks, leading in contrary directions.

She stopped. She looked left and right: back to the left and again to the right.

Her eyes shifted between the two.

Which should she take? Which was the correct one and which was the wrong one? (Unless, of course, both were correct—or could it be that they were both wrong?)

She felt the onus of the choice overwhelming her. She was standing in a clearing and the heat came at her from above and below, tumbling down through the trees and clawing its way up out of the ground.

Which should she take? The left, or the right?

There was no one to choose for her. For the first time in her life that she could remember she wasn't able to ask and have the answer given to her. It was *her* choice and hers alone.

One or the other.

It might have been life or death.

She felt her waterworks cracking open, and then dampness dribbling between her legs. The heat bared its teeth like fangs and snapped at her. White spots dropped in front of her eyes.

Left or right?

She had to choose, now or never, like life and death.

No one could help her.

The choice was hers.

Hers alone.

*   *   *

Crossing to the other pavement she was suddenly caught in the track of a car's headlights. She was dazzled by them for several seconds and stood in the middle of the street, fixed.

It was only when she saw the car was slowly moving towards her that she—vaguely—sensed danger.

Her legs moved beneath her. The enchantment was undone—and she ran for the blacked-out windows of Pandora's.

She remembered as she sat in the tea-room and looked over to the window. There had been days of late when she'd felt that she couldn't trust herself to do what should have been simplest: like crossing from one side of the street to the other.

She was sitting at her usual table. She opened her book, a collection of Elizabeth Bowen short stories she'd bought from a barrow. She turned the pages to find her place and wondered how it had come to be on a book barrow, if someone had been obliged to sell it, or hadn't cared for the stories: or maybe the book was blitz plunder? So many mysteries might occupy your mind in these days of wartime, your senses could be turned by them, for the worse.

'Thought you'd gone, Miss Wilmot.'

She looked up. ' "Gone"?' she repeated.

'Moved on,' the proprietor said. 'Gone to live somewhere else. Disappeared.'

She shook her head.

'They say there's lots doing it.' The man leaned his elbows on the counter, as if—the young woman thought—he was about to regale her with an oft-told tale. 'Changing their names, their identities. But folks disappear just walking along the street. Big holes under the pavement, step on the wrong one and down you go.' He nodded towards the window. 'They've found temples in the City. There's packs of dogs loose too, across the river. Barnes-way. And bonfires.'

His eyes returned to her.

'I don't know,' she said.

'No one knows nothing these days, Miss Wilmot. This hand doesn't know what that one's up to.' The man shrugged. 'It's luck. One minute you're sitting at that table, breathing—'

She had turned to another page and was trying to read from one sentence to the next. The man's voice cut across their sense. She didn't want to listen to him; she didn't want to hear words he must have spoken dozens of times before. He was only fishing for what he could discover about her anyway; she'd seen his lips mouth 'la-di-da' to customers when he must have thought she wouldn't see.

. . . gardens of palms sloping down to the sea.

'Do you like it, Helen?'

She nodded her head.

'I'm glad we came,' she said. 'It's hard to believe this is England. There might not be a war . . .'

Hadn't she said?

'There might not be a war . . .'

The man's voice interrupted again.

'Changed days for everyone, I reckon.'

She closed her book. She turned her head and looked across the room, towards the window. Her pale, glum imitation was watching from the other side of the glass. She had an angular set to her features she couldn't quite believe of herself. A good-ish coat, someone newly come down in the world, the pull of 'gravitas'.

She stretched out her arm to catch a strand of hair that had fallen on to her brow. The watching woman did likewise. She coaxed back the hair and the other copied her. Two silver bracelets slithered down two arms.

'. . . I repeat, Helen, actions have to be seen to be correct.'

'Oh, Father—'

'Such a thing seems to me most improper.'

'I'm sure I—'

'I have had to be two parents to you, Helen.'

'Yes, Father.'

Most improper, two parents, seen to be correct, yes Father, yes Father, oh yes

Then her eyes alighted on the newspaper lying on another table. Had it been there when she'd come in? But it must have been.

She pushed her chair back and stood up. She wanted something to read which her eyes could just skim the surface of and her mind scarcely needed to concentrate on.

She walked over to the table, conscious she was being watched by the man behind the counter. It was a copy of *The Times*, by some stroke of luck.

She picked it up and returned with it to her table. Momentarily, as she seated herself, her eyes met the proprietor's.

She spread the newspaper out on the table-top. She was aware the door had opened and closed and the weight of a man was crossing the floorboards and joists, but she didn't look up as she leafed through the pages.

She perused the 'Personal' notices on the front page; her eyes ran down the columns of print. At the foot of one someone had ringed an insertion with black ink.

'A LONDON GENTLEWOMAN REQUIRES THE DOMESTIC SERVICES OF A YOUNG LADY TO ACT AS HER CONFIDENTIAL SOCIAL SECRETARY'.

She re-read the words. She'd had no clear idea in her head of what sort of position she would like: perhaps 'liking' was beside the point, though, in these days when you took whatever job you could land yourself.

A telephone number was included. What exactly was a 'confidential social secretary', she wondered, and what were her duties? How many 'gentlewomen' were left in the world?

Re-reading the notice for the third and fourth and fifth times, she felt there must be a way of life which even a war and its privations hadn't scuppered: ladies would call themselves 'gentlewomen', they continued to lead social existences despite black-outs and night-raids, they still believed in the value of virtues like confidentiality, they held to the hierarchy of mistress and domestic employee.

She hadn't any qualifications of the secretarial sort, but how could anyone prove that she would not be able to perform a social secretary's tasks?

A few months ago she had been beyond such considerations. But these were changed days. And the longer she sat thinking about it, the more likely and appealing an opening it seemed. Her only doubt attached to the fact that someone had got to the notice before her and circled it with black ink.

It was dog eat dog in this new London—why not? Nothing was to be calculated on any longer, so people said. All day long the voices about her in the street echoed the question, 'What the hell?'

She placed her gas-mask case on top of the book of short stories. She pushed her chair back and got to her feet. She picked up the newspaper.

'Leaving?'

She looked over to the counter. The proprietor saw everything she did. Everything.

'No,' she said.

Another man stood at the counter with his back to her. For a moment . . .

The arrangement—if an air raid shelter could be that, and not just a dire necessity of the way they lived now—made her uncomfortable in two senses.

It always happened at night when there were only themselves in the house. Even the underground stations, hell-holes, wouldn't have caused this unease in her. Only her father and herself.

He lit candles, so that he could read his book and watch her over the top of the page. There was nowhere for her to look to escape his watching eyes.

Only her father and herself.

Once, as another part of London was taking the blows and as the rumbles carried for miles, he'd told her in their dug-out that she reminded him more and more of her mother. She'd smiled sadly, for decent and sociable propriety's sake.

The closeness disturbed her, the airless confinement like a tomb beneath the back garden.

'You'll be back?'

She blinked at the man.

'You're coming back?' he asked again.

'I—I'll be back.'

She smiled, hesitantly. She turned away, pushing the newspaper inside the folds of her overcoat.

'I . . . I've forgotten something . . .'

'Helen!'

With that she was running out of the shelter, back up the garden to the house. The droning of the planes filled her head, like angry wasps, a swarm of them.

She wanted the bracelet and the sketch. They were in the top right-hand drawer of the tallboy. She had time perhaps, just, before the planes reached the city. They had been lucky on previous occasions, and she always tried to think the best.

'*Helen!*'

Her father's voice called after her.

'*Hel-en!*'

She didn't look back. She ran with the torch. She felt she didn't want to return to that cell under the grass, not ever again, to that tomb.

'*Tomb*', '*womb*' . . .

In the womb she'd floated, almost free, in her mother's bloody waters. Down there, it was like death, without air or daylight: the weeping wax of the candles, the heat on her skin, London burning, her father pretending to read his book, telling her how she looked more and more like her mother—and herself, trying to see him as she must have done, at least in their first days together, with the eyes of adoring love.

She saw by moonlight. The telephone box was empty, and she pulled at the door and manoeuvred herself inside.

She picked up the receiver and, when the operator answered, she asked for the number. She heard the connection being made and waited for the receiver to be lifted at the other end.

The telephone box was directly in the track of a stationary car's headlights, and she turned her back to them, leaning against the dusty glass and forgetting that there must be danger on their account.

The operator's voice spoke again. She inserted a coin as instructed and pushed button 'A'.

'This is Miss Lazare's residence,' a girl's voice announced.

'Can I—may I speak to—to the lady of the house, please?'

'Yes, madam. Who shall I say is calling?'

'Oh, we haven't met. I saw—a notice—in the newspaper.'

'Yes, madam. I shall let Miss Lazare know.'

While she waited Helen looked back over her shoulder, towards the headlights, and tidied the scarf wrapped round her throat.

There was the sound of approaching footsteps from the other end and another voice was travelling down the line to her.

'Good afternoon. This is Miss Lazare.'

The tone to Helen's ear was civilised, refined, also business-like.

'Oh,' she said. 'Good afternoon.'

'I believe you wish to speak to me?'

'Yes.' Helen licked her lips. 'I—I happened to see a notice. In the "Personal" column. "Requiring the Services—"' She felt her mouth furring up. 'Perhaps—you've—?'

'The post,' enquired the voice, 'is of interest to you?'

Helen looked inside her purse and shook the contents.

'I thought—I thought it might be work I could do—'

The other voice rattled in her ear, sounding very close by.

'You have some experience of that sort?'

Helen pulled at the scarf. 'Oh,' she said. 'Yes.'

She heard the uncertainty and deceit.

'In that case,' came the reply, 'I suggest that we meet. Would that be convenient to you?'

'Yes,' Helen said. 'Yes.'

'My address is Number Seven, Michaelmas Passage, in Chelsea.'

Helen closed her eyes to remember.

'If you lose your way, I'm sure someone will show you.'

'When—when would—'

'Let us say tomorrow, and lose no time. If that is agreeable?'

'Yes.'

'I shall expect you in the afternoon. At four o'clock.'

'Yes. Thank you.'

'You can come?'

'Oh yes.'

'We shall meet then.'

'Yes. Yes, thank you.'

'Goodbye, Miss Wilmot.'

'Goodbye.'

Helen replaced the receiver. She picked up her purse, turned, and pushed her weight on the door. As she walked off, the newspaper lay where she'd left it, on the tray beneath the telephone.

That was attended to, she told herself. She wasn't sure what she might be letting herself in for, but apart from the ammo factories work was so hard to come by and she had to support herself, for a while longer at any rate. One untruth—such an unimportant one —couldn't matter, but for some reason it occupied her mind as she made her way along the pavement in the track of the headlights, back to Pandora's Tea Rooms. She didn't have a secretary's qualifications, not on paper, nor any proper, verifiable experience; now she realised how desperately in those moments she'd wanted not to lose the opportunity, and how easily she'd lied to secure it. A Scottish nanny used to tell her 'one wee fib begets another, Helen', but Nanny

Brechin had been scrupulously moral as these times were not; Nanny Brechin had scrubbed her charge's face and her own with Pears soap morning, noon and night and was the very apogee of inner as well as outer cleanliness, but at this juncture the only rituals that counted were those which enabled you to survive. Travelling the distance from Holborn to Chelsea and back every day might just keep her head above the rising waters.

She felt the heat inside Pandora's flushing her face as she walked back in. She hadn't been aware of it earlier.

She noticed the absence of the other man, that the proprietor was alone. He leaned on the counter with a newspaper open in front of him, seemingly not attending to her reappearance.

She sat down. A stage tune was warbling out of the wireless set.

'In our city darkened now—street and squares and crescent
We can feel our living past in our shadowed present.'

The book of short stories lay open, at one she hadn't begun yet, called 'Unwelcome Idea'. She didn't have any great wish to read at the present moment.

'Ghosts beside our starlit Thames who lived and loved and died,
Keep throughout the ages London Pride.'

From the pocket of her coat she took out a notepad and a stub of pencil. She scribbled down the name 'Lazare', in several spellings. She wondered—she didn't know why—if she ought to recognise that too in its variants, like the tune, from another set of circumstances, from another time than this one.

*

She saw from the ambulance: the house turned upside down and inside out, the walls blazing, the roof blown away. One wall still stood and curtains blew at a melted window, blew in the raging wind from the flames. Or so she seemed to remember.

'Her name is Wilmot,' someone was saying. 'Helen Wilmot.'
And then, hearing her name spoken, she blacked out.

*

In the room in Holborn she stood trying to decide.
This suit, that suit. Or . . .
Every time she had to choose, and on her decision rested the world's conception of her.

What was required for a gentlewoman's house in Chelsea?

Somehow the suits had survived the destruction. In the brown Donegal tweed she was prim, prudent, a governess. In the light grey serge she was smarter, more self-assured, halfway to being her own woman. In any of the suits she saw modelled in the magazines she might have been . . .

Might have been.

*

Once upon a time chiming moments would come to her, moments that silvered and sparkled when the rhyme and reason revealed themselves.

It would happen quite unexpectedly, for no reason. Suddenly she would see that everything about her fitted and belonged, and that she and her father belonged to the whole.

It couldn't have happened if her father hadn't been there too, beside her. Then they were the two halves of a perfect hole.

Looking ahead through the windscreen was like watching leaves fall, or snow, or seeing into the eye of a gathering storm: dizzying, entrancing, sending thoughts whirling a dervish dance.

Her eyelids were growing heavy. She felt as if her body had been filled up with soft, heavy sand inside; her legs weighted her like the trunks of trees.

She had the sensation that the road was holding them back, or trying to, making the wheels drag. She watched her father press his foot harder down on the accelerator.

The road went zig-zagging ahead of them.

The verges were offering up their crawling and hopping and scuttling things. Moths flitted past with pale wings; fireflies burned as brightly as sparks. A tree shook down a shower of pine needles; they splattered on to the bonnet and windscreen, then blew away.

She was aware of darkness on all sides of them, over them and underneath. It was massing itself behind the banks of vegetation, preparing itself—she was sure—for an ambush. It crowded behind the trees and prowled overhead where she couldn't see, ready to bring itself slamming down on the car's roof.

Her father's hands gripped the steering wheel tight, and she noticed how white his knuckles were. The red wand climbed on the black background of the speedometer—to 50, 60, 65. In her mind's eye she saw the car roaring along the road, over the hills and far away.

Vegetation reached out arms and scratched at the doors and the running boards. Insects flew into the grille and were dashed against the windscreen. Something thumped behind the rear wheels but she didn't look back, she knew the back window was filled with all that darkness in pursuit.

A straighter stretch of road had opened up in front. The headlights shone along it and she watched for the point where they couldn't breach the darkness, their vanishing point.

Her eyelids dropped. Her body was starting to slip down the seat. She felt she was filled with sleep.

She tried lifting her eyelids to watch the distance.

Slowly, from that vanishing point, an object appeared, white and resolute.

She blinked, several times. It floated above the road, in the track of the headlights. An owl . . .

The closer they came the more prominent its eyes seemed. She imagined she was being drawn by them, into *them.*

The bird floated with wings stretched, carried on currents of air. Its whiteness was drawing all the light towards it, towards the eyes under their heavy hoods.

The owl coasted, freewheeling on the air draughts, while underneath the car she felt the wheels were pulling clear of the force that had seemed to restrain them. She watched the perfect, sublime purity *of the bird's flight.*

Over to the right, she saw the moon, rising clear over some trees. Clouds swirled around it like smoke.

And then her head must have drooped, on to the back of the seat or on to her father's shoulder, and she felt the self that was inside her, like running sand, trickling back to the when and whence it had come.

Once upon a time she would also suffer the absence of that knowledge, glowing and warming—when the doubt was like a panicking bird, trapped inside her, beating its wings against her rib bones.

Then her father wasn't the wise king and provider. He was the dark spirit of woodlands and high places and Helen feared him as she lay awake in her bed on the top floor of the house in Kensington, above the street lamp and the creaking branches of the trees in the gardens.

Her terror was that all she was able to know of the world was what was offered to her, to her sight and touch. It was her father who had the other knowledge of what lay inside or behind the objects she could only see or touch the surfaces of. There was another, primary life and she had no access to it. *She* had no more life than the things did, and maybe *she* was a thing too: it was her father alone who could really and positively know what was contained inside her, behind her eyes and mouth and skin.

He saw through to another Helen Wilmot and it wasn't the one she offered to other people, to be approved of and to have the contact of their fingers, smoothing her hair or stroking the backs of her hands. Sometimes her father pretended that was how *he* believed her to be, no more than she appeared, smoothing her hair or stroking the backs of her hands: but she knew differently, that he was always seeing *into* every moment as she never could. That was why his eyes would grow so small and have such a bright light in them, why his brow folded into wrinkles, why his lips pressed tightly against each other.

There was another life and she had nothing to do with it. She never made contact with it, although it was just behind every object she saw with her eyes.

Sometimes, she guessed, it was history—or harm—or time to come.

Her father knew, and that was the difference between them.

He had the knowledge of the secret places, while she belonged to the floating wood and metal and glass surfaces of the secondary world.

*

By the afternoon Chelsea was wraithed in mist. It seeped up from the river, billowed like hot steam over rooftops, curled round chimney pots; it tore on lamp posts and railings, and lingered on the street corners ahead of her. Somewhere too, Helen felt the presence of the sun, a remote glow that was taking the worst of the chill out of the day.

She made her way through the confusion of weather, looking for the name 'Michaelmas Passage' on the flanks of buildings. She started to lose her sense of direction as the streets took sharp right angles and seemed to redouble on themselves. From nearby she heard a clock tower striking, four chimes.

She stopped to listen. As the notes died away, she was aware of someone—a shape—standing only a few feet away from her. She started when she saw it was a man, in an ARP warden's uniform, paying her very close attention.

She blurted out a question.

'Can—can you—help me?'

He didn't take his eyes off her.

'Depends,' he said.

'I'm—I'm looking for Michaelmas Passage.'

He hesitated before speaking.

'Down the lane,' he said.

' "The lane"?' she repeated, staring at him.

The man nodded.

'Over there.'

She looked in the direction of the nod, towards the other side of the street.

'The lane,' she said. 'Thank you.'

It occurred to her as she crossed the street—feeling the man's eyes were still on her—that she ought not to risk what looked like a narrow pathway between buildings, especially on instructions from a stranger. But there was no one else to ask, unless she knocked at a house door; the houses were unlit, though, everywhere seemed equally quiet and potentially hazardous, and she had no clues.

The lane was a paved alley between high walls. The stones sloped down into the centre, where there was a gutter.

She paused to take courage, then—unsure of whether she did right or wrong—she walked forward.

The mist was colder against her skin than she'd felt it all afternoon. She pulled up the collar of her raincoat. She listened to the echoes of her heels and seemed to be hearing two people, herself and another.

It was only an illusion, of course, and she tried smiling, to keep up her spirits.

Ahead of her she saw another street of brick houses. The road was laid with cobbles.

'Michaelmas Passage', she read as the echoes fell away behind her and she was left alone, walking unaccompanied through the gap between the side-walls of houses, with 'Michaelmas Passage' opening out to left and right of her.

Number Seven was on the other side of the road. She stopped to look: looking in the way her father instructed her.

It was a tall grey-brick house of the era of Hogarth. The middle and second storeys each had six windows; on the ground floor there were three windows on one side of a black front door and two on the other. The effect of unevenness was satisfying, Helen decided, even being in the uncertain frame of mind that she was.

The house sat a few yards back from the street. She walked towards it and saw there were two deep areas beneath black-painted railings, and—between them—a causeway of flagstones leading to the front door. It was a substantial house, built to impress.

Looking up at it, Helen suddenly felt herself discomfited, less confident in her abilities to bluff her way through an encounter with its owner.

She thought she caught a movement at one of the first floor windows and realised it was now or never.

She walked the short distance to the front door, between the railings and the area drops on either side. She pulled the shiny brass handle on the wall and heard the bell ring, sounding far away and muffled.

The door was opened by a young maid in uniform. Immediately Helen felt the sharpness of her eyes. The keenness and concentration in the plain country girl's face took her aback.

She smiled at her, more broadly than the occasion was warranting.

The maid spoke, without returning the smile.

'You're expected, Miss.'

Helen stood in the doorway for a few moments longer, summoning courage, before she stepped forward into the hall.

The door was closed behind her. She looked down at the black and white squares on the floor, then lifted her eyes to the smoky oil paintings on the walls: not portraits or landscapes but still life studies.

'Miss—'

Helen looked round.

'I—I'm sorry?'

'I'll take your coat, Miss.'

'Oh. Yes.'

'And your gloves and gas-mask case.'

'Yes. Of course.'

The maid held the collar while Helen slipped out of the arms. She remembered to ask for the coat, please, for one moment, and pretended to be looking for something in her pockets while she tried to disguise a slash in the lining. She handed it back to the girl, lining concealed, and smiled again stiffly as she walked off.

While she waited she checked her appearance in the gilt mirror on the wall, above the console table. She looked pale and seemed almost to float in these new surroundings, as if she wasn't correctly weighted or gravity wasn't doing its proper work. A nonsensical illusion, just a trick of the light; she knew that it was only her confidence betraying her—about to leave her in the lurch.

'I shall show you up, Miss.'

Trying to compose herself, she followed the maid up the broad staircase. She attended to what was nearest her, the walls: they were panelled like the hall's, in a dark wood that might have been fumed oak.

She took care to keep in the middle of the blue runner. There were three sets of stairs to the first floor, with wide shallow treads. Two Chinese vases—big enough to hold umbrellas—stood, one apiece, in each of the two corners. The light from the windows at the front and rear of the house was silvery grey with mist, and made her think of a sea-glare.

Under her feet floorboards creaked; the maid, by comparison, seemed to know where to position herself so that she gave away no clues of her presence. On the second flight Helen looked back and noticed what she hadn't before, a clock standing in the hall, the pendulum dragging inside its case.

Ahead of her, upstairs on the gallery, the furnishings appeared just as discreet and timeless in their taste. There was another gilt mirror and a two-chair-back settee with an embroidered seat, and a sofa-table with a Chinese green celadon bowl placed at its centre. She smelt beeswax, and wondered how many pairs of hands it took to keep the house in its peerless condition.

The maid led the way across the gallery. A Chinese paradise blossomed under their feet. The celadon bowl, Helen noticed, was heaped with dead petals and leaves dried colourless and crisp.

Helen watched as the maid opened a panelled door and stood back to allow her to enter.

'The drawing-room, Miss.'

Helen inclined her head and passed through.

*

They were the sounds and smells of a hospital, she knew: although she hadn't been inside one since the day her mother passed away.

The first and last thing she remembered was the house, turned upside down and inside out, and the walls blazing. It had gone up like a fireball, and time seemed to falter, then to bend and melt, like the glass in the window softening to liquid and running down the frames.

She was still standing on a sill, about to jump: she would always be standing in the rectangle of flames waiting to make her jump.

Now—*now*—was nothing to her. They tried to feed her, but the food had no taste, like the air she didn't want to breathe, which she resisted and struggled against.

She only heard and smelt, and they were the sounds and perfume of death.

*

The maid retired, and the door of the drawing-room closed.

Helen stood looking about her. The choice of furniture showed the same impeccable fastidiousness on someone's part that she'd been aware of on her way upstairs. There was a gleaming secretaire chest in some mellow churchyard wood, and a handsome escritoire of what looked like walnut inlaid with holly patterns; some books lay on top of another sofa table; a fine pembroke table occupied the space between two of the three windows. Some sabre-leg chairs stood against the walls, and for comfort there was a wing chair and also a couple of armchairs fitted with plain, sky-blue covers. The walls were hung with several carved gilt mirrors, including a convex one topped with an eagle above the fireplace, and a few innocuous water-colours—of church towers, and vistas of hill and sky. Half of one wall was covered by a tapestry, sun-faded and fraying at its edges: it showed a medieval chase, men on horseback in pursuit with hounds, spectating women framed between the trunks of trees —and, in the top left-hand corner, almost out of the composition, a white hart with its back turned to safety, facing in the direction from which its hunters will shortly appear.

Helen found she was shaking her head. The hart must have been waiting like that, in expectation of its death, for hundreds of years.

Suddenly the visitor sensed there was another person in the room and swung round. A woman was watching her and closing the door with one arm stretched out behind her.

'Miss Wilmot?'

'Yes. Yes, that's right.'

'I am Miss Lazare.'

Helen manufactured a smile and took in as much of the woman's appearance as she could at a first glance. She was elegant, somewhat hawkish (her nose was the sort that used to be called 'Roman'), fine rather than attractive. She was dressed in peacock colours, amethyst and aquamarine. The clothes were in the style of another age, the 1920s: the prime of her life, to judge now from the grey hair and the lines Helen saw beneath the powder as they approached one another. She was sixty perhaps, at a guess.

'So you found us, Miss Wilmot?'

Helen felt she should be recognising something, some quality in the remark, but she couldn't think what.

'Yes, thank you,' she said.

'Please,'—Miss Lazare pointed—'be seated.'

Helen sat down on the armchair as requested; she sank into the soft cushions and noticed that her interlocutor knew better and was perched upright and stiff-backed on the edge of the cushion.

Helen smiled. Miss Lazare returned the gesture, then looked away towards a pier-glass on the wall behind the pembroke table. Helen followed her eyes and saw them both existing quite apart from themselves, in another dimension.

'I should explain, Miss Wilmot. This is *not* my house.'

Helen tipped her head, the gesture of actresses in films who are eager for answers.

'It—it isn't?'

'I am a "tenant" here. I "lost" my last home.' The significant words were given the appropriate stress.

'"Lost"?' Helen enquired.

'In the last night raid we had.'

Helen meant only to show polite interest.

'Where was it?' she asked, quite ordinarily, but feeling that the skin was pulling too tightly on her face. 'If it isn't—presumptuous—'

She thought Miss Lazare hesitated.

'No, it's not presumptuous. I used to live in Kensington. In Rawlinson Gardens.'

To Helen, the answer was known before she heard it. She had lived most of her life only three or four streets away, in an area that had taken the toll of history and fortune that night.

'Number Forty-Nine,' Miss Lazare told her. 'That was.'

The woman smiled bravely.

'I'm sorry,' Helen said. 'Others—' She paused. 'The same thing happened to *them*.'

'To you too?' Miss Lazare asked, seeming to hear the implication in the remark.

Helen took a few seconds to consider what her response should be.

'Yes,' she said. 'Yes. To me.'

'It happened to where you live, you mean?'

Helen delayed again.

'My father's house,' she said.

'You lived with your father?'

'Yes.'

'Where is he now?'

Helen didn't reply, she didn't know how to; she was at a loss for words. She only shook her head.

'I'm sorry,' Miss Lazare said. '*I* lost everything. All that I had.'

She looked up suddenly—Helen was watching her—and at that moment the handle turned on the door and the maid walked in, carrying a tray.

The conversation reached to other matters as tea was served in front of the banked fire: tea from a black collied pot, and a plate of wafer biscuits.

'This is chrysanthemum tea, Miss Wilmot.'

Helen smiled at the information and felt herself ready to luxuriate in the atmosphere.

'Yes,' she said.

She pulled herself up on the cushion of her chair; she sat forward, fingering the scarf at her throat.

'Please help yourself to a wafer, Miss Wilmot.'

'Thank you.'

'A friend sent them to me. They're from a pastrymaker's in Perugia, so I was reliably informed.'

Helen lifted one from the plate, savouring the unexpected pleasure in these depleted times.

'Thank you,' she said, smiling.

She sipped some of the fragrant tea from the eggshell china cup and bit into the thin, vanilla-flavoured wafer. She noticed Miss Lazare watching her and she thought it her right, in the circumstances. She also caught the faint, sallow ghost of a smile that flitted across her face.

*

Afterwards she was shown the work room, the dining-room.

The outlook was north this time: the light seemed less sharp, less clear, and colder. Beneath the windows a sizeable, formally arranged garden ran to a grey brick wall perhaps a hundred yards from the house: there were intersecting gravel walks and geometrically-shaped beds edged with miniature box privets. Very little was blooming, and it seemed to Helen a garden designed for the rigours of meditation.

The room was furnished with the same restrained good taste as the drawing-room. A large mahogany dining table occupied the centre; all except a couple of the shield-back chairs had been placed along the panelled walls. There was a six-legged sideboard, and a small ebony chiffonier inlaid with ivory and silver. Standard lamps and a pair of table lamps on the sideboard were provided for the purposes of illumination; there was none at the moment, but the fire in the grate already coloured the room with an amber glow. A stuffed owl under a glass dome stared beadily at her from the mantelpiece. A baize-topped card table supporting a typewriter had been positioned between the two windows as if in anticipation of the most suitable applicant.

'I don't want to lose track of anyone, Miss Wilmot. Do you understand?'

Helen nodded dutifully.

'Yes. Yes, of course.'

'I lost my address books, diaries, my letters. I've written out names.' Miss Lazare indicated some hand-written lists. 'Now—it's a matter of time, and patience: sifting through telephone directories, street directories, making enquiries.'

Helen looked attentive.

'Did I ask you, Miss Wilmot?—have you done such work before?'

Helen dropped her eyes to the table.

'Yes,' she said, quietly.

'You have?'

'Yes,' Helen repeated.

She lifted her eyes in time to see Miss Lazare's: they were contracting at the untruth. The two women smiled at each other.

'Would you like to begin now, Miss Wilmot? I shall show you what to do.'

Helen nodded.

'And tomorrow I shall expect you at ten o'clock.'

Helen felt her surprise must be advertising itself on her face.

'If that is convenient?'

'Oh. Yes. Yes, it is. Thank you.'

'Now you are—joining the ship. As it were.'

They exchanged looks of curiosity, then polite smiles. Helen dropped her eyes again to the table-top. In the seconds of awkward silence she knew she was being watched by the woman who was now her employer; she was being studied, she felt, as if she were some new and strange, disorientated form of life, finding herself in a place and situation where her sort had never chanced to stumble before.

*

Helen sat down. She picked up the loose sheets of paper and leafed through them.

The name was fourth or fifth from the top of one of the pages. '*Richard Wilmot*'.

She stared at it, very hard.

A question-mark had been placed alongside, then a line scored through that and the name.

A very straight line, maybe drawn with a ruler.

Another man than her father called 'Richard Wilmot', obviously.

Of course.

With a question-mark beside his name.

And now she was joining the ship.

As it were.

*

The white hotel sits high above the bay. Over banks of rhododendrons and azaleas views reach to the horizon, to the cloudy land mass of suffering France.

The situation is splendid, and not—this is the hotel's charm—exposed. The lawns are sheltered by windbreaks of shrubs; the lower gardens are stepped into the side of the cliff. Palms and ferns grow in profusion, and unrecognisable flowers bloom in the temperate conditions.

Since the War began, last year, custom has picked up: the hotel has become popular with Kensington and St John's Wood types, glad to get away for a break, and with officers and their wives enjoying a few days of leave together. The spot seems far from their other concerns.

For minutes at a time Helen can forget, sitting in the sunshine with her eyes closed. Her father sits beside her, reading a book. The table is laid for tea: China tea, as they used to drink it. The porcelain crockery is fine eggshell, the cups are wide and shallow, and offer themselves to be cradled in your hands. This afternoon she's tried to sketch the table-top of tea things but the light has been too bright for her and she knows the perspective is wrong. So she closes her eyes and forgets, with her father sitting beside her reading his book. She has brought her own, an Elizabeth Bowen novel, but sometimes the effort of concentration required is too much: those mandarin sent-

ences meander and contort their sense. There are easier writers, but that one always stands at an interestingly oblique angle to the characters she's writing about.

Helen opens her eyes again. Again she glances over to the table furthest from her, where the young man who's been watching them sits. He has anticipated her this time, and his eyes are on the newspaper in his lap. He is perusing the front page of his Times with the most diligent application. She keeps her eyes on him for another few seconds, before she turns them back to her father.

He likes coming here and the hotel and its grounds agree with him, she knows: his face becomes less tense, even the knotty veins in his temple seem to benefit: he moves more freely, he doesn't hold himself with his London rigidity. At home in Kensington he is an older man in those horsehair rooms he inherited from his mother; it never seems to her that they are the proper surroundings for a man whose profession is the history of art. (Less improper, though, than that barn of a building in damp, haar-cold Grantchester they used to visit, the home of another authority on Delacroix and Ingres and looking as if it had been furnished with the unsold lots from a house-clearing auction.)

Here on the coast her father is relieved of the responsibility of being who he is: someone whose reputation is known and respected only in particular and rarefied circles, but who feels he is obliged to live up to that ideal of himself even when there is only herself to see. He is quite handsome still, she thinks as she considers him: well-preserved for a man in his fifties. He still has his strength, and his build is as she has always remembered it. Then, for a disturbing few moments, she wonders how other women choose to regard him: the wives and widows and spinster daughters who mesh the hotel's public rooms with their eyes, raised from tea cups and crochet and books.

From inside the hotel she can hear the polite strains of the trio playing in one of the lounges. She listens, and recognises a Coward song.

'Quite for no reason I'm here for the season,
And high as a kite.'

Suddenly she turns her head and she catches him, the young man at the furthest table, who can't lower his eyes to the newspaper in time. She smiles when she sees his confusion. Then she looks away, towards the rhododendrons and azaleas and the tops of the palms, uncertain why she doesn't want to let her eyes rest longer, to claim their victory.

She is aware that her father has lifted his head from his book and is looking at her. This place, she tells herself, is crossed with such glances, like trip-wires.

She closes her eyes and pretends she has neither seen nor been observed. But in the luminous darkness behind her eyelids the two images recur and superimpose themselves on each other: the young man sitting at his table, his attention focused on her, and her father, reading and not reading, his thoughts for once adapting from the abstract to the particular.

*

As she walked away from the tall house, along Michaelmas Passage, Helen turned her head and looked back.

She saw the two women—Miss Lazare and the maid—standing together, unsmiling, at one of the drawing-room windows.

Their eyes were most particularly trained on her.

*

Nine bombs dropped that night.

It was established later that they'd fallen to the eighth and penultimate one.

She was up in her room, reaching into the tallboy drawer for the bangle he'd sent her and the sketch, when she heard the first whistle, louder than her father's shouts and the screams of strangers from the square. Too late, almost inconsequentially, she realised that she'd turned on the light to see by and had forgotten to cover the window.

Then came the quake, and she knew at once that the roof had been blown away and the walls behind her were collapsing.

With the first impact the whole upper portion of the house at the front must just have tumbled into the street, like toy bricks kicked over.

In her bedroom at the back the floor and ceiling juddered and she was knocked clean off her feet and thrown backwards. She was dazed for several seconds. Spread-eagled on her back, she looked up.

There was a huge, ridiculous hole in the opposite wall, the slubbed silk paper was in tatters, the ceiling dipped crazily and cracks were bursting it open. Through where her father's bedroom should have been, she could see the tops of trees and the white stucco fronts of houses on the far side of the square. Nonsensically the light bulb still shone above her in the dust-storm; it swung crookedly on its wire, with its shade at a tipsy angle.

It was another few seconds before the blaze started. She watched the flames suddenly roaring up the height of the house at the front. There was another quake, which must have been more of the building crumbling and falling on to the road. She could hear the last agonised screams of the people in the car they later found, crushed flat underneath. More of the roof collapsed, in a maelstrom of dust and dirt; through the hole she saw beams somersaulting down, dragging fire and trailing cascades of sparks.

She crawled uphill to the door, rubbing at her cuts and aches. She could hear the fire crackling at the bottom of the staircase and felt its vicious heat.

On her hands and knees she slithered back down the tilting floor, to the window at the back of the room. She was clear-headed enough, just, to know it was the only hope of escaping she had.

She scrambled to her feet, pitching forwards. She clutched at the curtains hanging from the broken pelmet and yanked them back. She found the sash cord and—choking for air—she tugged at it.

Nothing happened.

She grabbed at the handles of the window and pushed and pulled with all her strength. She shook the frame, battered it with her fists. The bottom sash was stuck fast.

She ran back into the room. Everything was on the floor, in a fog of dust and grime. She seized at a flex and pulled until a heavy gilt lamp base rolled out from beneath a chair. She lifted it; she took her aim, swinging it at the end of its cord—then, dodging back at the last second, she flung it at the window.

The glass exploded and flew everywhere. It covered her with a glitter like frost she hardly felt, like sugar coating on her soiled mackintosh.

She swung the lamp again—and again and again—at the biggest shards like icicles, till she knocked them out and they fell into the pit of garden.

She dropped the lamp. She looked over her shoulder and saw the front of the house—or where the front of their house should have been—being devoured in the blaze. Flames licked at the wall of her father's bedroom; through the hole she was being watched by a mad orange eye.

Above her the ceiling heaved. Suddenly the heat was baking her.

She climbed up on to the window-sill and stood balancing herself with her arms spread out, hands grasping the side of the sash. The garden was sombre and still, like a country garden, absurdly: only patterned here and there by the tragedy as shadows prettily flickered across it.

She heard voices, growing fainter but more terrible. Then the floor juddered again, the planks underneath were ripping and splitting and showering blocks of parquet round the room. Foul, ancient dust blew up.

She crouched into a ball with one hand holding on to the window frame, the other pulling an end of curtain over her head. There was a third great wrench in the structure of the house, which must have been the staircase falling in.

She tried standing up. The heat was clamped to her, like a burning second skin. She looked round again from the window and saw a blazing beam from upstairs filling the doorway. Black smoke was billowing in.

Her eyes stung. In seconds the sourness and stink was a metal claw pushing on her chest, wanting to pummel and pound the life out of her.

Up on the window-sill she raised herself a few delaying moments on the balls of her feet. With the tops of her fingers she kept her balance. Her eyes were streaming, and she closed them.

With her eyes still shut—one, two three—she jumped.

The last thing she was alive to was her body meeting a surface simultaneously taut and giving. In a split second she knew what was happening, she was passing through the conservatory roof. Like an aerial dive. There was a panic of cold colder than ice, then the searing sensation of some scorching heat, such a scalding deadly heat she could feel it like the thinnest, sharpest blade of a knife, slicing beneath her skin and carving it clean off the bone.

*

By contrast, her father must have died instantly.

*

At some point on the next morning she left her father sitting in a deck-chair on the top lawn and went walking in the hotel's grounds.

She took the sketchbook with her: she was conscious that her artistic ability, her being artistic, was one of the qualities by which people judged and interpreted her, 'read' her. She must, at the very least, look the part.

She also felt that her two years' training at the art school ought to *have equipped her for rather more than* this—*a sketchbook clutched under one arm as she followed the winding footpath on the cliffside —but she believed too that life hadn't properly declared itself to her yet, its colours still had to settle and fix.*

A light breeze had got up while she was on the terrace. She'd laid a white chiffon scarf on top of her hair and tied the ends loosely under her chin. Her father had asked her where she was bound for.

'I want to find a view.'

She'd watched his eyes alight on the sketchpad: not quite trusting her, she suspected.

'I've somewhere in mind, Father.'

Beneath the level of the top lawn she lost the polite melody of the string trio playing in the sun lounge. She descended into stillness.

The footpath serpentined downhill beneath the palms and sprays of tropical grasses.

She passed the oriental bamboo grove.

Somewhere close by, water dripped.

She found her spot, on a low wall beside the path, with a panorama through trees of the brilliant blue of the bay. She perched on the warm stone. She placed the sketch pad, closed, on her lap.

Unseen by her, the silent observer of the past few days stood studying her from a point on the cinder path further up. He watched as she lifted her face to the sun and untied the knot under her chin with a flick of her wrist. She shook out the scarf and laid it on the wall beside her, then she turned her attention to the vista of trees and sea and sky.

She opened her sketchpad. A breath of wind rustled the pages and spread them like a fan. She watched and let the pages open where they would. She was holding a pencil and scrutinised the point.

She looked away at the prospect. A yacht was crossing the bay, white sails bulging with wind. She tapped the pencil on her thumb, and seemed uncertain where and how to begin.

The sea glinted and sparkled. It met the sky on an invisible line of horizon, sweeping up into a fading shamiana of blue, like a tarpaulin to sail by.

At which moment it happened that the breeze returned. Beneath the wall the high pines creaked and, noticed only by the young man, the white chiffon scarf went flying.

In the event—as he told her afterwards—all he had to do was stretch out his arm and open his fingers to catch it. He stared, feeling like a vizier in a tale where people travel on carpets. The chances of his catching it must have been minimal, he realised: he took it to be an omen of the day's beneficence and good favour.

She looked up as she heard his footsteps approaching on the path. When she saw who it was, her eyes tightened.

'*Excuse me—*'

She closed the sketchpad.

'*I don't believe you've noticed,' he said, pausing and holding one arm behind his back. She relaxed the muscles of her face.*

'*I'm sorry?*'

The man brought his arm forward and showed her the scarf in his hand.

'*I might have decided to keep it—' he told her.*

She felt her cheeks were firing with embarrassment.

'*—if I weren't so scrupulously honest, that is.*'

She smiled, to make the remark seem not to matter to her at all.

'*The age of chivalry—' She cleared her throat and lowered her eyes to the scarf. '—isn't dead, I see.*'

He held out the scarf and she accepted it from him.

She placed it on top of the sketch-pad.

She heard the silence of the garden: like a hole opening up around them.

'*Why should you have kept* this*?' she asked him, and ventured a smile as she glanced up at him.*

He shrugged, looking down at her.

She turned her head. She simply nodded, feeling the heat on her cheeks.

'*I'll remember the sunshine,' he said. 'And that music they're always playing.*'

Her eyes returned to him. She asked the question before she could consider the wisdom of it.

'*You're on leave?*'

He clicked his heels together. 'Awaiting my instructions!' he replied, in a pretend-pukka accent with a bull-in-his-mouth.

She smiled, less gauchely.

He glanced past her, to the pines and the sea, and the soft perfect blue of sky that was only a trick of multiple aeons of gaseous light, an absence of true verifiable colour.

He stood watching, concentrating for the moment on that vacuous element of absolutely nothing, while Helen, sitting on the wall, watched him with all her powers of attention.

Far beneath them, on a branch of one of the pine trees, a single songbird twittered, briefly filling the cliffside with sound as if the garden were an echo-box.

*

Helen woke in another year, she sprang up in her bed.

She stared ahead at the shapes and masses gathered in the room.

Why was she here?

Then, through translucent strata of time, she remembered, in the middle of this night.

*

The next morning she made her way back through the confusion of weather to 'Michaelmas Passage'.

With a start she saw the same man in the warden's uniform whom she'd asked for directions the day before. She kept her eyes trained in front of her and walked straight past him.

It occurred to her as she crossed the street—feeling the man's eyes were on her—that she ought not to risk the narrow pathway between the buildings a second time.

She paused at the entrance to the lane to take courage, then —unsure of whether she did right or wrong—she walked forward.

Between the high walls she listened to the echoes of her heels on the uneven stones and seemed to be hearing two people, herself and another.

It was an illusion, of course, it could only be, and she tried smiling, to keep up her spirits.

*

A whistle of screaming air, like her inside being pulled out through her ears, then rubble flying and an orange flame scaling the wall like a genie.

Voices were wrapping words round her.

A

     Couple

            Of

               Days

                    We're

                         Just

                              Waiting.

*

Helen stood at the dining-room window.

Miss Lazare was outside in the walled garden, walking on one of the gravel paths. She was sombrely dressed, in a black coat and a black hat with a shallow bowl and broad rim, like a fedora.

She had been traversing the gravel for several minutes, quite slowly, this way and that. She was looking down at her black shoes, as if it was *their* choice where she walked next.

Helen couldn't decipher her expression from this distance. All she was able to tell was that she wasn't smiling. She was like someone burdened, with a possibility or a memory or a secret that was weighing like a stone on her conscience.

She turned, this way and that; she would walk for so many steps before she changed direction again.

It was hard to believe that she had the freedom of this house, Helen thought, to do—in theory, at least—whatsoever she wished. She wasn't a captive confined behind the wall with no command of her circumstances; she wasn't a prisoner obliged to tread those mathematically-plotted gravel paths between the flower beds as some compulsory method of exercise.

So why, Helen asked herself as she watched from the window, why should she now be having any doubts on the matter, when she had been willing to take it on trust from the beginning—from the first moment of reading the newspaper notice in Pandora's Tea Rooms —that this gentlewoman must be a superior being empowered with the management of her own destiny?

*

Over the top of his book Mr Wilmot saw them returning and the young man taking his leave.

His eyebrows drew together as he resumed the story of Washington Square.

Later, as Helen walked with him on the top lawn, he tackled the subject.

'Talking,' Helen answered in reply to his question. 'We were just talking.'

'Talking about what, *might I ask?'*

'About this and that.'

Helen let her father take her arm under his.

'And is this to become a habit? You are to go about talking to strangers?'

'But who's a stranger and who isn't a stranger?'

As the words left her mouth she wasn't sure what she meant by the remark.

The tic pulled in her father's cheek.

'I'm twenty, Father, almost twenty-one,' she said. 'This is the nineteen *forties. Plenty of women have left home by my age.*'

'But—' Her father's voice curved against her cheek, as if it meant to trick her. 'But you *haven't?*'

She drew her head away.

'Do you mean you'd want *me* to?' she asked.

'You didn't say anything about leaving home.'

'When?'

'When you went to art school.' His arm still held hers. 'It makes practical sense for you to be where you are, Helen. With me.'

He shook his head.

'This is a foolish conversation,' he said. 'A foolish day. A foolish time to be living through.'

They continued walking. They both turned their heads at the same moment to the view of scintillating sea.

'Here,' Helen said, 'it's so far away. For a while.'

She filled herself with that vista of blues, colours running into one spectacular, bedazzling melt, a vast silver sheen on the sky.

'Will there ever be an end to all this?' she asked.

Her father laid his hand on her wrist.

'We can only live,' he said, 'as normally as we can.'

Behind them both, at a discreet distance, the young man stood on the terrace; he failed to see the outlook of glittering sea and sky, his eyes otherwise sun-blinded.

*

The door of the dining-room opened and Helen swung round in her chair. Miss Lazare stepped into the room.

Helen looked towards the window: it seemed only seconds before that she'd been watching her pacing the gravel path.

Miss Lazare walked over to the fireplace. She held out her hands. 'Heat!' she said, directing her eyes at the table as she passed.

Helen smiled unsurely, too brightly, and she felt her effusiveness was another minor deceit committed.

For the next few seconds Miss Lazare seemed to be looking right through her. Helen shifted uncomfortably in her chair.

Miss Lazare turned back to the fire in the grate.

'How are you faring?' she asked.

'Quite—' Helen rustled some papers busily. 'Quite well, thank you.'

'You have everything you want?'

'Yes, thank you.'

'Miriam will bring you something to eat.'

Instinctively Helen wanted to refuse.

'I—I don't eat much. Thank you.'

'But we must attend to your needs, Miss Wilmot. Luncheon *and* tea.'

Miss Lazare looked over her shoulder at her new social secretary.

'Tea is a ritual here, Miss Wilmot.'

She smiled very briefly.

'We do have a system for our days. Although—technically—I am only a tenant of this house, and Miriam alone has the running of it. Things being as they are, you understand?'

Helen thought herself called upon to nod.

'System, Miss Wilmot. If I didn't take care to organise our activities here, then chaos might—very probably *would*—ensue. Or disillusion, or despair.'

To Helen the words had a ready-made ring to them. She wondered if perhaps she wasn't the first 'social secretary' after all, and someone else had sat here at this table obliged to listen as she was doing.

'Everything has its place,' Miss Lazare continued, moving back from the fire. 'Let us say, we are choosing to be wise *before* the event.'

She smiled again—the same brief smile—and recrossed the room. Helen followed her with her eyes.

'Now, Miss Wilmot, I have to leave the house in the afternoon. Miriam will bring you tea.'

Helen felt it only courtesy to reply. She wasn't sure that she wanted looking after, having to accord to someone else's ritual.

'Thank you,' she replied, and heard her own insincerity.

'Chrysanthemum tea, Miss Wilmot. Don't forget.'

Miss Lazare stopped before the table, blocking the light from one of the windows. Her shadow fell across the table, on to the papers.

Helen stooped over her work. She pretended to be consulting the index of a street directory.

After a pause—a considering one, Helen felt—Miss Lazare passed on her way and the shadow lifted from the table. The door closed.

Immediately Helen turned and looked back, towards the window which had the better panorama of the garden, where she'd stood earlier watching.

Puzzlement at something which she couldn't determine was drifting like a woolly grey nimbus among all the other thoughts in her head.

*

At four o'clock, as the clock struck downstairs, Miriam brought tea into the dining-room. An echo of chimes reached them from outside.

Helen watched the girl lay the tray of tea things on a small table beside the fire and noticed for the first time that she was quite shapely under her maid's black pinafore.

'You didn't eat much of your lunch, Miss Wilmot.'

'I—I wasn't very hungry, I'm afraid.' It was a lie. 'Settling in . . .'

'We're not troubled with the rations here.' The information was offered very matter-of-factly.

'I shall try better.'

'Take some tea, Miss Wilmot. The mistress is very particular.'

'Yes, I shall. Thank you.'

'She's gone out.'

Helen put down her pen.

'Yes,' she said.

The maid stood studying this new recruit to what her mistress had called 'the ship'.

'Will that be all?' she asked.

Helen crossed her arms on the table top; for some reason she was embarrassed—she felt she was required to be embarrassed—by the question.

'Yes,' she said. 'Yes, thank you. Everything—'

She didn't finish. The maid passed in front of her and made her exit from the room.

Helen sat looking at the door for several seconds. Then she stood up and walked across to the side-table next to the fire. She lifted the collied pot, hesitated, then poured.

She picked up the saucer and cup. Why chrysanthemum tea, with its slightly fusty, greenhouse taste?

She put the cup to her lips and tasted.

Her face clouded.

*

The sun shining on the white walls of the hotel makes Helen's eyes ache. She and Burton slowly tread a straight line across the top lawn.

'You seem to know this part,' she said.

'Well, I was born not far from here. About a dozen miles away.'

'Did you grow up here too?'

'Till I went to school. And it was home when I came back. I knew it less well then.'

'Do your family—'

'Nobody lives here now.'

'Oh.'

'I just thought I'd come back.'

'You used to come here? To this town?'

'When I was small, for the day, to play on the beach. Sometimes I cycled down.'

'While I was—' She smiled to remember. '—I don't know what —looking at the fossils in the Natural History Museum. Or my father was showing me improving paintings.'

'Weren't they?'

'"Improving"? Not—not morally. They improved my "aesthetic sense" perhaps. I'm not sure what the point of that was. When there was going to be a war at the end of it—to complete my education.'

The lawn sloped steeply and their legs ran away with them down the ramp. They laughed, and Helen gulped for breath.

'It's quite close by,' Burton said.

'I—I'm sorry?'

'The village where I used to live. I could show you.'

Helen's smile stuck.

'And I could show you Cloud Hill.'

She didn't recognise the name.

'That's the hill,' he said. 'The village is at the bottom.'

'Oh.'

'Come and see it. Won't you?'

'I . . .'

'You've got to see Cloud Hill. It wouldn't take long.'

'I don't—'

'We'll go in the car. I've got petrol. We could make a picnic of it. You can see three shires from the top. It's bound to be clear.'

Burton's face composed itself and a more serious expression replaced the smile.

'We should use our time,' he said.

Helen cleared her throat.

'I'd like to go, really.'

'Well, then?'

'I'm not sure,' she said.

'You're "not sure"?' He sounded crestfallen, dispirited.

'I—'

She looked at him, deliberating.

Then she nodded, slowly. Her smile reappeared.

'I—I would *like* to go, yes,' she said. 'Yes.'

He caught her smile and the seriousness lifted, the moment was floated free.

'That's settled, then,' he said. He was buoyant again, she saw, recovered.

'Nothing more to be said,' he told her. 'We're going to Cloud Hill.'

She smiled, but warily. Immediately afterwards an instinct caused her to look back over her shoulder, up the fall of cropped lawn towards the hotel.

As she stood looking, trying to find which room was her father's, her eyes started to hurt and blur with the glare off the white walls, but she hardly even noticed. In the weeks that followed, though, she did remember: then it seemed to her that pain and impaired vision must always have been the unconscious condition of her life.

*

Her father had attempted to educate her in artistic matters.

'It's a matter of seeing, Helen. Knowing how to. Opening your eyes and seeing what is truly there.'

Sometimes it had seemed to her that that wasn't what he meant at all, that 'seeing' and 'knowing' had to do with what lay behind the picture, in the historical details of biography.

But he was talking in a general sense, she knew, and it hadn't all to do with Delacroix and Ingres and Watteau and David and the paintings he sometimes took her along to examine in dank, unheated, ill-lit country houses. ('Palaces of Wind, Helen, as Coleridge would say.')

It was as an attitude to life that he meant it, and so she understood: that people only live with the familiar, inside a circle of activities reduced to a routine. They look with their eyes, but what they see tells them nothing; it adds not a whit to whatever comprehension they already have.

Sometimes she'd thought she needed glasses because her head would ache when she read too late in the evening, and among the contraptions in the oculist's consulting rooms, with the outside world curtained off behind heavy green velvet drapes, she'd realised as she hadn't before how complex was the mechanical miracle of sight, that it wasn't to be abused or made so abysmally little of.

The oculist had advised against glasses, and her father had told her the judgment confirmed the man to be honest at least. 'Don't read for longer than ninety minutes at a stretch by artificial light' was the oculist's prescription for the headaches. 'During the day,' her father suggested, 'sit by a window if you have close work. Every so often lift your eyes and look outside.'

So she had done. She had developed the habit of trying to look beyond herself.

Once she had let a palmist in the street study her hand and the expression in her eyes was a magus's searching for stars. The woman had mumbled, told her she had laryngitis and couldn't speak, and handed her her money back.

The title of the paper her father was working on when the bomb dropped and killed him had happened, by no accident, to be 'The Unobscured Vision of Bastien-Lepage'.

*

The scene needed figures.

Helen lifted her eyes from the page in front of her to the sunlit lawn outside.

It was the palms she was having most difficulty with. Through the window they had a density and there-ness they didn't have on the sheet of paper; as they were drawn they looked as if she must have imagined them, half-remembered them, with the leaves too light and fragile and feathery.

But those hot weather trees had outlasted transplanting to another hemisphere and the very worst English winter salt-storms.

'I really—'

She held the crayon tightly between her fingers as her father started to speak. He had been untypically quiet, monosyllabic, at lunch and she'd known her announcement had taken him quite by surprise.

'—I really do not think this is—at all suitable—*behaviour, Helen.'*

She swallowed.

'Actions,' he said, 'actions have to be seen *to be correct.'*

He had seated himself in the chair behind her. She wasn't sure how, perched on the window-seat, she was going to maintain her composure. She would have preferred them to be discussing the matter, not in a bedroom, but in one of the hotel's numerous public rooms: then she could have believed she was only meaning to do as anyone else might have done in her situation. Alone with her father she always lost confidence in herself.

'They must be seen to be correct, Helen.'

She knew she had to feign unconcern, that the incident shouldn't be allowed to overwhelm and depress her, it was gossamer stuff.

'It's only to look at Cloud Hill,' she said, lightly enough. 'I don't expect—I don't expect we'll stay long.'

Her father's reply was—ominously—delayed.

'It seems to me you have made up your mind already.'

She stared hard at the crayon.

'He asked me,' she said.

There was a longer pause before her father began his persuasion in earnest.

'I have had to be two parents to you, Helen.'

'Yes,' she said quietly. 'Yes, I know that.'

'I really—I really do not believe that your motoring to this place would be in anyone's best interest.'

She held the point of the crayon above the paper.

'It's wartime,' she said.

Her father sighed.

'Might I ask what that has to do with the matter?'

'Everything will—' She hesitated. '—be seen—to have been different.' She concentrated on the tip of the crayon. 'Different,' she repeated.

'What do you mean?'

'I mean—I mean that no one knows. About what's going to happen to them.'

'That doesn't excuse anything,' her father rejoined.

She felt her face sharpening, honing to a point.

'Don't you trust me?' she asked.

The question seemed to momentarily confuse her father.

'I—' He coughed into the back of his hand. 'Those fellows—with that kind of life—'

'He's fighting for our King and Country, Father.'

'Soldiers, I mean. Or airmen. In his case.'

She knew what her reply must be.

'Yes, Father. But that's—"circumstances".' The crayon cut across the page. 'There are thousands having to fight, hundreds of thousands—'

Her father sighed again.

'But they come back—on leave—and they think—they think they're all heroes.'

She smiled.

'Oh no,' she said.

'Oh yes,' her father replied, quite firmly. 'Oh yes. Home from the sea, home from the field. Except that it's the air. It's as old as legend and myth. Homer.'

Helen shook her head at the comparison.

'Not Homer, Father. Cloud Hill. He was brought up near it.'

'And he can't leave the past alone, I suppose?'

Helen's eyes lifted from the page. She looked sideways at her father.

'He just wants to show me,' she said, speaking plainly and distinctly.

'And so the two of you go gallivanting off?'

Helen looked away again. Was there any point in continuing? Was any good to come from resisting him?

My father, hallowed be thy name, thy will be done, till kingdom come.

And there—when she looked—they were, on the page: two figures sketched in, crossing the top lawn, crossing it on that wayward diagonal, inhabiting the scene and recomposing it around themselves, lending it scale and perspective like a third dimension: the 'human interest' was there too, of a kind, and reason and imagination must be equally satisfied.

*

'This evening a friend is calling by, Miss Wilmot. We shall be having a glass of sherry. Would you care to join us?'

Helen was caught unawares. She had closed her mind to any invitation of a social nature.

'I—'

'My friend will be leaving early, so you shan't be detained, I'm sure.'

'I—It's—'

'It's no inconvenience, Miss Wilmot. I feel I must offer you

Her father pointed, to the peeling wall behind the altar.

'There, Helen, can you see?'

She took several steps forward, out of the sunlight flooding the nave.

'Yes,' she said. 'Yes, I can see it.'

The scene, pre-Perugino, materialised on the stone. The colours were pale, bleached by centuries of sun.

The disciples sat at a long table, and Christ presided in the some hospitality, and this is an opportunity.'

Helen nodded.

'Perhaps I should be offering you dinner. I'm convinced that you don't eat enough, Miss Wilmot. Another time? Let us say my concern for you is a practical one.'

Helen smiled.

'Now that you know we shan't detain you unnecessarily, I shall tell Miriam—'

And so the matter was settled.

middle. Some of the details were lost, where the plaster had flaked away, but the whole was there in its essence, and Helen wondered how she could have failed to see.

From another part of the church she heard singing. The meticulous harmonies of the plainsong and the sight in front of her and the enveloping warmth from the stone kept her rooted to the spot.

In the unalloyed pleasure of the moment she turned round to find her father.

He stood several feet away, viewing her as if—as if she were an object herself.

She felt herself colouring.

For a few seconds he seemed not to realise. He wasn't looking at her face, but at her legs, her bottom under her skirt. His eyes were very tight in his face, and —she thought—hard.

Then as his eyes moved upwards he noticed she was looking at him. His eyes opened wide, then it was his turn to colour.

Immediately she turned away to save him his embarrassment. Mystified on this Umbrian afternoon.

*

At ten o'clock the next morning she was ready for Cloud Hill. She waited inside the hotel's vestibule until she saw the car, then she pushed through the revolving doors and walked out on to the top step.

He approached slowly, having to negotiate the other cars parked along the crescent driveway. She took her time walking down the steps, preparing the first words she would say to him. After spending at least half of the past hour in front of mirrors, she knew she looked not like her usual self, and she felt a little unreal and unsteady. She'd tried to persuade herself that today she wasn't Helen Wilmot, she was a stranger to her ordinary self, as if she might be reassured on that account. Now, as the moment approached, she realised this other, rounder-faced person she had become was as nervous of what was to follow as her father's sharper-featured daughter she'd left upstairs.

The car drew up in line with the bottom step. She smiled in response to the smile from inside, the most brilliant smile she could manage. The passenger door opened and she felt that, after all, events were as easy and painless and unthinking as in a dream.

So it seemed for a few seconds as she paused, to try to make the realisation last, the smile still bright.

It was as she reached the second bottom step that her confidence (if it was) left her. An instinct caused her to look back.

The revolving doors were turning and she watched, unsurprised, as her father emerged: the stranger's father too, it transpired.

He stood looking down at her. Their eyes met—then his looked past her, to the waiting car.

Behind her she felt the keenness of the third pair of eyes as they watched the confrontation. She saw muscles pulling in her father's neck and she understood they'd both of them come to a point where none of the familiar markers applied any more.

The car's engine throbbed beneath the bonnet flaps. Time seemed to stutter as she hesitated, caught between her father and the man with the means to transport her somewhere else. She was conscious that, for the second time she could remember in her life, she was being offered a choice, an option of alternatives, and she had to decide alone.

Behind her, the engine thrummed. Looking up the flight of shallow steps she saw how the veins in her father's temple and forehead stood out.

She occupied the middle ground, between what seemed to her now to be two different lives.

*

Miss Lazare's friend had a look of long-ago, even before that of her own hey-day. She was wearing a violet silk dress edged with black lace, and a musquash wrap; her thinning grey hair had been finger-set in marcel waves. She held her head very straight and still and her long jet earrings hardly moved as she spoke—Helen was fascinated to watch.

Her name was Miss Somerville. She lived in Bath.

'But nowhere is safe now, Miss Wilmot,' the visitor explained. 'I feel as safe here in London, I think, as I do in my own city.'

Helen nodded sympathetically.

'I fear we've suffered badly, my dear.'

'Do you know James Saunders?' Miss Lazare asked. 'Oh—but he's in Bristol.'

'We're not far from Bristol. I know a number of people there—but not *your* gentleman.'

'It just occurred to me that you might.'

'In Bath there's rubble strewn across some of the streets.'

Miss Lazare shook her head.

'Vandalism, Evelyn.'

'Do you know Bath, Miss Wilmot?'

'I—I've been there. With my father. It's—very—'

'If there's time left, you must come and see my house.'

'My friend has a beautiful house, Miss Wilmot.'

'But I expect your services here are indispensable, my dear, are they not?'

'Certainly I'm very grateful to have Miss Wilmot on the premises, Evelyn.'

Several seconds of silence followed.

'If I might say so, Lavinia, I think you have ordered things very well here.'

'I feel I must do *some*thing, I must make a start.'

'Is—is Miss Wilmot of the same persuasion as ourselves?'

Helen looked between the two women, who were both watching her.

'I think she—she sees the wisdom of it. Do you not, Miss Wilmot?'

Helen demurred, then mumbled 'yes'.

'I don't think Meredith and her crowd care, not really,' Miss Lazare continued. 'They still carry on as they did before. They see no reason to change the habits of a lifetime just because—'

Miss Somerville said 'of course', and nodded her head sagely.

'Well, that's one way of looking at the business,' Miss Lazare declared. 'Their lives were like parties before. Meredith, God bless her, was never one to give up easily.'

'Not Meredith!' Miss Somerville said, and laughed.

'Now, Evelyn—Miss Wilmot—I think we require a little more alcoholic sustenance. Notwithstanding.'

'*Notwithstanding*'? The conversation was beyond Helen's grasp.

She thought some words were being very quietly and discreetly exchanged as Miss Somerville followed their hostess to the drinks table: probably a pitying explanation of her own father-less condition. Old friends enjoyed 'sotto voce' confidences—she used to watch her father muttering remarks to his, which weren't intended for her hearing. Maybe the true pity of her situation, even more than her now being alone and homeless, was never having had the confidantes to trust with the private and personal information she might have wanted to entrust to them.

*

From the top of Cloud Hill Burton pointed to where the three shires lay.

Afterwards—walking a little way downhill—they found a sheltered vantage point protected from the wind, and ate the contents of the picnic hamper.

When they'd finished Helen tidied up. Burton suggested they stay on awhile. He told her they should enjoy the view.

It was a magnificent prospect. The country unrolled like a crinkled vellum map, to far woollen forests. Closer to, toadstool trees fastened down the fields like buttons. Streams were like slashes in the green, to the silver under-lining. Toy villages lay beneath them, ready to be rearranged at their will and returned to a box when they had both done with them.

They were sitting a few feet apart on the grass. Burton rolled up his sleeves; he offered her the use of his straw sunhat, but she declined with a smile.

That gave her an idea and for several minutes she sketched him in the hat, reclining on one arm.

She showed him the result. He approved. She closed the sketchbook hurriedly, she didn't know why.

'There are rings beneath the grass,' Burton said, nodding over his shoulder. 'Like ramparts. Centuries and centuries old. Tens of centuries.'

She shook her head incredulously at the information.

'They used to worship the sun from up here. And did whatever else they did.'

'What was that?' she asked. 'Do you know?'

'Probably a little side-line in sacrifices. As was their wont.'

'Here?'

'It must have been meat and drink to them. If that's the expression. But Death—it wasn't an abstract. Just the passage to somewhere else. A corridor.'

'In life we are in the midst of death?' she said.

'I suppose so.'

'What a gloomy conversation.'

'Let's stop, then.'

'Yes.'

They both smiled: he first, then her.

'We don't need to talk,' Burton said.

'No—'

'Anyway—I used to feel this place didn't want you to.'

'How do you mean?'

'I used to feel a great silence lived here. And words weren't any use, because they couldn't describe it.'

'Silence?'

'As mysterious as history is.'

'We mustn't talk about history again—'

'It was as if this place knew all about the past and also knew all about what was going to happen. Somehow it was—it was outside time. And here you were in another element.'

Helen smiled, cautiously.

'I think it's a beautiful place,' she said. 'To look at. I should never have known about it if you hadn't brought me.'

Burton shook his head.

'No,' he said. 'No, perhaps you wouldn't.'

They continued to sit apart, listening to the chirruping of insects in the grass.

Helen leaned forward, tracing the outline of a pink's petals with her fingertip.

'But I did wrong,' she said.

'What's that?'

Burton stretched back on one elbow; with his other hand he pulled down the brim of his straw sunhat.

'Coming,' she said quietly: speaking so low that she knew he wouldn't be able to hear her.

'Thomas Hardy,' Burton began, 'when he was old he remembered being a child, wearing a big sunhat. Pulling it down and trying to

*make himself invisible. Peering through the weave of straws: seeing
but not being seen.'*

Helen smiled.

'It has been a lovely afternoon,' she said. 'Really.'

Burton heard the remark. He pulled himself up.

*'I hope there'll be others,' he said, turning back the hat's brim.
'You don't seem—I don't know—you don't seem sure.'*

*Helen picked a stalk of cow-parsley and shook it in front of her
face as a fly-whisk.*

'Nothing's sure,' she said. 'Nothing's ever that, is it?'

Burton sat up and clasped his knees.

'You're very English, Helen. Very restrained.'

She examined the head of cow-parsley.

*'This is England,' she said. 'Deep England. I haven't seen as much
of the world as you have.'*

'But you can imagine it, can't you?' he asked her.

'Can I?' she replied, and laughed.

*'Oh yes. You've an interesting head inside. I knew that straight-
away.'*

Helen shrugged her shoulders.

'Well, well,' she said.

*Burton fell on to his back. He folded his hands under his head and
lay looking up at the sky.*

'This is the highest point for miles. And miles, and miles.'

*Helen gazed down across the near distance of fields and copses. A
long black car was moving like a Dinky model along a twisting
ribbon of red road. A church wore its steeple like a dunce's cap.*

*'I like the height,' Burton said. 'Nothing—nothing seems impossi-
ble on a good day.'*

Helen sat on her heels watching him.

'Why Cloud Hill?' she asked.

*'I don't know. Maybe one'll appear and come down—and trans-
port us, safe into the blue beyond? Do you think?'*

'I shouldn't mind if it did,' she said, happy to be saying the words.

*'No.' Burton rolled on to his side and looked over at her. 'No,
neither would I.'*

*On an instinct Helen avoided his glance. She reached out her hand
and retrieved her sketchbook. She didn't want to lose any single part
of the day, she wanted to forget nothing of what was happening to
her.*

*

She is living in a house with a thatched roof and pink plaster walls, in a glade of autumn trees. Smoke curls lazily from a chimney. In the dip between hills behind the house lies the sea.

She is always outside this house as well as inside. She sees everything, herself included, with an objective eye. She sees herself as her husband does, because she believes *she* knows him better than he knows himself. She feels her spirit is everywhere, in this house with pink walls that is her delight and dream of a home.

She remembered the view from a journey on a train. She had sat looking up at the panel of sepia photographs beneath the luggage rack, at one in particular, which showed a cottage with plaster walls, set in a glade of autumn trees. Smoke was curling lazily from a chimney. In the dips between hills behind the house lay the sea.

In the frame of mind she found herself in that day the view was suddenly familiar to her, she was looking at her journey's end.

She lifted the sketch again to the light. It was a passable likeness. But now she had nothing to compare it with, and the image had become the actual.

She listened to what she could hear through the curtains of Holborn's nocturnal life. She'd passed through in the mornings and afternoons on the days when she had classes, and the place had intrigued her. The dusty streets and the vegetable barrows and the women in turbans and men in shirt-sleeves always seemed to have nothing to do with the life she came from and returned to. Some of the students had rooms in the area and spoke of it either affectionately or disrespectfully, but never without some feeling. She thought that there you must be put in the way of life's buffetings and you couldn't hope to be indifferent to the experience.

And now, somehow, here she was.

She laid the sketch carefully in the drawer and pushed on the handle, and Christopher Burton, wearing his Thomas Hardy sunhat, was returned to the darkness.

*

A marble knight and his lady and another knight lay, hands clasped, on the tops of their memorials.

Burton told her they'd gone down to the plague and childbirth and the Saracen.

'They say the abbey's haunted.'

She turned and looked at him.

' "Haunted"?' she repeated.

'So they say.'

'Don't you believe it?'

'Look at their faces—'

She stopped and examined the woman's thin, bony features.

'I don't think,' he said, 'they would have given up without a struggle. Do you?'

'Why should they haunt us, though?'

'I suppose, because we can see their faces.'

For several seconds Helen was silent, and thoughtful.

'Maybe it's we who haunt them,' she said. 'Just being here. And they have to go through it all again.'

' "Through it"?'

'The plague, and the child-bearing, and the Crusades. All just for our benefit.'

She nodded her head, agreeing with what she'd just said.

'That's their fate,' she told him. 'For as long as this abbey stands.' She smiled at her words. 'Alive for half-a-century. And another seven centuries of never being allowed to forget.'

She walked past the marble Crusader. She glanced at the pressed palms, and at a butterfly that had settled on his right hand gauntlet, and she wondered for how many years she would have the memory of today, their day together, he in his Thomas Hardy straw hat, she in cream cotton.

*

'A few weeks sometimes.'

'That long?'

'If they've courage for it.'

' "Courage"?'

'To hold out.'

'Or "cowardice"?'

'Whichever. It's a manner of speaking.'

'How much longer?'

'Some days. Perhaps.'

*

'Here is your Mr Burton, Helen.'

Helen and her father were standing in the palm court making the first of the arrangements of the day: when they would meet for lunch, after Helen had done some sketching and after her father had had his hair cut by the hotel barber.

Mr Wilmot beat his book against his leg.

'I thought our paths might cross.'

Helen looked between the two men. She had been trying to make her plans for the morning sound casual and untoward, straining to keep her voice steady.

Burton nodded.

'Good morning, sir.'

Helen watched her father draw himself up straight.

'Good day,' he said, in what she recognised was his chilliest tone, calculated to repel.

With that he walked off. Helen and Burton were left looking after him, then at each other.

'I expect it's yesterday? Cloud Hill?'

'Yes. Yes, I'm afraid it is.'

'Maybe it brings it back to him?' Burton suggested.

'"Brings it back"?'

'Going places. With your mother.'

Helen looked over into one of the room's ferny corners.

'I don't know. Sometimes I think I don't understand him at all. Not as I should.'

They stood back, to allow a couple of elderly guests to pass, and were conscious of two pairs of squinnying eyes claiming them.

'I—'

Burton lowered his voice. The room caused strange and unexpected echoes.

'A letter came this morning,' he said. 'A War Office letter, I mean.'

Helen stared at him. 'Oh.'

'It's—Well, it's pretty sudden. I've got my flying orders.'

'Your flying orders?' she repeated, in a voice she didn't trust to hold.

'They're talking about Burma—maybe. Fleet Air Arm stuff. I've got to report back.'

'Wh—when?'

'As soon as possible. I'm taking the train up, tomorrow morning.'

Helen nodded.

'I was wondering,' she heard him say. 'If you would have dinner with me tonight? Please. It won't be like the Ritz—'

She gulped noisily, only meaning to swallow.

'I—'

'Can you?' he asked.

She shook her head.

'My aunt—my father's sister—' She paused for breath. 'She telephoned us yesterday. To—' She stared at a point on the shoulder of his jacket. 'She—she's asked us to visit. For dinner, this evening.'

She was trying to keep her face straight, not to let it show what she was feeling, not to flag her distress to him. But she couldn't, and her composure broke.

The room swam, tilted with all its ridiculous ferny and palmy frondescence. She felt his hands on her arms, he was supporting her.

'Just tonight,' he was asking her.

'I can't,' she was telling him.

'I must see you.' He spoke the words quickly. 'Down in the cove. Beneath the garden. After dinner, then. Whenever you like. Midnight. I'll wait. There'll be moonlight—'

'He—he said we have to.' The voice she was hearing wasn't hers: it cracked and wouldn't hold. 'He said—'

'There won't be time tomorrow,' he was telling her.

She knew that, she knew.

He leaned closer, till she could feel his breath on her ear, the words hot and curling their way inside, into the tubes, into the tunnels of memory.

'There's no time,' he was saying. 'There's no time—'

*

Somehow she was back at the card-table in Miss Lazare's dining-room, in the house that wasn't properly Miss Lazare's.

The morning's task was typing replies to letters from friends, social invitations (some of them declined) and a batch of enquiries from suppliers keen to have such a faithful customer's favour again.

It was unthinking work, except when a word would catch her up every so often and she would have to peer closely at the script and try to come on the term from various angles. The replies were largely formal and automatic. Even the letters to friends had a strangely disinterested and uninvolved air, as if they were really only by way of a receipt: they seldom suggested a meeting, and imparted relatively little about her present circumstances. What information there was was conveyed in stilted, spindly prose: 'This house in Michaelmas Passage is merely a temporary arrangement, although for how long I am bound to be here, I cannot say. But you, Sybil, know about such matters as well as I: all of us being, as it were, in that same boat together.'

While she typed Helen was occasionally aware of her eyebrows meeting and her brow furrowing, puzzled as to what manner of solace the letters gave to recipient and sender. It was with the stricken—those in the same position as herself—that her employer seemed most in accord: was she envious of those whose lives had been less dramatically altered by events than hers? A few times she mentioned friends who had been 'lost', 'taken from us, but not —thank God—for ever'. Others, surviving the common trials with good grace and clearly hale and hearty in spite of all, were seen to have fewer claims on her now, their appeal was dimmed and diminished—'Beatrice, I've only just noticed after all these years, flitters about on the surface of things', 'I spotted WW one day, just in passing; she looked indecently well, I thought, glowing with the knowledge that she's in the rudest of health, as if her mind could think of nothing much else', 'It's so odd that Gilbert can only talk about how much this now costs, or that, and do you remember when it used to cost only so much, those were the good old days. If he had any sense he would be grateful but I sometimes wonder if that isn't a wholly false premise'.

At least the letters weren't too prudently discreet, and it made the job a little more interesting than it might otherwise have been. To Beatrice and WW and Gilbert, the disapproval was concealed: the letters talked blandly of Chelsea, made vague social gestures, they must meet when she had her affairs sorted out, when she could plot her activities by a diary, when she returned (her favourite delaying tactic) from the country.

The clatter of the typewriter keys filled the room. Helen's eyebrows met again. *She* hadn't been told about any proposed visit to the country, but it was how those of Miss Lazare's kind lived. In time, she guessed, guests would come here, to spend a night or two in Michaelmas Passage, when London was safe and they were all living normal lives again.

*

It was several years since Helen had visited 'Wychwood'.

She found everything was just as she remembered: the lane that carried them downhill, the banks of creamy meadowsweet, the trees entwining overhead to make a green tunnel, the screeching from the rookery, the slow sinking sensation in her stomach as the house came into view—pebbledash walls first, then the mismatching thatched roof, and the muddle of outbuildings where she used to wander as a child, after her mother died, with nothing to do, among the mangles and hoes and tennis rackets with broken strings. She was never cheered to see 'Wychwood', least of all now.

Her father tried to sound encouraging as he steered the car between the gateposts and gravel flew up under the car. This evening she didn't have a daughter's faith in him: they'd come thirty miles on a visit that was hardly convenient to them, and it had to be this evening. Her Aunt Catherine had never been the most warmly hospitable of people, although most probably that was owing to her nature—secluding herself so far from anywhere—rather than to her feelings for her brother-in-law and niece, which (Helen gave her the benefit of the doubt) were probably true enough and as keen as she was capable of having for anyone. But (Helen surmised) she would not have considered thirty miles of back roads such a neighbourly distance that she would have blithely issued them an invitation without some other purpose than familial politesse. It had occurred to her during the solemn drive inland that her father might actually have solicited the invitation, so that their absence would be observed by all in the hotel's dining-room.

She was feeling uncharitable and in very low spirits as they got out of the car and walked towards the open front door and her waiting Aunt Catherine. She planted a cold kiss on her cheek, as seemed expected of her. Inside the house was as dull as she remembered: dark panelling, stained wood floors, dim lamplight in the warren of low rooms with narrow windows set high, solidly Edwardian furniture with something of a censorious air that wouldn't have been out of place in a mayor's parlour.

In the dining-room they sat at the table beneath a low-wattage bulb inside an over-sized fringed shade that had been retained from the recent days of gas. Helen's eyes strained in the gloom. Her mind strained with the effort of conversation and she could think of almost nothing to say. Her thoughts were elsewhere, and she caught only an occasional word or phrase.

She noticed the concern showing on her father's face.

After the rabbit terrine had been cleared away, and the plates set down for the main course, she didn't open her mouth again. (Later she realised that her aunt must either have failed to notice, or been unusually diplomatic in witholding comment.) The middle course was disposed of to the accompaniment of her aunt's chatter and her *father's carefully judged responses. God help me from being old and single and profligate with words, she thought: although 'garrulous' wasn't exactly her aunt's condition, being too slily observant of others to ignore their social failings and permit them in herself. This evening she was attempting to say the right and proper things and determinedly talking over the silences.*

'I must say, Richard, Helen is looking better than I have seen her for a long time. Sea air has done her a world of good.'

Helen watched the maid as she piled the plates on a wooden tray.

'London isn't healthy,' Miss Addington continued. 'It never was healthy. As you know, I am not a city person.'

'Oh, I'm quite used to it,' Mr Wilmot replied. 'Louise became used to it too, in time.'

'She certainly didn't inherit her enthusiasm. Or else—'—Miss Addington smiled bleakly—'—or else I would have it as well.'

Mr Wilmot smoothed the linen napkin on his lap.

'City life has its compensations,' he said. 'Even in a war.'

'You know, Richard, I do worry about you. And—'—Miss Addington glanced in her niece's direction—'—and also about Helen, of course.'

Helen focused on the wax runs on the unlit candles in the silver sticks.

'You shouldn't worry,' Mr Wilmot said.

'That's all very well to say,' Miss Addington replied, with some tartness. 'But even if I shouldn't, I do.'

She then tried to smile away the vinegariness, but Helen told herself she saw through that ruse. It was her father who, as ever, was required to placate.

'Of course we miss this—this abundance of fare, Catherine.'

Miss Addington warmed to the compliment. 'Morality is a little —"slacker" here, shall we say? In certain respects.'

Her smile was in general forgiveness. Mr Wilmot smiled, less surely. He looked across the table, towards Helen. Her eyes were fixed on the silver shafts of the candlesticks.

'Hallam Park is like a little Eden to us here, although I ought not to admit it.' *Miss Addington allowed her spine to rest against the chair's straight back.* 'I turn a blind eye to Mrs Winch's kitchen door conversations—or a deaf ear, should I say. Perhaps it's best that I don't know all who come to this house.' *She laid her hands flat on the table's mahogany.* 'All I do know is, I found a pheasant hanging in the larder on Tuesday and I thought of you, Richard.' The hands were crossed. 'And Helen, of course.'

'We have appreciated it. Very much.'

Helen didn't speak.

'There is a fresh stilton to come: and some walnuts Mrs Winch has pickled.'

'It's very good of you, Catherine.'

'Oh, it's purely selfishness on my part. I've enjoyed having company in the house. It's been quite a change for me, I can tell you.'

Mr Wilmot turned his silver napkin-ring. He looked first at Helen, who was watching the spent candles, then at his sister-in-law on the opposite side of the table. Their eyes engaged.

'Do you—' Miss Addington asked, 'I've been wondering, do you have to go back tonight?'

For the next few seconds Mr Wilmot's face shrank on its bones. He looked briefly at Helen; she had heard and sat tight-lipped. He attended to his silver napkin-ring.

'You could stay, both of you, couldn't you? See my garden in the morning, when the mist has lifted from it. Inspect my dahlias. I have some Mavis Shoesmith chrysanthemums.'

Miss Addington glanced surreptitiously in Helen's direction, then responded to her brother-in-law's milk-and-water smile.

'The rooms are aired,' she said. 'I took the precaution of having Sara warm the beds the past couple of nights.'

'Of course—our rooms are waiting for us at the hotel. But . . .'

(There was a short pause: momentarily longer than it should have been, Helen was realising.)

'The lanes are so dark,' Miss Addington said, 'I'm sure there's no pleasure to be had in driving at night. Quite the contrary. I should only worry about you both.'

The misery was gathering on Helen's face. Her father and aunt affected not to notice; they talked across her.

'You can sleep under thatch,' Miss Addington said, rising and surveying the table before the next course of the meal was served. 'That would make a change for you both. You'll hear our owl, but at least we have no mice. And—you can paint it all when you get back, Helen, can't you?'

Neither wished to hazard Helen's moonchild stare, and didn't.

'What a very pleasant evening it's been,' Miss Addington continued, removing some items of cutlery.

Then her face acquired a more solemn cast.

'It was here you met Louise, do you remember, Richard?'

'How could I forget?' Helen heard her father reply.

'You know, I don't believe I ever saw her look more charming than she did that afternoon.'

Helen gazed miserably at the reflections of silver on the table's waxed top. The owl hooted and she heard its echo in the wooded cove beneath the cinder-path up to the hotel. The figure of a man stood beneath an umbrella pine, breathing hard. Moonlight was chilling the sand with shadows.

'Afterwards I felt I'd known,' Miss Addington said, removing a mat, 'known about the two of you. A blood instinct, let's say. Of course—' She seated herself again. 'Of course the folk in this corner of the world are famous for being clairvoyant. I expect that's because we're so inward-looking. Geographically-speaking.' She pointed towards the window, to what lay behind the drawn curtains with the pattern of stylised trees and foliage like a dense forest. 'I mean, the coombs, those dips and dells outside, and having to live in their shadows.'

*

She returned with the letter to her bedroom.

She placed it on top of the dressing-table and walked round the room several times, summoning the courage she knew it must take to open the envelope and read what was written.

She looked out the window, down on to Monmouth Square.

She waited till she might steel herself, but her patience abandoned her first. She picked up the envelope and ran her thumb beneath the seal.

Her knees felt as if they would buckle and her legs give way under her; she had the presence of mind at least to sit down before she had read more than the first few words. As her eyes sped from line to line, she lost all sense of herself, this time and place were nothing.

'. . . All in all, though, it could be worse, and I suppose I don't have so much to complain about. There isn't the waiting there used to be, days and days of watching the sky and never knowing when something was going to happen. This way keeps us occupied, you're too busy to think forward or back.

'Most of the time, that is. But sometimes I invent: from here I can undo what took place, or what didn't take place, I can change the plot, I can work a different ending . . .'

*

A hooded black shape hovered just outside the range of her vision.

Sometimes it was in the corner of her eye, at other times it was somewhere over her face but she wasn't able to focus on it.

From somewhere else a savage light was drilling through her.

'Who—who are you?'

The words were being spirited out of nothing.

'What's that now, dear?'

'Who—who—?'

'I'm Father Williams.'

How sure the words sounded, how sure.

'But—'

' "But", my dear?'

'Why—?'

' "Why?" ' The word came back, heavier, ownerless.

'What—?'

'There, now. Don't be exciting yourself there, Helen.'

Helen?

'You're among friends.'

Among—

'We're all friends.'

—friends.

She didn't know. It was hopeless. Hope-less.

The black shape fell into a corner of her eye. The light skewered her, spiked her like a lance.

*

In an age before, a child plays in the private gardens of a London square.

Over her shoulder she can see the tall white house where she lives with her father. Her bedroom is on the top floor, and next to it is the nursery window. Nanny Hine's bedroom faces the other way, on to the backs of the houses on Gower Row. From upstairs Helen can watch the world passing beneath her: the other occupants of the square, the ladies and gentlemen and their children, the housekeepers, the nannies, the cooks, the maids, the delivery-men, the messenger boys, the road-sweepers. All the world passes in a day. She can see over the railings into the gardens, and now—at ground level—she imagines herself watching from the bedroom window, seeing the person who is herself looking backwards over her shoulder.

But thinking in that way is hard work and she can feel her head stretching to fit in the thoughts. She runs forward instead, to the pond.

She looks, as she always does, at the forgotten stone dolphin on its plinth, drily frolicking in gauche, unbecoming mid-air.

She picks up the cane, stretches out an arm over the rim, and pushes the cane's tip against the keel of her model yacht.

The effort causes the yacht to careen in a different direction. She stands watching as its prow clears a mush of sodden leaves.

The yacht loses its momentum and as she decides which side to catch it from, left or right or in front, she notices again the woman in the veil.

She was here one day last week, and another time the week before that. The hat and black veil hide her face. As she did on the two previous occasions, the lady—a lady rather than a woman—paces one of the gravel walks, her face concealed but turned in her direction, to wherever she happens to be. She wears a dark grey coat and black gloves and black stockings and shoes. With the black hat and trailing veil, the absence of colour is disturbing. But Helen only has to look behind her to see home, and that is a comfort to her.

Today Helen stares back at the stranger, knowing she is being watched by her, as she was last time and the time before. The lady doesn't turn away, but carries on, placing one foot in front of the other.

Then, from the silence Helen realises that the lady presses so lightly that the gravel makes no sound: not as it does when she runs along it coming in or leaving, scattering it.

The woman continues to watch. Helen stares, and tries to invent a face for her from the missing features beneath the fall of black tulle.

*

Helen was checking her typescript when she heard the voices again.

She laid the sheets on the table-top, stood up, and walked across the room. She turned the handle of the door very carefully, prised it open no more than an inch, and put an eye to the crack.

They were leaving the drawing-room: a pale, out-dated quartet in their 1920s attire. She'd had only the briefest of introductions from their hostess earlier, and she hadn't had time to take them in.

Miss Lazare led the way, and—aquiline mien and paradise hues notwithstanding—seemed the least extraordinary of the group. The others differed from her in having even more pallid, almost greenish, drowned complexions. There was a foppish young man wearing a black velvet suit, with a horse's face and a poet's lank hair falling on to his high forehead. He was followed by a society lady of Miss Lazare's vintage, wearing a silver turban and brass-coloured cocktail dress and black lacquer on her long nails. She was followed in turn by a thick-set, middle-aged man dressed in what appeared to be a morning-suit, and with his neck imprisoned in a high wing-collar.

They were all laughing—at some prior remark—and they descended the staircase in high, mirthful spirits. Helen waited for the older man's head to sink from view before she opened the dining-room door and tip-toed across the gallery to the banister rail.

She looked down into the hall. The quartet stood directly underneath her on the chessboard of black and white tiles while Miriam hurried off to fetch their outerwear. The equine young man delivered his words with a backward toss of the head, as if he were neighing.

'Miou, my dears,' he said, 'she's simply too scandalous to live!'

The lady in the silver turban interjected.

'Biting the hand—'

'Miou—'—the solid man in the wing-collar interrupted her in turn—'Miou is one of life's enhancers,' he announced.

The younger man rested his hand on his hip.

'Explain yourself forsooth, my dear Charles.'

The reply was offered readily.

'She is one of those flaming celestial bodies around whom the rest of us—'—the others began smiling and laughing in anticipation —'are fated to revolve—'

'—endlessly!' the younger man cut in, and brayed with appreciation at the judgment.

Miss Lazare was smiling too, and shaking her head.

'Mad creatures!' she said.

'Ah, none madder,' the man with the look of a poet replied. 'Had we known better, methinks, should we ever have gone to Rawlinson Gardens?'

'You are an ingrate, Howard—'

Howard feigned shock and effrontery.

'But that is a dispersion on my dignity, madam!'

There was more laughter, then the other man spoke.

'Sinclair *will* insist on his dignity. To the bitter end.'

'And beyond!' came the instantaneous reply.

The lady in the silver turban called 'Meredith' clapped her hands with their slender fingers and pared black lacquered nails like talons of dried gore. She spoke through her laughter.

'Talking of dispersing—'

Helen stood at the banister rail watching. While Miriam returned the guests their outerwear, her mistress exchanged a parting kiss with each.

As he wrapped a black muffler round his neck, the younger man asked the other.

'Whither goest thou, Charles?'

The older man shook out a white satin scarf.

'Ad conciliabulum Alberti,' he said. 'In omnibo.'

The lady in the brassy dress held her arms out backwards to Miriam, preparing to receive. She continued to smile.

'No Will-o'-the-Wisp mislight thee,' she said.

The younger man tied a knot in his muffler, and replied over it.

'And shooting-stars attend us—'

Thereupon all three guests started to don capes. The younger man's was black velvet with a silver chain; the society lady's was of fur; the older man's was the tweedy Inverness variety.

When they appeared ready to depart, the man called 'Charles' undid the clasp of an instrument case and removed a violin and bow.

The others seemed unsurprised, and to take it as a matter of course. The horsey young man picked up the empty case. The older man placed the violin under his chin, raised the bow, and—allowing Miriam a few moments to reach the door and open it—he serenaded the trio from the house.

They trailed their laughter behind them, along the street.

Miss Lazare stood between the jambs, calling after them for a while; then, when they ceased to call back, she stepped into the hall and Miriam finally, firmly, closed the door.

Miss Lazare returned to the middle of the hall. Her expression was suddenly solemn. As Helen watched from upstairs, she stopped in her tracks, apparently lost in thought.

Miriam approached her from behind; she seemed about to rest her hand on her mistress's arm, but then must have thought better of it. She walked off without a word, to the back quarters.

Miss Lazare watched her leave. A door closed, then she turned her face towards the high mirror wreathed in gilt acanthus leaves that hung from the wall by a dolphin's tail above the console table. She walked towards her reflection; she leaned over the table's marble top, reached out her right arm and—Helen was just able to see —touched the features of her face in the glass with her fingertips.

From outside on the street, through the shell of plaster and brickwork, the Pied Piper music carried faintly, a tune that Helen knew she should recognise.

*

Later, standing looking at the dull grey lacklustre Thames and swallowing long, deep breaths of fresh air, she remembered what it was: the same Coward melody the trio would play during every recital in the grand hotel above the sea.

'Ev'ryone's here and frightf'lly gay,
Nobody cares what people say.'

*

Helen saw her father from the other end of the street.

They were both running for the house. Hail stones ricocheted off the pavement.

There was something melodramatic, almost absurd, about the situation, and she started to smile, then to laugh.

They reached the front steps within a couple of seconds of each other. Her father was smiling, perhaps because she was laughing so girlishly. At the age she was.

They ran up the steps together. Her father pulled the key out of his pocket and pushed it into the lock. She leaned on the front door with her shoulder and they both went tumbling into the hall at exactly the same moment.

They held on to each other to prevent themselves falling.

Funny, she was thinking—funny strange and peculiar—how he laughed like this so seldom, as if he was really meaning it.

They stood together in the hall, laughing into each other's face. They stood like that for maybe ten or twelve seconds.

It was long enough for her to feel the pressure of his hands on her elbows, to see that his eyes had—yes—the uneasy, glazed suspicion of guilt in them.

He did take his hands away, but he was a fraction too late in doing so.

They continued smiling, but finding other reasons for it, shaking the rain from their coats, stamping their feet, knowing they were upsetting the harmony of the house with their party behaviour and the dampness dripping from them. Mrs Clark would have to clean the floor again, and she would ask them if they'd never heard of umbrellas for goodness' sake.

That thought might have been in both their heads at the same instant. They smiled again.

And then the danger was past. They moved apart as they took off their mackintoshes. She held hers out at arm's length to give him.

'I'll hang them up,' he said. Unnecessarily, of course.

'Oh, thank you,' she replied.

She found herself in the mirror above the console table, looking flushed and bedraggled. There was a medieval sharpness about her face she had surprised several times of late, a legacy from the mother who survived in one silver-framed photograph on a side-table in the sitting-room.

She watched her father as he made his way from the hall, walking slowly towards the back quarters.

The danger was over, for another day. Danger? She knew—there was the forbidding unity of blood between them to tell her—that that was precisely what it had been, and that he knew too.

She might leave, live out, share with another student. She might. There was more than her physical comfort in the house to be considered.

But thereagain . . .

And somehow she never did, and she failed to hear the voices in the kitchen talking about them both beneath the stairs, the indiscreet moments when they called her what she'd once heard spoken before, through the nursery wall by Nanny Hine in one of her queenly rages, 'Miss Pretty Puss', 'Daddy's Little Girl'.

*

Somehow, the next morning, Helen found herself back at the house in 'Michaelmas Passage'.

There was a hiccup in the system at the mahogany table in the dining-room. A page was missing from a sheaf of papers. She didn't wish to say, and was careful to disguise her confusion.

'Have you mislaid something, Miss Wilmot?'

Helen looked up. It had been the thought in her head. A few times it had occurred to her that her employer was more cognizant than she seemed, in all her harmless green-and-blue bohemian eccentricity, to be. In their shared paper-work she was frequently a step ahead, an answer ready for her before the question had quite left her mouth. Even Miriam conducted herself as if she might have the gift of seeing through excluding surfaces.

She was aware of Miss Lazare's attention as she fanned out the pages and checked again.

'I—'

There was no point in dissembling.

'There's a page I can't find,' she said.

'You can't?'

'I had it yesterday. I'm sure I did.'

Miss Lazare lowered her eyes to the correspondence in front of her.

'There were pages on the sideboard,' she said.

Helen stood up, passed behind Miss Lazare, and crossed to the sideboard. There were loose papers lying on the top; she sifted through them.

'Is it there?'

'It doesn't—' Helen turned round and addressed the words to her employer's back. '—it doesn't look as if—'

'Then it must have dropped down behind.'

It seemed very unlikely—a shallow lip of wood ran the length of the sideboard at the back—and Helen thought it wasting time even to look. She reached out her hand and felt in the gap between the sideboard and wall with her fingertips.

*Some*thing was there.

She caught whatever it was—a piece of paper—and retrieved it between two fingers. She tipped her head to read it and saw that it was the missing page.

She turned and looked at Miss Lazare, who sat at the table with her back to her, occupied in double-checking one of the letters.

The explanation might have been quite innocuous: an inspired guess, because something like it might have happened before.

Might have . . .

Helen was conscious that her face was creasing with puzzlement.

*

In the afternoon work stopped at four o'clock and Miss Lazare led the way through to the drawing-room. She seated herself in the wing-chair, which had been angled towards the banked fire in readiness; she indicated the arm-chair opposite, also half-facing the fire, and Helen lowered herself on to the cushion. She was grateful for the rest, finding that having to decipher page after page of the barbed-wire handwriting made her eyes ache. The drawing-room would have been better for the purpose: even now the room was unlit, except for the flames in the grate, but she could see quite distinctly.

Miss Lazare seemed to be reading her thoughts.

'I like the river-light,' she said.

Helen nodded.

'When the fog lifts,' she continued, 'I swear you can smell the sea some days.'

Helen looked across to the high windows.

'Did—did you never want to live here?' she asked, now curious to know.

'*Here*?'

'Before, I mean. To live in a house in Chelsea.'

Miss Lazare smiled down at the carpet.

'It's too late now to think of that,' she said. 'Of what might have been.'

'But you like it here?' Helen asked.

'Yes. Yes, I *do* like it. Not that I have a great deal of choice in the matter.'

Helen nodded.

'It reminds me,' Miss Lazare said, 'of a sea-port. It's all angles.'

'Like a Cornish fishing village.'

'Yes, I suppose it is.'

'When I was a child,' Helen said, remembering, 'we—my family —we used to go to Cornwall, for holidays. To hilly little towns, with lanes and high walls and always a harbour. Everywhere smelt of the sea there, even when you couldn't see it. You could taste salt off your skin.'

Miss Lazare looked up.

'Perhaps,' she said, speaking slowly, 'perhaps you could taste salt off your skin *here*, Miss Wilmot. Do you think?'

Helen caught the concentration of the older woman's eyes as they fixed on her. She smiled, embarrassed.

'I—I really don't know, Miss Lazare.'

She felt the remark unsettling her, but in the event she hadn't time to dwell on it. Suddenly Miss Lazare got to her feet as if on a signal. She walked across to the door and opened it, and as she turned back round Miriam entered soundlessly with the tea-tray.

Helen sat watching, her eyes flicking between the two of them.

The tray was set down. Miss Lazare stood examining herself in a pier-glass.

'But the stairs are steeper for Miriam,' she said, pulling at a strand of hair. 'She probably curses our fate every time she has to come up or go down. Isn't that so, Miriam? "Why *here?*" you're always asking yourself, I have no doubt.'

The maid straightened up, eyeing the tray.

'Why indeed, ma'am,' she said.

'Because—'—Miss Lazare smoothed the arc of one eyebrow—'—because London is not as it was, Miriam, and we find ourselves in other times. Thrown on their mercy.'

She paused momentarily before continuing.

'They say there are pockets of air under the pavements and if the stones have been loosened you might step on one, the wrong one, and just—vanish.'

'Beneath the ground?' Helen asked.

'It has happened. The earth is throwing up its mysteries. They've found a statue of Mithras, the sun god, from the Roman age. Apparently he's smiling.'

Miss Lazare smiled into the mirror.

'Time,' she said, 'is out-of-joint. Nothing now is to be reckoned on.'

'Yes,' Helen confirmed. 'There are dogs running wild just across the river.'

She saw Miss Lazare's eyes staring at her in the pier-glass, then the courteous social smile was reapplied beneath.

'After the War started, Miss Wilmot, London turned into a city of stories. People would tell you all about themselves, what had happened to them. As if they were afraid *not* to tell you, and the moment would pass—and the chance would be lost.'

Helen was thinking of a reply—she was even wondering whether the stories people told need be true ones—when Miriam interrupted.

'The lovers go under the railway bridges at night.'

'A bank was shelled,' Miss Lazare said. 'Paper money blew like autumn leaves. There are convicts playing with children in the crypts of churches.'

Helen spoke. 'There are bonfires burning. So I heard. And foxes in Mayfair.'

Miriam's arm shot out in the split-second before a cup started to slither off its saucer.

'These are—'—Miss Lazare concluded—'—these are unseasonable—and un*reason*able—times.'

Silence.

Miriam took a few steps backwards.

'I should let it sit a couple of minutes, if you will, ma'am. To infuse. If you don't mind.'

Miss Lazare smiled.

'Why should I mind, Miriam? Why should I concern myself about a couple of minutes?'

Helen watched Miriam make her exit from the room. Miss Lazare waited for the door to close.

'I don't expect Miriam will want to go on climbing those stairs for ever,' she said. 'But that problem will be attended to when it occurs. After this War, there won't *be* maids any more.' She turned back to the pier-glass. 'They're a dying breed.'

While Miss Lazare stood contemplating her reflection, Helen got to her feet and walked across to the window. These exchanges made her anxious and restless, although she didn't know why.

The bottom sash had been pulled up two or three inches and she could almost imagine she smelt the salt sea. She stood in front of the window and what she then saw startled her.

On the pavement directly beneath stood a middle-aged city gentle-man—more or less of the age her father had been when another version of history caught up with them both—dressed in a bowler hat and fitted overcoat and leather gloves. He held his head high and was looking up at her.

Helen stepped back. She'd noticed the smile: encouraging, flirta-tious.

She withdrew, and caught Miss Lazare tracking her in the mirror. She felt her face burning.

Lowering herself into the armchair she knew she had to speak, if she was to have any choice left to her.

'How—how long did you live in Rawlinson Gardens?' she asked, in a voice that would carry.

Miss Lazare turned round.

'Oh.' She opened her hand, palm upwards, as if she were weighing time in it. 'Twenty years, nearly.' The hand swept over her hair. 'It was thought to be quite a smart house. I gave rather smart parties. People of fashion came to them. You are too young to remember that, Miss Wilmot.'

'Number Forty-Nine?' Helen asked.

'Yes. Yes, that's correct.' Two hands attempted to secure a comb that had worked loose. 'Do—do you know the area?'

'I lived quite near. I used to. In a square.'

The comb was pushed back into the roll of hair.

'You were brought up there?'

'My mother died, when I was eight. I lived with my father.'

Miss Lazare's face stiffened—then she elongated her mouth to a dry smile.

'The parties, they're a thing of the past, of course,' she said.

'Do you think of them a lot?' Helen asked.

The smile stayed fixed in place.

'*Then*, Miss Wilmot, I didn't dwell on the past.' She looked towards the window. 'I didn't need to. But later you learn that you also dwell *in* the past.' She took several steps towards the light. 'If I close my eyes, I can *be* there.'

At that moment, for no clear reason, Helen felt a surge of confidence and confidentiality.

'If *I* close my eyes,' she said, 'I—I can fly!'

Miss Lazare was at the window. She reached forward and pulled down the sash. She had just turned away when there were sounds of a disturbance from the street: running footsteps, raised voices, a dog's barks.

Helen was intrigued. She felt she must surrender something—her decorum—but she wanted to see, to discover what was happening.

Miss Lazare spoke as she turned her back to search for something in the escritoire desk, but Helen didn't hear. She stood up and walked across to the window; she looked out and opened her eyes wide at the sight.

A fraças was taking place: an elegant but violent pantomine. The gentleman who had smiled at her was involved in fisticuffs with a man of a lower order, wearing a cap and holding a dog on a string. The gentleman's bowler was lying on the cobbles. As Helen watched, the gentleman aimed a punch at the jaw of the other man, who managed to duck and then responded by slamming his available fist into the older man's stomach. The gentleman staggered forward, his gloved hand clutching at his abdomen. The dog's barks turned to yelps, then howls.

Behind her, Helen realised that Miss Lazare, quite unconcerned, was speaking to her.

'Well, we shall add the name to our list. Now, Miss Wilmot, it is time for our tea. Chrysanthemum tea.'

Can't she hear? Helen thought: doesn't she know that two men are meaning to knock the daylights out of each other just outside her house?

Not 'her' house, of course, '*the*' house. Maybe that was why she wasn't attempting to interest herself, because she was only a tenant here after all, on the loosest kind of mooring? Or was it because of her dignity—

Helen felt she didn't want to be obliged to have to point out the obvious. Then when would her job be done?

'Tea, Miss Wilmot?'

Helen smiled, through the howling.

'Yes, thank you,' she said, and walking back towards the sparking fire and the open arms of the chair she put the open-ended randomness of other people's lives behind her.

*

Miriam held the door open.

'Goodbye, Miss Wilmot.'

'Goodbye.'

Helen walked out on to the pavement, pulling on her gloves. She turned left, river-wards— the way she'd come—and covered a few yards.

Then she stopped. Another route was suggesting itself to her.

She did an about-turn, and started walking in the opposite direction. She passed the house, quickly, and set her sights on Kensington by her own internal compass.

'I HAVE WATCHED YOU, HELEN, ACROSS THE LIFE CLASS, MANY TIMES, BUT I HAVE FELT UNABLE TO DECLARE MYSELF TO YOU.

YOU ARE BEAUTIFUL. I KNOW I AM IN LOVE WITH YOU.

I CANNOT EVEN TELL YOU WHO I AM—EXCEPT THAT MY GENDER IS YOURS, HELEN.

PERHAPS I SHALL NEVER BE IN A POSITION TO TELL YOU, TO YOUR SWEET FACE. MY LOVE IS NOT TRULY WRONG BUT SOCI-ETY COUNTS IT A SIN. MINE IS THE LOVE THAT DARE NOT SPEAK ITS NAME.'

*

Approaching Rawlinson Gardens, Helen was remembering walks with her father or Nanny Hine and journeys in taxi cabs or, later, on the tops of buses. Since the end of peacetime the streets had been moonlit, eerie, like places she had never been to before: like the cities she used to dream about in her sleep when she was a child, travelling to them as those-who-had-to-prove-themselves in fairy-tales would

145

make journeys to the other side of the known and familiar to bring back some rare object or knowledge. Since *that* night of moonlight with the wailing air raid sirens she'd felt she hadn't completed the return journey: *almost*—to within sight of the known and familiar —but not quite.

Everything might have been as it used to be: the name plate, and the lettering of the words 'Rawlinson Gardens', the railings, the house on the corner, the gate to the area steps at Number 11 made fast with chains and padlocks, the chestnut tree in the gardens that overhung the road at a certain point and dropped spiky husks in autumn, which car wheels flattened. 'Rawlinson Gardens' had always been the long way home, if ever there was a reason to delay: when she had a grudging school report, when her father had distinguished professional company in the house that she knew was going to intimidate her, when she had doubts about giving so much of her time to her father.

The houses were solid, imposing, and well-maintained in spite of circumstances. She followed the numbers, through the twenties and thirties, looking up into lit ground floor rooms. In one house a husband and wife stood woodenly at a fireplace exchanging the day's news, in another an elderly man was filling a younger man's schooner with decanted sherry; his neighbour through the wall, a harsh-faced woman, was fixed by an item in a newspaper; *her* neighbour, a little boy in pyjamas, sulked moodily at the window while, in the house next to his, a young woman in an evening gown and drop earrings laughed uproariously at something an invisible companion was telling her.

Helen was feeling no particular envy to be in one house rather than another; she suspected it had been her lot in life to be a looker through windows, a watcher in the darkness. The matching of her parents had decided that.

She saw the makeshift fencing from fifteen or twenty yards away. Curiously, she sensed that the air had a sudden chill in it, as if it was meeting the absence of something.

In the event she discovered that there were houses missing after Number 47, and that the absence was a deep, expansive hole in the ground, already seeded with the first quick-growing grasses.

Three houses (she deduced from the numbers on either side of the gap) had gone.

She stopped in front of where the middle one, Number 49, must have stood. She reached her hands out for the fence.

Once or twice in the throes of typing she had entertained a sly doubt that perhaps—just possibly—Miss Lazare was not who she claimed to be, that Rawlinson Gardens and her supposed misfortune there might not be the whole truth. Now she felt relieved to know that the story of her life and situation must be proven by the evidence. She imagined a quiet smile lifting the corners of her mouth.

At that moment she realised she wasn't alone. She turned round. An old man was standing on the pavement behind her; he was looking at the site and shaking his head.

'Terrible thing!' he said. 'Looks like someone knocked a great giant's tooth out.'

She nodded.

'How did it happen?' she asked. 'Do you know?'

'Caught the tail-end of a raid. There were some folks in the middle one. Got bombed out.'

She nodded again, and turned back to the empty lot.

She heard the man clucking his tongue on the roof of his mouth. She let him finish before she put her question to him.

'Do you know—whose it was?' she asked.

'Oh, don't know names, love. Just know everyone in that house got themselves killed.'

A couple of seconds lapsed, were lost, before she swung round.

'"*Killed*"?' she repeated.

'They pulled 'em out. Two of 'em too burnt to say *who* they were, not properly. "Women"—that's all.'

'Are—are you sure?'

'They were women?'

'No.' She shook her head. 'No. About the people all being killed.'

The man looked at her for the first time.

'Sergeant told me. Number Forty-Nine. Got in the papers too. Terrible time it was.'

Helen pointed.

'*This* house?'

The man looked past her.

'It's not a house *now*,' he told her.

She shook her head.

'No,' she said. 'No. No, it's not.'

The man clucked his tongue again.

'I heard—' she began.

'You heard something, Miss?'

The 'Miss' dismayed her.

She shook her head. He must have been mistaken.

Slowly she backed away, from the site and the man. If she hadn't found him here—or if she hadn't come—she wouldn't need to be concerning herself, she wouldn't be giving it a second thought.

She saw him looking at her, calculating who she was, why she had to know. She smiled to him, another of those too wide, daylight-bright smiles.

*

A mummified figure lies on a hospital bed. An electric light stares down from the ceiling, like an eye.

Then darkness. She smells, very faintly, the night-light burning in its jar. Camphor-ish.

Sounds and voices, disembodied, float about the white-tiled room and she can't tell night from day. She wishes she could live further and further inside herself, not in the room but in her cocoon of bandages, inside her head, behind her eyelids which she tries to keep closed, except when she starts to doubt and thinks the room may have disappeared or *she* may have imagined the walls and floor and ceiling out of herself and *become* the room.

And the window. Sometimes it's there and sometimes it isn't. She opens her eyes to sunshine, closes them, then opens them again and a moon is sailing free of clouds, clean and clear and pure as a hole in the black sky, and it grows and grows till it fills the window and might smash the glass like a fist.

*

She found she was being spoken to. For a moment . . . But it wasn't him.

'Is Rawlinson Gardens so interesting?'

He was about the same age, he had the same build, and a war tan. It wasn't *his* voice, though, but a Londoner's. He was carrying a rolled-up copy of The Times.

'I—The person who lived here—Number Forty-Nine—'

'What happened?'

'I—I don't know—'

The man smiled at her. She looked past him, over his shoulder.

'Days are getting colder,' he said.

'Yes.' She nodded. 'Yes, they are.'

'Can't get used to it. The weather.'

She started walking. His feet followed hers.

'You can't?' She spoke it as a question, not really attending.

'That's another world.'

' "Another world"?' she said distractedly.

'I've been out east.'

' "East"?'

She stopped still and looked at him.

'Burma. Never thought I'd get back.'

She studied his face, quite brazenly, and saw that it was sensitive as well as intrepidly smiling, capable of being hurt.

'That's not a posting, it's a sentence,' he told her. 'A death sentence, I mean.'

'You've—?'

'Everyone hanging on for grim life, just for leave. But I had to see the old place again, didn't I?'

'It—*it*'s different too,' she said.

'Not all of it.' He pointed with his newspaper. 'Still some leaves on the trees, see? Thought I'd have had my fill of them. Trees. Jungle dreams at night.'

He smiled.

'I knew someone—' she said, and paused.

'In that house?'

'No. In Burma. He—he flew.'

' "Flew"?'

She didn't reply.

'It's hell,' he said.

'It—it happened quickly. He wouldn't have had time to realise. They said.'

'Best way,' he told her. 'Out like a light then. By the way, I'm—'

'Fowler', she heard: 'Colin Fowler' or 'Robin Fowler'. Or 'Corin Fowler' possibly.

He offered her his hand. She took it.

'My name's Helen Wilmot.'

'Hello, Helen Wilmot.'

He smiled again as he let go her hand.

'Thought I'd go for a walk,' he said. 'Care to come?'

'I—' She fixed on his rolled newspaper. 'I—'

'You've other plans?'

'No,' she said.

'Well, then. If there's nothing to stop you—'

'No,' she repeated. 'No, there's nothing to stop me. Not now.'

*

The lady stood beneath the trees, her face hidden by the trailing black veil of her hat.

Helen held her father's hand tighter. He walked slowly, in the direction of the gate. He wasn't looking at the lady, it was as if he couldn't see her, the stranger in the black hat and veil.

Helen tucked the yacht beneath her arm. She held back, so that her father came between her and the figure watching them from under the trees.

She couldn't resist a glance over her shoulder as he steered them both towards the gate and the road and the house on the other side. She couldn't help herself.

They were still being watched.

Even the assurance of her hand inside her father's didn't mean to her all that it usually did. She felt that even that might not make them safe, if the lady didn't want them to be safe.

In stories one person could put a spell on another, and most often there was nothing you could do about it. Sometimes behaving well and being kind could undo it, but only sometimes.

She wished she was seeing from the future, and reading the story complete. But, she realised in these moments she was destined not to forget, that would only have told her 'what must be', not how she might turn events and shape them to a happy ending, wishing bad back into good.

*

'You should give it up.'

'What?'

'You're far away.'

She nodded. She replaced the tea spoon in the saucer.

Pandora's had seemed the only place to come: back to her usual table. Over his shoulder she noticed the proprietor watching them both vigilantly.

'Something troubling you? Is it the job?'

She smiled at the question but didn't reply.

'How long have you been coming here?'

She shrugged. 'Two or three weeks. It's all right. Except there's no one to speak to.'

She corrected herself.

'There *was* no one to speak to.'

'I don't think I can believe that,' he said.

'How long—' She let her eyes rest on his face. 'How long do you have?'

'Oh. A few days.'

She felt her face falling.

'There's never any time,' she said. 'Is there? Except for all the wrong things. Like—like having to work.'

'Have you got to?'

'I have to live. I need to live on something.' She swallowed. 'That's only—well, common sense. No?'

He smiled.

'Should have got married, shouldn't you?'

'I missed the boat,' she said.

'It's the boat's loss.'

Their eyes met. Then she looked down at the cup and saucer. She pushed them away from her.

'It's such strong tea,' she said. 'I can't drink it.'

He was watching her hands. She shook her head.

'There's no time,' she said.

'There's *some* time. A little.'

'There are no *words* left. Except for all the wrong things.'

'And what would you say, Helen Wilmot?' he asked her. 'If you could.'

*

'. . . *I have another aunt, my father's sister: she lives in Devon. She's married, and I have cousins. They're very scatter-brained— everything's a mess. My father thinks they're very—his word is "unruly". He can't hear himself think there. I'm sure I could go down if you could tell me when you might be back. They're in Dartmouth.*

What I have to say seems to me so dull: yet there's so much I do have to tell you and I don't know how to begin, I don't know how I could put it all down in a letter. Even all my father's famous knowledge couldn't tell me that.'

*

They stood outside Pandora's, on the common pavement.

'I should be getting back.'

'It was good of you to—'

'I've been going there in the afternoons. To Rawlinson Gardens.

Tomorrow—' Fowler hesitated on the word. 'I could see you again,' he said.

'I don't know.' Helen shook her head. 'Not the Gardens.'

'Somewhere else?'

She looked about her.

'One of the bridges?' she suggested, vaguely.

'What about Chelsea Embankment? The Tate?'

She nodded.

'Yes,' she said. 'Yes, that'd do very well.'

A car's tyres hissed along the street.

'It's been—' Fowler clutched his newspaper. 'Well, I've enjoyed it. The chat. Very much.'

'Yes.' Helen smiled. 'Yes. So have I.'

Fowler smiled.

'Goodnight, then,' he said, starting a slow retreat.

'Goodnight.'

She watched him as he turned round and walked off in the direction from which they'd just come.

Still watching, she took several steps towards Pandora's. She moved into the smear of yellow from behind the windows and felt—as she always felt—that she was being reclaimed.

She watched as shadows took possession of their living prey; she listened to his footsteps, growing fainter and further away.

It was then, suddenly, that she perceived the loss of him, to the very limits of herself: she experienced it like suffocation, as if a strength far greater than hers held a smothering bag of feathers to her mouth and she was gasping.

*

The next morning Helen timed herself to be late. She heard a church tower striking quarter-to-ten as she began the walk up from the Embankment towards the maze of back streets.

She had surfaced to the day feeling confused and cheated in some unspecifiable way, also defiant, that she *wouldn't* be confused and cheated. She remembered her journey back to Holborn, and what had preceded it, her words with the old man in Rawlinson Gardens.

He might have been wrong, but he'd seemed so sure. *If* he was correct, then . . .

Was *this* 'Miss Lazare' a counterfeit? What other explanation was there?

She wondered if her parents had known in advance, when they'd given her the christian name of her maternal grandmother for her middle name, 'Alice'.

'In another moment Alice was through the glass, and had jumped lightly down into the Looking-glass room. The very first thing she did was to look whether there was a fire in the fireplace, and she was quite pleased to find that there was a real one, blazing away as brightly as the one she had left behind. "So I shall be as warm here as I was in the old room," thought Alice: "warmer, in fact, because there'll be no one here to scold me away from the fire. Oh, what fun it'll be, when they see me through the glass in here, and can't get at me!"'

She tugged very hard on the front bell pull. Miriam opened the door, nodded without speaking, and closed the door behind her.

'. . . the pictures on the wall next the fire seemed to be all alive . . .'

Unpeeling her gloves she felt perverse enough to smile, as if nothing were the matter. She stretched her mouth very wide.

'. . . and the very clock on the chimney-piece (you know you can only see the back of it in the Looking-glass) had got the face of a little old man, and grinned at her.'

'The mistress is expecting you. She went up at the usual time.'

'Am I late?' Helen asked, attempting surprise.

She looked over at the clock in its case: it had stopped, and the hands pointed to seventeen minutes to three.

She removed her coat and scarf, and Miriam took them from her, along with the gas-mask case.

'How long have you worked for your mistress?' she enquired.

Miriam held up the coat, and Helen noticed the slash in the lining showing: deliberately so, perhaps?

The reply was short and evasive.

'Quite a long while.'

This time there was no address to the social distinction between them both.

'How long is that?' Helen asked the question bluntly, without feeling she needed to make a subtler approach. 'Did you work for her in Rawlinson Gardens?'

The girl walked off, not supplying her with an answer. Helen stared after her. At last the situation was declaring itself: a serving-maid believed herself as good as some of her betters.

Helen walked up the staircase, with her hand on the banister rail. She crossed the gallery and turned the handle of the dining-room door. Inside she saw Miss Lazare was already seated at the table. They exchanged smiles, and Helen realised she was only betraying her own intentions.

'Good morning, Miss Wilmot.'

'Good morning.'

'I've gone on ahead.'

'Yes,' Helen replied, meaning to sound curt.

She pulled out a chair and sat down.

'Some more names came to me,' Miss Lazare said. She handed across the sheet of paper. Helen took it and gave what she meant to be a cursory glance at what was written down. She laid the sheet to one side of the work awaiting her.

'I've this stuff to get done first,' she said, brusquely.

'Yes, of course.' Miss Lazare smiled. 'Whenever you can. There's no hurry.'

Replies had to be written to some long-outstanding letters, and Miss Lazare proceeded to dictate while Helen copied.

After five of them Miss Lazare said she thought that was enough for present and she would be most grateful if they could be typed up this morning.

'I've left them for so long,' she said. 'I have a guilty conscience today.'

Helen didn't offer a response. The words sounded like dinner party talk: people have consciences on some days and not on others, as if it were like a visitor who called occasionally.

Helen lowered her head and attended to something else. She swivelled her eyes leftwards as Miss Lazare suddenly pushed her chair back and stood up. She kept the lower half of her torso in her sights as she walked towards the pembroke table where the telephone sat. She was reaching out her hand to lift the receiver when the bell started to ring. Helen jumped, but Miss Lazare seemed not at all surprised. She picked up the receiver and immediately began talking, without needing to ask who was calling.

'James! It's been an age!'

She uncurled the flex.

'Who on earth told you? Sybil?'

She pulled the receiver further from the telephone.

'But you missed the party.'

Helen stared as she listened.

'What's that? Oh, night of nights. Where *were* you?'

The flex was pulled tight.

'Oh, Bristol,' she repeated.

A voice explained, rattling out of the earpiece.

'I see. I see.'

Miss Lazare shook her head.

'Absolute hell, darling!'

And then Helen was remembering, something that had been lost to her all this time.

*

She was standing inside the telephone box not thirty yards from Pandora's, the receiver held to one ear, the newspaper clutched under her arm. A car's headlights were dazzling her through the glass, and she turned her back to them.

The maid summoned the mistress of the house. The words she was listening to were delivered in superior, elongated vowels. *Let us say tomorrow and lose no time, if that is agreeable.* Oh quite. *You can come?* Yes, yes I can come. *We shall meet then.* Thank you, thank you. *Goodbye, Miss Wilmot.*

*

'She knew my name.'

Fowler stared back at her.

'What's that?'

'She called me "Miss Wilmot".'

Fowler scratched his head with his rolled-up *Times*.

'The first day, when I phoned her. She said "Miss Wilmot".'

Helen stopped in her tracks.

'Well, that's your name,' he said.

She shook her head.

'But I didn't tell her. She *knew*, though.'

'Maybe you *did* tell her? And you've forgotten you—'

'No,' she said and shook her head again. 'No.'

She started walking, hardly aware that Fowler was beside her. And yet, if there hadn't been the prospect of reaching him at her working day's end, she mightn't have had the courage to believe her memory of events was the correct one.

She spoke her next words very quietly.

'I wasn't supposed to notice. To see. I can't go back there now.'

Fowler didn't seem disturbed that she should say it.

'Just give it up, then.'

She sighed.

'It's a job. There aren't many.'

'Oh, there are.'

'Not the "right" ones. The kind one's supposed to have.'

'Appearances?' Fowler said, and she couldn't judge his tone.

'Are you surprised?' she asked him.

'You don't—'

'With a father whose career was art history? *I* don't think it's surprising,' she said. 'How we appeared was very important to us—to him.'

'Well, now you have your own priorities to decide.'

'And there's the money—'

'Well, there's always that.'

'You see, then?' she said. 'Nothing's so simple.'

He held her arm.

'You look tired, Helen.'

'The whole city's tired. Tired to death.'

'One day it'll be over.'

'When?' she asked, and slipped her arm through his.

'It has to be finished *some*time. Everything comes to an end.'

'"Everything comes to an end"?' she repeated, pulling her coat tighter about her.

'Of course it does. Cheer up!'

She forced a smile.

'That's better!'

She continued to smile. She was grateful for his comfort.

'All those people,' he said, 'with long faces down into their coats.'

She nodded.

'I have to ask you—' he began.

She turned her eyes to him.

'—if you think I'm forward?' he asked her. 'Not "proper"?'

It seemed to her to be a very serious question.

'"Forward"?' she repeated. 'No. No, I don't think that.'

'Everyone's got to *use* their time,' he told her.

She nodded.

'I'd guess . . .' he said—and then he hesitated.

'Yes?'

'I was wondering—maybe you—haven't lived such a lot?'

She looked at the pavement in front of her.

'Inside my head,' she replied, 'I think I have, yes.'

Their footsteps sounded together, in perfect time.

'Two people, Helen, out of this drifting city . . .'

They walked on, their movements in tandem. Other couples passed them.

'It's like—'—Helen tugged at the lapels of her coat—'—it's like the dark side of me,' she said.

'What is?'

'Going there. Going to Chelsea. I don't see how I can any more.'

*

The topic recurred—Miss Lazare and her curious, displaced existence in Michaelmas Passage—as they made the lazy, roundabout journey back to Holborn.

In the course of their perambulations they went into a pub and had something to eat, cold ham ends and pickles; they sat against a wall, next to the fireplace and away from the crowd of locals, Fowler drinking his draught and she sipping at her sweet gooseberry wine. There was too much noise to speak above and they didn't try. The general jollity had a forced ring to it, to her ear, and she felt uncomfortable. It might have had to do with the wan yellow light from the grubby glass pudding-bowl shade on the ceiling, or perhaps the gooseberry wine rushing to her head was partly to blame. From her sitting position people's heads seemed too big for their necks, and in the orange firelight those nearest to them looked lantern-jawed and moon-faced. They made a joke of everything, and she wondered if that was the clue to surviving: even a story about a ceiling that had collapsed on an amorous widow and widower in their seventies, who were raptured to heaven 'in flagrante'.

When they were coming out, she looked up at the signboard above the door. She pointed. ' "The Hart",' she read aloud. Another joke, she thought, which somehow excuses all the ones inside. Perhaps her father's instinct had been the correct one, that she was better off without the world, and she'd failed to understand at the time.

Fowler took her arm. She felt his eyes were on her more and more as they walked back to Porteous Street: she puzzled if he could have some conception of the thoughts that were in her head, and wanted to disprove them, if he could. Or was she ascribing to him powers that she was *willing* him to have?

They stopped when Pandora's came into view. A car passed, its headlights cutting through the slits of their covers.

'Well . . .'

'Don't go,' she said.

'I've—'

'Please!' She held on to his sleeve. 'I don't think—'

He nodded.

'Once,' she said, 'when—when my father was alive—'

He smiled.

'You never met him?'

'Your father?'

'No. No, not—'

She shook her head and he perceived her meaning.

'It seems—a long time ago,' she said. 'We did things differently then. He was going to meet me—in the gardens—beneath the cove—'

'You have to forget. Forget all that, Helen. Do you hear—?'

' "Forget"?' she repeated. 'How? How do—?'

*

She knew by now which floorboards on the staircase creaked and which didn't. She led him up, whispering to him where he should place his feet.

In her room, with the door quietly pushed to, she hesitated about what to do. What came next?

She left it to him to dextrously unbutton her blouse. He folded it back over her shoulders and then rested his hands there. He pulled her towards him, very gently.

She looked at his mouth. One hand left her shoulder and the fingers picked back loose strands of hair from her face.

She couldn't stop looking at his mouth. All physical feeling in her seemed to be sending pulsations to the fulcrum of her body, the needing hollow between her legs.

She was remembering everything in those moments: the different corners of heat in the hotel gardens, the warm exotic scents of mimosa and frangipane, the coolness of shadows beneath the palms, the precise degree of blueness in the bay as her eyes perceived it, how their footsteps sounded on the cinderpath, the pitch of the solitary bird's song, the constant echo of the water drops.

Between her legs meanwhile she seemed to be awash, liquid, made for lushness and fertility.

In the interlude of time afterwards it seemed the easiest and most natural course for events to be taking: not as she'd always imagined it must be, the point to which everything in her life had intended her. Merely, she was in a corridor, and all it did was continue, uninterrupted, with no apparent end to it . . .

As they lay in the narrow bed, she tried for a few moments to dream they were in any other foreign, romantic location. The white moonlight shining round the edge of the curtains ribbed the ceiling, and it could have been the play of water shining from a canal on to a palazzo ceiling. Holborn might have been Venice, or Paris, or Rio, but she also knew that the exercise was redundant, since the evening wouldn't have happened exactly like this if she hadn't had the prospect of returning to this room alone, in a war-plagued city where other people conducted their existences so enigmatically, and in a time-slip where they were all victims of their conditions, past, present, and future.

'What's this?' she heard him say.

She extricated her arm and held it up. He turned the bangle on her wrist.

'It was a gift.'

'From Burma?'

The word had been spoken.

'Yes.'

'They sell them in the streets there. In dark little booths of shops.'

She didn't think she wanted to hear about its history.

'I wish I'd had someone as pretty as you to buy one for.'

She closed her hand and eased the bangle over the knuckles. She was passing it along her fingers when, from down-river, a sound of droning reached them.

'They're back,' she said.

They lay listening. Then, at some point, he was kissing her again.

He nuzzled into her ear. As he moved his weight, the bed groaned.

'What if Mrs Reilly hears us?' she said. She caught the absurd anxiety in her voice.

'It's the end of us!' He spoke in a parody of fear and concern she knew she deserved.

She let her head sink into the pillow and tried to relax the wires she could feel straining inside her neck. It was as if the tension had passed to there from the fork between her legs, where now she seemed to have no feeling left.

'What's *your* landlady like?' she asked him.

'Mrs Spode?'

She moved to allow him to lay his arm beneath his head.

'Dear Mrs Spode is like a dragon guarding her cave. She gives the impression that the twentieth century hasn't been invented: and she prefers to live in the last one, thank you very much. In her youth. With the memory of *Mr* Spode.'

Suddenly—over the running feet on the pavements— she remembered the story they'd been telling in 'The Hart', about the elderly couple interrupted in their love-making and transported to kingdom come: delivered through passion.

'It's a ghost house,' he said.

She watched the growing diagonals of shadow on the ceiling, seeming to oust the fugitive light from the street.

'Houses always are,' she said. 'Only it's worse now.'

'Why "worse"?' he asked.

She remembered another time, the marble effigies in the abbey chancel.

'There are so many of them now,' she told him. 'Ghosts.'

She heard him smile.

'"All I see around me",' he said, '"is change and decay".'

A shiver passed through her.

'I reckon the ghosts have the best of it.' He spoke in a whisper. 'Don't you think?'

She knew that, if he could see properly, she must look confused, muddled. His eyes were watching hers, but it was too dark for her to decipher their expression; she found it hard to visualise even, from the past few hours, when she could always bring back with perfect recall every gesture and inflection from a couple of years ago, from those days of intense sunlight that had defined each merest second of time. Perhaps now it didn't matter what she, or he, saw.

In all probability he wasn't looking at her anyway as he lifted himself, bent over her face, and covered her mouth with his.

*

She made her way back to Michaelmas Passage through the confusion of weather.

Morning mist lingered on the street corners ahead of her. She felt the presence of the sun behind clouds, a remote glow that was taking away the worst of the chill.

She entered the gully between the high brick walls. Her heels echoed the length of the alley and she seemed to be hearing two people, herself and another.

*

She was sitting at her work in the dining-room and had just heard the bedroom door close on the floor above when Miriam hurried up to the gallery outside with the news.

'The car has arrived, ma'am.'

'Yes, Miriam. I'm ready.'

The maid dropped her voice. 'Oh, *must* you go, ma'am?'

Miss Lazare (if she was) replied in a decided, even, gentle tone of voice. 'Everything has been got ready for me, Miriam. I can't disappoint now.'

The dining-room door opened and Helen feigned to be busy. Miss Lazare coughed drily.

'I have to leave you now, Miss Wilmot.'

Helen looked up.

'Oh—Yes, I see.'

The woman's mouth sucked in air. The fingers of her right hand played with the clasp of her bag and it struck Helen that the occasion was making her nervous. She had never seen her with her face made up; there seemed to be too much of everything, powder and lipstick and cheek colouring. The room smelt of her perfume, trailed like scarves.

'You know what's still to be done, do you?'

Helen passed an eye over what was in front of her on the typing table.

'Yes,' she replied, 'I think so.'

'It all explains itself, I expect.'

The remark was accompanied by a martyr's smile.

'It—it seemed the most sensible thing to do, Miss Wilmot. In the circumstances. To get everything ship-shape again. It—it concentrates the mind very well. Don't you find?'

Miss Lazare had opened her bag and was examining her appearance in the mirror of her compact.

'Of course, there's still so much left to do,' she said.

Helen sensed the statement was made to the reflection as much as to her.

'I went to art school for a while, when I was young—'

Helen narrowed her eyes at the information.

'I thought I might have made a career of that,' she continued. 'But . . .' She opened her mouth and inspected her teeth. 'Well, I seemed to be best at what I did.' She closed the silver compact. 'Bringing people together. That was a gift too, perhaps.' She smiled, rather wanly. 'Perhaps.'

The clasp shut on the bag.

'You see, that was my freedom, Miss Wilmot. That was my life.'

'Yes,' Helen heard herself say.

'My mother died when I was a child. My father had to be two parents to me, Miss Wilmot. I hope I did my best. I was the woman of the house, I smiled for our guests. And . . . it carried on from there, I suppose.'

Helen was standing stock still, listening to every word that was being said.

'Life chooses for you. Have you noticed that, Miss Wilmot? Even you with your youth—'

Helen saw her own reflection and Miss Lazare's, in the pier-glass, sharing that cold glassy image of a room exactly similar to this one.

'My father, as they say, was a man of consequence.' Miss Lazare smoothed an eyebrow with a fingertip. 'My mother died in a riding accident, or so the story was put about. She may have *willed* it to happen, but we didn't think about that. We couldn't: we didn't dare to think about it.' Her finger smoothed the other eyebrow. 'At any rate, *her* duties became mine. The woman who fell from the horse and struck her head on cobbles and may have done the deed deliberately, I filled her place. And sometimes—' She paused. 'Sometimes I thought I saw the sense in what she'd done, or what she *might* have done. When I was performing like a mechanical doll. Which was the easiest way often enough, as *not* thinking is often the easiest way. Don't you find, Miss Wilmot?'

The older woman fixed the younger one in the mirror, as if she were expecting an answer.

'I—' Helen cleared her throat. 'Sometimes,' she said. 'Yes.'

'We live by custom, by rote. A dream of existence.'

Helen listened. The words sounded as if they had been spoken before, in other circumstances.

'It's in the unconscious that the proper life is lived: unpredictable and otherwise. Don't you think?'

Helen could only think to nod. Maybe she'd read the words in a novel, or come across them in a biography, and was repeating them from memory? She sounded like an actress performing in an indifferent play, speaking just as she was bid.

'Well, Miss Wilmot . . .'

Miss Lazare straightened her black velvet and mink beret, then pulled at the slain heads hanging from each shoulder.

'Time, as they say, waits for none of us. I shall leave you to your work now.'

'Yes.'

'Miriam is here.'

'Yes.'

'Goodbye, Miss Wilmot.'

Miss Lazare offered her hand. Surprised, Helen accepted it. It was the first time they'd had physical contact of any kind. Helen felt the strength in her fingers, like a drowning woman's.

She waited until she could hear heels on the floor tiles in the hall downstairs before she walked through to the drawing-room. She could still breathe the perfume.

She stationed herself close to one of the windows. The front door of the house opened and she watched as the woman emerged and, with slow steps, approached the long black car parked at the kerb.

A chauffeur was seated in front, on the far side. The back door was open. As she pulled it wider, Miss Lazare (if she was) glanced backwards over her shoulder, towards—Helen supposed—Miriam standing in the hallway.

Then, hitching her furs, she turned away. She lowered her head and climbed into the back compartment of the car, closing the door behind her.

The engine growled to life, first gear was engaged, and the car pulled away from the kerb. The front wheels were directed into the middle of the street, and the car departed, rolling sedately over the cobbles.

It was in the very last seconds, as the corner was being turned and Helen was stepping back, that she had cause to continue looking.

It seemed to her that her employer was not alone in the back of the car, that—yes—the shape of someone else was just visible through the oval of back window.

In the next couple of seconds the car had gone and there was no way for Helen of confirming if she had been right or wrong. She might only have been imagining it, she realised as she returned to the dining-room: but thereagain why should there *not* have been another person in the back of the car?

It was the look she was remembering as she tried to attend to the typewriter keyboard in front of her: the parting glance over one shoulder, to Miriam standing in the doorway as acting custodian of this house of which they were only tenants. She hadn't been able to see an expression on her face that might have told her what she was thinking or feeling.

Neither joy, she was sure, nor the other puffball fancy of these days—hope—too cobwebby light to lay hold of.

*

In the nursery above the square and the pond and the beleaguered stone dolphin, the curtains have been drawn against the dark and wind outside. A gas fire sizzles in the grate. The gas in two wall brackets sputters and the pink light wavers inside the gauze.

It's 1929 in the streets of London. In electrically lit rooms flappers dance the first hours of pleasure away, in ordinary homes newspapers are raised and darns worked in the heels of husbands' socks, beneath wind-tunnel bridges the lost and hopeless argue about best berths under weeks' old newspapers stiffened by frost, and in various counting offices about the city heads are bent over ledgers and cigarettes are smoked to stubs as companies and uncommercial businesses—with a will of their own—prepare to come crashing down on the morrow.

Helen is eight years old. It's late, well past her usual bedtime, but her father is 'out' tonight, 'visiting friends' after the recent confinement of mourning for his wife. Nanny Hine is in an excusing and indulgent mood, having done as nannies are given to do and drunk a little more than is quite seemly. Even so, Nanny Hine is fully in charge of herself, and Helen has caught only an occasional trace of her breath's sourness. By this point they're sitting in the two armchairs with the singing springs, on opposite sides of the fireplace. All evening Nanny Hine has been 'fidgety' (a Nanny Brechin word), unable to keep still until now. Even now, though, she cannot settle into the hold of the armchair in one position for longer than a few seconds. At last she pulls herself forward with knees apart and stocking tops and suspenders showing, fixes Helen with her eyes, and licks her lips as she sorts out the words to speak.

'Shall I tell you a secret, Helen?'

' "A secret"?' the child repeated.

'Yes, a secret.'

Nanny Hine nodded her head, and Helen nodded hers too, but less surely.

'You see—' Nanny Hine lowered her voice. 'The thing is, Helen—' She paused, in part for dramatic effect, in part because of the delicate

*nature of what she must impart. 'I—I saw your dear mother last
night.'*

Helen's mouth fell open.

*'I knew you wouldn't believe it,' Nanny Hine said. 'Being your
father's daughter too.'*

'My mother?' the child repeated.

'Your mother, *Helen.' Nanny Hine nodded her head. Then she
stopped nodding it, because she didn't think that she was making the
admission sound solemn enough.*

'Yes. She was in this room.'

The child seemed to be struggling for air.

'Here?' she said.

*'Yes. Here.' Nanny Hine dug her elbows into the squashy chair
arms. 'Why not* here?*'*

Helen stared at her.

'My mother's with the angels now,' she announced quietly.

'Oh. She is, is she? I see—'

*Nanny Hine smiled: one of her less successful, too sickly sweet
smiles. She sensed that she must advance slowly and patiently in this
conversation, but she felt the girl's assurance—coming from her
father—riling her.*

'You don't know, *though,' she asked, 'if she's reached them yet, do
you?'*

'My father told me,' the girl replied.

*'Your father told you?' It was Nanny Hine's turn to repeat,
parrot-like. 'Your father said? And how come he's so cock-sure?'*

Helen returned her gaze without blinking.

'He knows—*everything.'*

*'No one "knows", Helen.' Nanny Hine was damned if she was
going to be got the better of by a child. 'No one knows. Not till it
happens.'*

'How—how do you know?'

'I used my noddle,' Nanny Hine said.

'How?'

Nanny Hine screwed up her eyes for a confidence.

'You can't—'

She pulled herself forward on the cushion of the chair.

*'You can't disappear all of a sudden,' she said, 'just because you
die. I won't.'*

Helen stared. Her mouth had dropped open again.

'But how?'

Nanny Hine felt generous enough with her wisdom to spare another smile.

'People are too big and important and alive just to suddenly become—nothing. Go out, "like a light", like they always say. But that's not what they really mean. Look, I'll show you.'

And with that Nanny Hine pushes herself out of the chair. She is still a woman in her forties, but time has not been kind to her. Every year that comes to her she carries more weight, and her legs have started to sag with the load. In a chair and wearing a straight face she has a measure of dignity, which is why she is seated as often as possible: then she can effect her purpose with the very minimum of effort. Standing up she feels she is ripe for ridicule; being vertical causes her to use the sharp edge of her tongue a good deal and to waste her strength and energy in acting out her fits of pique. Tonight, however, she is beyond all such concerns as she crosses the room and turns down the light from the wall brackets, then returns to the fizzing gas fire.

Helen sits expectantly and wide-eyed in the fire's shine.

'A person,' Nanny Hine says from her standing position, 'is like that fire. They're glowing and alive. Then—I don't know what, an "accident" let's say—something happens, the life stops, the energy. The gas.'

At this point Nanny Hine bent forward, and layers of flesh bunched into rolls as she reached down for the tap on the fire. The hissing became softer as she gave the bib a sharp tweak to the right. Very slowly the room started to dim.

'The fire goes out, see,' said Nanny Hine, 'but it doesn't all vanish. Does it now?'

Helen peered at the cooling gauze.

'There's a glow left behind: as if the fire—it's refusing to go out, it won't die. So, think what it's like after all those years a person's alive, how they want to die even less. And they leave a bit of their energy behind, in the room. And if you look for it, you can see it. The glow of a person.'

Helen was shaking her head. 'No,' she said, sounding fearful. 'No.'

'It's not frightening,' Nanny Hine told her from on high, her bandy legs turning invisible. 'You're not to be afraid.' She stared at the child. 'Helen? It's beautiful, do you hear me?'

Tears shone in the girl's eyes.

'Maybe ghosts live for years: maybe, Helen. If some terrible pain

166

has come to the person, and they have to suffer so much, and suddenly they're giving out so much energy at last. Sometimes it's years, or months. A few weeks, some people say: then the person gets very faint. Your mother'll just be here for a little while, because she didn't suffer so much in the end, even though she was such a delicate little thing. But she didn't want to die either, Helen. For a few days she'll be here with us.'

Unbeknown to both of them, the scene was being witnessed, by Mr Wilmot, who stood in the doorway watching.

' "Here"?' Helen repeated.

'I can feel,' Nanny Hine told her, 'she's here now. Somewhere about. It's called "passing over".'

One of the wall lights went up. Nanny Hine spun round, snorting for breath.

'Get out of this house!' Mr Wilmot roared at her.

'What—what's that?'

'You heard, woman.' Spittle flew. 'Pack your things and get out.'

'You haven't—'

The other wall bracket was turned up. Mr Wilmot's face was white with anger.

'But you can't do that to me,' Nanny Hine said.

'Yes, I can.' The voice bellowed and was aimed like a punch in the stomach.

Helen started to cry.

'Not to me,' Nanny Hine said.

'Oh yes. Oh yes.' The words rumbled.

'What'm I supposed—'

It was too much for Helen's father. He exploded. 'I don't care what you do. Out, I said!'

'I've—I've nowhere to go.'

'Just get out! Now!' The words were choked out. 'And don't come back, woman.' Helen saw the rage contorting her father's face. 'Never—never—darken our door again.'

*

From the window Helen watched as the car bearing Miss Lazare departed. It rode the cobbles at a steady, sedate pace, occupying the middle of the road.

Between the last houses of Michaelmas Passage and as the front wheels rounded the corner Helen noticed the woman's face turn to take a last backward look.

Then the car was gone. Helen blinked. She stood at the window a few moments longer. The street stayed empty.

Just audible from the other side of the river was the baying of dogs.

*

Nanny Hine's packing up was done in high, angry dudgeon as Helen got herself ready for bed.

The woman's voice travelled through the wall to her.

'Pretty set-up this is.'

'Who does he think he is?'

'Daddy's girl, and don't think I don't know what that means.'

'Gets me out of the way anyroads.'

'Not a word of thank you.'

'Don't think I don't know what's going on.'

The words were being spoken for her benefit, Helen realised as she lay between the cold sheets: not really for her 'benefit', though, but for her harm, her undoing.

'Oh, I know all right,' the voice continued, as if it was sounding through a hailer. 'I've learned a few things in my time, Mr Know-It-All Wilmot.'

*

Miriam entered the dining-room without knocking.

'I have to check the fire, Miss.'

'I—I don't think—'

'Mistress's instructions, Miss Wilmot.'

She looked as if she had been crying; her eyes seemed rubbed red. Otherwise, Helen thought, I would tell you in no uncertain fashion to kindly announce yourself before barging in.

The house was irritating her with all its mysteries. She felt she was about to be defeated by what she didn't understand.

The girl poked at the fire. Helen returned to the window, drawn to it in spite of herself. She was remembering the black car's departure.

'I'll bring you up some coals, Miss.'

Helen turned round. She caught sight of the mantelpiece owl cowering beneath the dome; it perched, shoulders hunched, on a twig, preparing for the moment when it would smash out of its glass tomb.

'I'll go down and fetch them, Miss. The coals.'

'Very well, then. If you must.'

'I have to keep it stoked. Mistress's instructions. "Attend to Miss Wilmot". Those were her very last words to me.'

*

Nanny Hine left in the evening. The door next to Helen's bedroom slammed, the bathroom door slammed, the door at the top of the staircase slammed; finally the front door in the hall banged shut with majestic, awesome finality.

Helen watched from her bedroom window. Earlier she'd seen the closed door of the study and knew that her father sat inside, reading a book or allowing her to think that he was, waiting like her for the unpleasantness to end.

It had ended, at last. Helen craned forward and saw Nanny Hine—without her starched uniform now, wearing dark clothes like the rest of London—teetering down the steps, swaying on her bow legs with the effort of carrying her suitcase. On the pavement she stopped under a streetlamp and turned her head and looked up at the window. Helen drew back, out of her range of vision, but a moment or two too late. She waited till she heard the heels scraping on the pavement before she leaned forward and looked down again.

Years later that parting glance would recur to her in her troubled sleep: the woman's expression was neither sorry nor chastened as it ought to have been, but—defying the requirements of the situation —quite unrepentant, unblinkingly aware and matter-of-fact. With the years she imagined that one or other of the eyebrows rose fractionally, as if posing a question—'Which of us do you believe, Helen Wilmot, your father or me?'—or as if she was leaving her charge with a warning: 'Ignore what I've told you at your peril'.

The child had stood at the window watching her trudge the length of the street. On the corner she didn't stop or hesitate or betray herself by a backward turn of the head. Her mind was made up, resolved, even if her body reeled under the weight of the suitcase: laden (her father discovered later) with various trophies purloined from the house by way of material compensation (they included her mother's silver-backed hair brush, a paperweight of blue Venetian glass, a pretty porcelain figurine of a lady in a bustle dress, and a carriage clock).

On the few occasions in the future when her father ever spoke of the woman again, he referred to her (while Helen pictured the intimidatingly black-and-white starched uniform) as 'The Thieving Magpie'.

She stopped typing in mid-letter—'I told Stephen I'd seen her in Piccadilly, but he said that was impossible, the ambulance had already come for her. The excitement of these weeks has weakened her heart, and Marcus is beside himself with worry, as if he has some sure inkling . . .'

She looked over at the telephone, and remembered the timely premonition of the call, as if Miss Lazare was connected quite otherwise to her friends, on a grid of forethought and anticipation.

Helen pushed her chair back and got to her feet. Knowing what she wanted to do, she crossed to the door, opened it and passed through, out on to the gallery. She reached for the balustrade and looked down into the hall. The clock, she saw, was covered with a length of white cloth. She felt her brow wrinkle as she turned away and made for the second staircase.

On the first tread she went up on to the balls of her feet. As she moved to the second, third, fourth steps, her hand trailed on the banister rail.

The floor juddered, the planks underneath were ripping and splitting and showering blocks of parquet round the room. Foul dust blew up from years ago.

There was another great wrench in the structure of the house, which must have been the staircase falling in.

She looked round again from the window and saw a blazing beam from upstairs filling the doorway. Black smoke billowed in, and her eyes stung.

Up on the window-sill she raised herself a few delaying seconds on the balls of her feet. With the tips of her fingers she kept her balance. Her eyes were streaming, and she closed them.

With her eyes still closed—one, two, three—she jumped.

Helen paused on the staircase. She lifted her hand off the banister rail and held it out in front of her. She turned it different ways. It showed no evidence of injury, the skin was quite whole.

The delay was only momentary, and she started climbing again. At the top of the staircase she looked down into the well, to the chessboard of black and white tiles on the hall floor. She listened for sounds beneath her but heard only her own breathing.

She crossed the top landing, with her destination clear to her. Her hand reached out to grasp the brass knob of the door handle. She pushed—purposefully—against the weight of panelled wood.

The door opened noiselessly and Helen looked ahead, into a room flooded with grey river-light.

She hesitated before, cautiously, she stepped inside.

She had to screw her eyes up against the brightness. A floorboard creaked under her as she moved from one foot to the other, and she glanced down. It groaned again, like the twitching beam of a sailing ship.

She side-stepped the plank and proceeded on tip-toe. The other boards were mute and she felt the knot of breath in her throat uncomplicate itself.

She crossed to the dressing-table, attracted by the sheen of metal and glass and by her three selves walking towards her in the three mirrors. She shared their meek smiles, and then lowered her eyes to examine the objects laid out on the gleaming wood. There was a silver-backed hand mirror, and a silver comb, both engraved with a florid 'L', and a hair brush with an ivory back and handle. She lifted the mirror and felt its weight and mass, then in turn she picked up the comb and the brush. (Had they survived the blaze? Wasn't everything supposed to have been lost?) She examined the two bottles of toilet water and the tub of talc.

She replaced the objects and left them as she had found them before advancing towards her reflection in the mirror of the wardrobe door.

She pulled the door open. The wardrobe was cavernous inside. Clothes of another age drooped from hangers; thirty hangers perhaps. She pushed them along the rail.

She explored beneath the trailing dresses and gowns. Part of the space was taken up by a rack of shoes. The rest provided storage for several band-boxes.

She removed the boxes and looked into them to find the one she wanted. She undid the lid of the fifth and last and from inside she lifted out a rimless black hat, like a small cloche, with a full veil of black tulle attached.

She stepped back and turned towards a cheval glass. Watching the effect, she laid the hat on top of her head and, trying to remember the original impression as best she could, she

Her mother used to accompany her to the gardens, and tell her of days when the poor dolphin had once spouted clear water from its mouth. She would sail the yacht for her.

Seeing the lady in the veil afterwards made her think of her mother—or, rather, of the aunts and great-aunts and family cousins who had come so sombrely clad to the house for the funeral, draped in the long swathed the veil over her face and shoulder.

She stood looking at herself. They weighed almost nothing, the hat and the veil. Widow's weeds. The tulle smelt faintly, very faintly, of lilac.

She unwound the veil and removed the hat and returned them both to the band-box.

shrouds of black netting that were the accepted fashion in mourning at the time.

The lady would walk slowly on the gravel, looking over at her with her face invisible. She never approached any closer than the bush her mother used to tell her was a lilac, and one of the plants which helped to bring the bees and butterflies to these gardens in the middle of the world's greatest city.

In a queer way, it had seemed to her that the lilac shrub was sanctioning the stranger, it must be the clue to how the veiled lady 'belonged'.

Behind her, unnoticed by her, the door of the bedroom had opened—and, through the crack, Miriam watched.

The box was laid in the wardrobe, and the door was closed. Helen looked round about her, then she crossed with a few light, soundless steps to the chest of drawers. A brass box sat on top: a jewellery box, she realised, as she lifted the lid.

Inside there were some rings, a necklace of coral beads, and a broken string of pearls. The more valuable items must have been kept elsewhere, in one of the drawers maybe.

There *was* something else, though. Helen's mouth puckered when she saw, not quite understanding at first.

From beneath the strings of beads and pearls she extracted—

*

She took the package to her bedroom to unwrap it, ignoring the suspicion in her father's eyes.

The box was lined with pink tissue paper, and inside that was the bracelet.

She took it out. It was heavy, a thick, solid round of silver; a dragon was engraved on the outer edge, a beast with ten legs in pursuit of its own tail.

She smiled, and eased it over her hand on to her wrist. She held up her arm and watched the bangle fall almost to her elbow.

It gleamed in the sunshine of that spring morning, from that time which seemed lost to her now, in her Chelsea days, from the other side of time and flux like a river.

*

The keen river-light in Miss Lazare's bedroom, at the top of the house which was built like a ship, couldn't disguise that the bangle from the box was the double of her own.

Standing holding it in her hand, she thought it must *be* it, that she'd left it on the premises and Miss Lazare had put it there for safe keeping. But she'd been wearing her bracelet in bed the night before, and she'd buried it in one of the drawers in the chest this morning, thinking today not the day she should be wearing it.

When she looked again the silver seemed more scratched than her own, or perhaps that was a trick of the light, she was uncertain. The dragon was chasing its own tail, exactly as hers did, ringing her wrist.

She peered at the maw, and counted the legs—ten—and failed to see that the door of the bedroom was still open and that other eyes than her own were watching.

If she *had* been aware she might not have done as she did, which was to drop the bracelet into the pocket of her cardigan. It seemed at that moment the only possible course of action for her, and guilt had no part in it: either she had to prove the absence of the other bangle, or else—

People bought them in Burmese street markets, she'd been told: cross-legged men squatting in back rooms had been making them all their lives, and *they*'d learned their craft from others before them, and so presumably it went on, generation after generation deep into the onion of time. There might be others in London, she might have passed their wearers in the streets: the secret sisterhood of the silver dragon.

She shook her head. It made no sense. No sense at all.

She closed the lid of the jewellery box while, unnoticed by her, the bedroom door was pulled to. It was a simple brass box, prosaically engraved with shorthand arabesques, not what she might have thought of as being a likely repository of confidential truths of time and space.

She shook her head again. No sense at all. She tried to smile.

*

'Guess who I *saw*, then?'

Helen lifted her head from her crayon drawing.

'Well, miss, who do you think?'

Nanny Hine confused her when she claimed to be so wise and wore that lop-sided grin.

'Far from here he was.'

'Who?' the child felt obliged to ask.

'Why, your dear old dad, of course.' Nanny Hine twisted the smile even more. 'Not so old, though. Not too old for getting up to no good.'

'"No—no good"?' Helen repeated.

'Well, I can't say. But usually if there's a lady in it, it means no good. And him in mourning too.'

'"A lady"?'

'Oh, very fine and fancy, I'm sure. Not just any lady. For your dad. Walking about Chelsea, near one of his cronies'—what does he call them?—their "studios". I should cocoa.'

'Who—?'

'A dandy lady. They're fine and fancy there, all right, in Chelsea. Like china ladies in shop windows.'

'"Chelsea"?'

'Probably thinks it's nice and far away. For strolling about the lanes. In his mourning. Too far for Nanny Hine to know.' The smile caught on a tooth. 'But I've got my friends too. Nannies stick by each other, Missy Wilmot. Nannies' code. Just so happens I know someone Chelsea way—with eyes in their head—for cooing doves.'

'"Doves"?'

Nanny Hine's mouth still smiled but her eyes had contracted and caused two mirthless little sunbursts of wrinkles.

'What're you drawing?'

'It's—'

'Here, let's see.'

'It's—'

'A bridge? Fancy now, there's a coincidence.'

Helen was uncertain what the long word meant.

'They've got bridges at Chelsea. Ever been there, Helen? I'll take you some time. Lots of interesting sights for little girls in Chelsea. And nannies too. Nannies who work their arses off while fine and fancy ladies sip tea all afternoon, la-di-da tea—not the kind you and me drink, though.'

Helen didn't know which question to ask first.

'What—what kind of tea?'

'How should I know? How'd I know something like that?'

Helen stared at her drawing, which suddenly didn't seem as convincing as she'd thought it was.

'I never told you this, Helen.'

Helen looked up. She saw the smile had gone.

'Don't say Chelsea to your father. D'you hear?'

Helen nodded slowly.

'Don't ever say Chelsea to him. Maybe we'll go. Just us.'

Helen stared at the point of her crayon.

'A drawing expedition,' Nanny Hine said. 'If we do. But it'll be our secret. Yours and mine. And your ma's—'

'What?'

Nanny Hine heard the alarm.

'You can tell your ma. In your sleep. That you went to Chelsea.'

Helen shook her head.

'Wouldn't she like to know, then?'

She stopped shaking her head and kept it still.

'It's nothing to her now, though, is it?' Nanny Hine asked. 'Poor soul.'

And that—because circumstances didn't allow them to discuss it ever again—was the beginning and the end of the matter.

*

Helen was sitting typing when Miriam opened the door, carrying the tea things.

Helen immediately fixed her.

'Your mistress knew my name.'

Unperturbed, Miriam crossed the room and laid the tray down on the side-table next to the fire.

'When I phoned,' Helen told her, 'for the first time. I didn't tell her. But she said it.'

'I don't know anything about it, Miss.'

'I didn't tell her. I would remember, wouldn't I?'

'Maybe you did tell her.' The cup and saucer rattled. 'Miss.'

Helen shook her head.

'No. No, I didn't.'

'Maybe you're imagining she said your name.'

'I'm not imagining it.' Helen affirmed the point as positively as she could.

'I don't know, Miss, I'm sure.'

With that the inscrutable Miriam recrossed the room and departed.

Helen waited until the door had closed, then she stood up and walked over to the tea table. She picked up the pot from the tray and strode across to the window. She threw up the sash. She removed the lid of the pot and looked inside.

Very purposefully she tipped the pot upside down, shook it, and watched the contents pour down on to the gravel.

*

She returned to the typing.

'. . . Chelsea is a change, quite a pleasant one given the circumstances, and having to take what one can get. We're prey to the mists, of course, which are never done, but somehow the place suits it. Often I'm reminded of Cornish fishing villages . . .'

Helen recognised the borrowing, but had no feelings that the remark should have been appropriated from her. She was wondering what the purpose of the letter was, if anyone was ever going to read it with any sort of interest.

She was also thinking of Miriam, charged with the running of the house. She believed she had not only been stolen from by Miss Lazare but—rather more the issue—lied against by the girl.

As she continued typing, she realised she should have been more forthright, she should have forced an answer from her. The girl had been indifferent to her concern, insolent even.

Helen stopped typing. It occurred to her that she'd never been below stairs. Where better to confront the girl and corner her?

She tried typing more but she couldn't rid herself of the picture in her head—Miriam in the kitchen, eluding the answer to her question. She decided that going down was the only recourse she had: she wouldn't rest until it had been done.

All she allowed the girl was a single rap on the kitchen door. As it swung open she saw her turning round, looking startled: behind her she noticed a man's shape, disappearing from the room. For a moment Helen almost lost control, mistaking the form for one she thought she knew . . . Then she recovered.

'Who is it?' Miriam asked.

Helen smiled. The question was superfluous. Obviously the girl was delaying: mark of a guilty conscience.

At the same time she was puzzled, that it should have been a man: her suspicions had been otherwise.

'So, here you are,' she said curtly.

'Miss Wilmot.' The girl flattened down the front of her apron. 'Were you wanting something?' she asked. She had regained her equipoise. 'I'd have answered the bell.'

'Am I out of bounds?'

'This is the kitchen, Miss Wilmot.'

Helen smiled tepidly.

'The engine room? Of the ship?'

She looked round at the laying surfaces of the room. She spotted the caddy of tea and the teapot. That infernal chrysanthemum tea.

'I'm leaving now,' she said, not having decided the matter previously. 'I'm going home.'

'Very well, Miss.'

'I've hurt my eyes reading.'

Their eyes met. Helen's glanced away.

'Will *you* lead the way, Miss?'

A dismissal. Helen turned her back on the kitchen and marched off towards the stairs.

In the hallway she waited while her coat and scarf and gloves and gas-mask case were brought from the cloakroom.

Miriam handed her the coat. She was to dress herself now, but that saved her the indignity of the slashed lining. The gesture even had the effect of calming her.

'It feels colder today,' she ventured. 'Don't you think so?'

'I hadn't noticed, Miss.'

'*I* think so.'

She folded her white chiffon headscarf and placed it on top of her hair.

'Do you plan staying here for long?' she asked, pulling the knot tight under her chin, wanting to know.

'I don't understand, Miss.'

Of course not. Of course not.

'In this house?'

The answer came pat.

'That depends.'

'Everything *depends*, Miriam,' she said.

'On my usefulness, Miss Wilmot. How long I'm needed.'

'Oh.' Helen couldn't resist a stab, a twist. 'In the Brave New World, you mean?'

Miriam's face was a blank.

'I should think,' Helen said, meaning to be cryptic, 'I should think there will always be a place for you.'

'I can't say, Miss Wilmot, I'm sure.'

'No.' Helen adjusted the scarf before picking up the gas-mask case. 'No,' she said, 'maybe not.'

Damn her, she was an idiot and nothing better.

'I shall let *myself* out today, Miriam.'

She was turning for the door when the maid spoke again.

'You've forgotten something, Miss Wilmot, haven't you?'

Helen looked back. The bracelet! Her heart hurt, slamming against her chest.

Miriam brought one hand from behind her back. She held out the pair of gloves.

'Oh'. Helen took a long, slow, deep breath. 'Yes.' She took the gloves. 'Thank you.'

'For the cold.'

'Yes.'

Helen felt her eyes too coy to look at the girl directly. The girl stood saying nothing while she pushed her hands clumsily into the gloves. Now all she wanted was to be gone, somewhere else. Even back in that room, unloading what was in her pocket. It didn't matter any more that her questions hadn't been answered, that maybe they wouldn't be, *couldn't* be. She was determinedly not thinking of the time to come, when the questions would expand and grow in her mind until they entirely filled it, like fog, like a miasma.

She walked towards the door. She reached out for the handle, turned the ball in her palm and pulled.

Why should a house require so little security, it struck her, in these times especially? Anyone might walk in and do as they would, sample the comforts, cast eyes on some covetable object . . .

'Have you remembered everything now, Miss Wilmot? To take with you?'

Helen spoke quickly. 'Yes, thank you.'

She hurried outside.

'Goodbye, Miss.'

Goodbye, goodbye, good*bye*.

*

She waited for him on the cold Embankment, for what might have been hours. Cars and buses drove by, so many of them that she thought they must be re-passing her on their return journeys. She felt she had the eyes of the world upon her.

She only left when she realised that the light was draining from the sky and that some of the cars, with caps on their headlights, were slowing down and the men driving them were staring at her. Their intensity made her prickly and uncomfortable.

Prickly cold. She was numb with the cold.

She walked off, directing her gaze at the pavement. To her surprise, her eyes were dry.

The paving stones held her upright. She was amazed at that.

She saw no bonfires this evening, she couldn't hear any baying dogs. All the stories were confounded.

She wondered if she hadn't wished the man into being: if, all her life, she hadn't just seen what she'd wanted to see.

The point beyond that in the argument, she realised, was to question whether *you* weren't only as other people chose to 'see' you, you were an invention of their expectations.

She shook her head and looked sideways: a car was moving off from the kerb, the driver's hopes thwarted. All over London their wives were preparing make-do suppers in kitchens, while other women hadn't a notion where and how to start to fulfil their bodies' physical requirements. She felt that, curiously, her own bodily cravings were over now and it was her soul she was chiefly concerned for: her spirit that endured beyond the body's caprices.

*

In a square she stood behind railings watching a girl of seven or eight or nine running over gravel and grass, chasing a white balloon. A man's voice was calling from one of the houses.

The balloon eluded the child's fingers. It started rising towards the railings.

It couldn't have been easier for Helen, she simply reached out her hand and caught the trailing string.

The girl ran up to the railings.

The girl's eyes and Helen's met. A look was exchanged between them that might have been recognition, calm and quite unastonished.

The man's voice continued to call from the house across the road.

Then Helen gently tapped the balloon. It floated up, clear of the railings, and began to fall again.

The girl lifted up her arms, stretched her fingers, and—as if she could have no more important object in her life—took hold of the end of the string.

*

She wouldn't give up all hope, not yet, and she kept looking out for him, all the way back to Porteous Street.

Past Pandora's she dug into her right-hand coat pocket for her key. It wasn't there, where she always kept it, but—for some reason—it was now in the other pocket.

She shook her head.

Beside her, on the pavement, she noticed the long fall of her shadow. She saw it was starting to obscure her, her shoes and her legs and the skirt of her coat.

She lifted her eyes, drawn by the two uncovered headlights shining ahead of her. They dazzled in the street's light dusk.

The car was moving towards her.

She recognised it, from the radiator grille and its position in the middle of the road.

What was it doing *here*?

She stood back against the wall as it came closer.

She saw the chauffeur's cap, but not his face. She noticed that the colour of the upholstery on the front bench was dove grey.

As the car passed her, cleaving the air with a sigh, she thought she could see two figures in the back compartment, behind the partition glass. The one nearest to her appeared to be a woman.

But the car was travelling too quickly and the light in the street was too uncertain for her to be any more positive than that: two passengers perhaps and one of them a woman, to judge from the softer outline of the clothes.

The event, other than that, was a mystery.

Helen stood watching the car—the oval of back window, the red tail lights, the gleaming black bodywork—as it swung down the darkened street, undeflected by all the cracks and potholes. For a moment it was like a daring, disdainful bird of foreboding, the white owl turned into a rook-black omen: then the brake lights winked on the corner, the indicator stick glowed, and as the wheels moved into the corner the car was returned to the condition of the actual and material, or whatever this state of being was which she and it inhabited.

*

'Just the two of us,' said the woman who used to be Nanny Hine. She smelt of lilac-scented talcum and strong humbugs. 'That's nice now, isn't it?'

She turned the key in the lock and the door squeaked open.

Helen thought it was the dingiest room she'd ever seen. There was a bed, and a fireplace without a grate, and some ornaments set out on the high mantelpiece. The Meissen lady, was it, from her mother's dressing-table?

A painting of flowers hung on the wall above a chest of drawers.

'Yes, just us two together again. That's *very* nice, Helen, isn't it?'

She'd been sitting in the gardens in the square when the gate from the street had clattered open and in had walked someone she hadn't expected to see ever again, instantly recognisable even without her uniform. 'I thought we'd have a chat, you and me, Helen. And you can come and see my new home. My sort-of-home.'

'Like it?' the woman was asking her. 'Not what you're used to, of course.'

'It—it's very—very neat.'

The woman laughed at the word.

'Me oh my! "Neat", are we?'

She laughed again.

Helen looked away to the window, to the view of grey brick houses opposite.

'You don't look very approving, missy.' The voice was sharper. 'It's not like your father's place, of course, is it?'

Helen stared at some feathers in a jar.

'Well, is it?'

She didn't know what to say.

The woman dropped into the room's one armchair.

'The Ritz it isn't. But then I don't give myself fancy airs. Not like some folks I could mention. Very superior, high-and-mighty they are.'

They'd seemed to travel miles to reach here: first the bus, then a long walk for blocks, trying to keep up with the strides as her arm was nearly pulled out of its socket.

'Some people think they know everything . . .'

The conversation had gone no further. At that moment the door opened and in walked a man in a raincoat. His eyes stared. He took his pipe out of his mouth and pointed it at her.

'Jesus Christ, what've you done?'

'What do you think I've done?'

'You're—you're bloody mad!'

'I know *what I'm doing*. And I'll thank you to—'

The man grabbed her hand and hurried her out of the room and down the stairs. Afterwards she had a memory of rosebuds on the wallpaper and a picture of Jesus under crinkly, wavy glass: afterwards, when she was back home in Monmouth Square.

The man put her on the bus and gave her a sixpence.

'Just forget you came here,' he told her. 'Forget all about it, will you?'

She looked down at him from the platform at the back.

'It didn't happen,' he was telling her.

Of course she knew that that couldn't be.

'Just a mistake,' he said. 'Don't think another thing about—'

The bus carried her away. Lights shone out of a tea-room and she felt it was the strangest day, to be in this other London she knew nothing about. In every street there was another London: in every different building, that meant, in every house, in every room.

She didn't know why it had happened.

When he asked her she told the man with the cap and leather satchel where she wanted to go.

'Number Twenty-One Monmouth Square, please.'

'Blimey!' he said. 'To what do we owe this—'

'Let her be,' a woman told him good-naturedly from the seat behind.

'I'm going to Buckingham Palace,' the man opposite said. 'Drop me at the gates, James.'

Someone laughed. The other passengers' faces split into smiles.

All these people, all these streets, all these Londons. For a few moments Helen was dizzy, nearly sick, feeling how small she'd shrunk, like Alice, just in an afternoon, seeing the same pink sky she always watched from the nursery window colouring the whole city that wasn't only hers now but everyone's.

*

Helen drew the curtains in her room. She turned the knob on the wireless with a twist of her wrist and, after the set had warmed, the room filled with a song.

'Once there was a thing called Spring,
When the world was writing verses like yours and mine.

All the boys and girls would sing
As we sat at little tables and drank May wine.'

She took off her scarf and coat, and dropped them on to the back of the armchair. From the pocket of her cardigan she removed the bangle. She held it up to the light and inspected it, then she placed it on the mantelpiece, between the porcelain figure of the lady in her crinoline and the model ship in its bottle.

She opened the drawer of the chest, hoping against hope, but inside she saw the bangle she'd left there in the morning. She took it out. She held it up to the light and inspected it, then she placed it on the mantelpiece, between the china lady and the sailing ship in the bottle.

'Now April, May and June
Seem sadly out of tune,
Life has stuck a pin in the balloon.'

She walked over to a table in the corner of the room and, for something to do, rearranged several peacock feathers standing in a stoneware jar.

'Spring is here, why doesn't my heart go dancing?
Spring is here, why isn't the waltz entrancing?'

Not having all the objects around her which she'd grown up with disturbed her some evenings. But even in Monmouth Square most of her mother's things had disappeared from the house during her last illness and after her death. It was as if her father hadn't wanted to be reminded. The dressing-table set (except for the silver brush, which Nanny Hine had made off with) and the Parisian leather vanity case and the shoe portière had all gone, and most of the jewellery and clothes: having them might have helped her to *believe more* in her mother, given some substance to the nebulous images she barely remembered. But her father had decided for her, that that was not to be.

'Stars appear, why doesn't the night invite me?'

In this room of her own, she walked across to the bed and sat down. She felt her face taut. With one foot on the floor, she lay back. She started unwinding the scarf at her throat.

*

'Not long.'
  '*How* long?'
  'Who can say?'
  'It must seem like forever.'
  'It's as well we don't know.'
  'So soon, and never soon enough.'
  'We're just waiting.'

*

She knew what to do.

The next morning, as the bells of a church were pealing nine o'clock, she was standing outside the public library where she would be able to supply herself with the answers.

She was alone. No one else in the city seemed to care if they found the answers or not. She'd slept badly and she had to haul herself up the steps when a woman's shape moved behind the glass and the doors were opened.

She filled in a slip of paper with her request and waited at the issue-desk. The reading room was empty; it had been decided that she didn't merit having the lights turned on.

The bound volume of newspapers was brought to her. As she reached out to take them, she caught sight of the bracelet on the woman's wrist, disappearing beneath her cuff. It was silver, a bangle—

She snatched at the woman's fingers. For a moment they offered no defence but as Helen tried to pull back the cuff of the cardigan they tugged free of her grip. The woman stared at her, in consternation, then—the silence seeming to add to the offence she'd suffered—she scowled.

Helen turned her back on her and made her way to a carol carrying the heavy tome of newspapers. She sat down and dropped her load. Its weight resounded round the room.

She felt leaden, drained. She opened the volume at random, read the dates at the top of the pages, then worked forward. She found the date she required and slowly turned the pages of that day's edition. Her eye caught a word, a name, and she peered closer at the column of print. She looked back to the beginning of the paragraph.

'Three houses in the west terrace sustained severe damage in the raid. The owners of Numbers Forty-Eight and Fifty confirmed that those houses were empty at the time the bomb exploded. It is believed that all the occupants of Number Forty-Nine met their deaths in the ensuing fire. Seven bodies have been recovered from the site.'

She stared at the last sentence, tried reading it again to make sense of it.

She shook her head, unable to believe what she was thinking.

Then, in another column on the same page of Home news she noticed a report of the damage done to a neighbouring square on the same night.

She turned to the next day's edition, to the columns of deaths. There she re-read one she knew by heart: Richard Parry Wilmot, husband of the late beloved Louise, devoted father of Helen.

She inspected the 'L's listed, then moved on to the following day's edition. Suddenly her heart seemed to stop as she recognised the name and photograph above an obituary notice. She held on to the edge of the desk and dared herself to read what was there.

'The death has occurred in tragic circumstances of the distinguished musician, Mr Charles Castell. He was widely regarded as one of the country's most accomplished virtuoso performers of the violin. In another capacity, Mr Castell was also a noted composer of solo concert pieces for that instrument.'

The man in the photograph wore a wing-collar and was in profile. She shook her head again, as if to rid herself of a ludicrous fancy. She might have been about to smile, but stopped herself. She bunched her right fist tight.

Above her, sunlight slanted through the panes of the dome's cupola and fell earthwards in a sepulchral shaft. She glanced up, as if in expectation of wisdom, a revelation. She waited, as patient as a saint, while her mind hummed with the implausible and impossible.

In a moment she unbunched her fist and slammed her hand down on the desk-top.

She needed to know that she was actual, present, in the here and now.

The blow to the desk left her hand and her arm hurting. But spirits suffer in hell . . .

She opened her mouth and let the cry fly out of her.

'I'm here!'

And another.

'Tell me I'm not here!'

She looked round the room that was like a mausoleum. She was expecting angry looks, a chill reprimand.

That would have proved *some*thing to her.

But not even the woman behind the counter was there. No one

stared back at her, no one accused her of disturbing the peace.

The library was empty, except for her solitary self.

*

Outside an 'All Clear' was sounding.

Helen stood in the middle of the street and watched as the underground station offered up its saved human cargo.

People hurried along the pavements, back to their business. No one spared a second look for her as she stood staring.

Everyone was carrying a gas-mask case, and it was then she realised she hadn't brought hers.

The scene as she stood spectating was like a film stopped and suddenly re-started. A drey hauling a cart turned the corner, car engines spluttered and whined. A tin slop bucket was emptied from a doorway and the contents sluiced the high pavement and ran down into the waiting gutter.

*

Then she ran for a couple of blocks in the cold without stopping, gulping down fresh air.

On a corner she almost collided with a man but dodged him in time and steadied herself; he spun round as if he was passing through a revolving door. In other circumstances she might have smiled, laughed even, but not in these ones. Later, stepping off a kerb, she had to jump back to avoid a whistling cyclist who didn't seem to see her. She nearly lost her balance and only kept herself upright by reaching out for a lamp-post.

She tried to concentrate, but it meant putting everything else out of her mind and she didn't see how she could. She even had the madcap fancy that somehow the circumstances might have been capable of imagining *her* into being . . .

She was passing a shop window that was criss-crossed with a latticework of black tape, and she stopped. She laid her hands on the two supports of the green wooden window frame, leaned forward, and—most deliberately—she breathed on the glass.

She stepped back, admiring the island she'd mapped with the hot air from her lungs. She watched a woman walking towards her and saw that she was taking care not to look or else had truly failed to notice. She might have drawn her attention to the vaporous evidence on the diamond lozenges of glass on the shop window, but she needed more than a puzzled or pitying or fearful look for confirmation of her living and breathing being.

In another street she spotted a telephone box. It was unoccupied and she hurried towards it. She tugged at the handle on the door, pulled the dead weight back, and manoeuvred herself inside. She lifted the receiver, shook some coins out of her pocket, gave the number—sounding breathless—had to repeat it because the operator couldn't hear, and waited for the connection to be made. The operator replied, and she plugged a coin into the box and pressed button 'A'.

'Hello. This—this is Miss Wilmot. I'm—I'm afraid I'm unwell today. I can't come. Please tell—I—'

She dropped the receiver on to the cradle. Her eyes searched the street but saw nothing of what was there.

She leaned forward. Selecting the pane closest to her mouth, she made a circle with her lips and, superstitiously taking care not to make contact with the surface, she breathed on the glass. Another island formed, moist and tropical.

She was inspecting the result when, at her shoulder, the telephone started to ring. She jumped, as if she'd taken current. She stared at the telephone, horrified.

Somehow she found the door and blundered her way out. She turned in all directions, then began to run, anywhere just to get away. Her heels scraped on the pavement. Behind her, the ringing continued, rising high above her footsteps and the traffic noise, serrating her nerve ends like the teeth of a saw.

*

Later, tiredness weighted her like sand.

It didn't matter to her where she went, and she lost all her bearings.

Her movements were like a dream to her. She only became conscious of what was happening as she turned a corner, past a man playing a hurdy-gurdy. She'd taken several steps when she heard the tune: 'London Bridge is falling down'.

She looked back. The man stood beside the machine pumping it hard, his cap pulled low on his brow; at his feet, attached to a length of string, a mongrel dog sat surveying the passers-by.

*

Back in her room, she lay on top of the hard, lumpy bed, staring up expressionless at the ceiling.

How did the ceiling keep standing with all its cracks and chips?

From outside she distinguished separate qualities of sound: the muffled traffic roar on Theobalds Road, thumps as a football was kicked against a wall, radio voices bleating in another room.

Over these she started to hum a tune: the same one she'd heard from the wheezing hurdy-gurdy.

'London Bridge is falling down,
Falling down, falling down,
London Bridge is falling down,
My fair lady.'

*

At the end of the afternoon she found the house from his description of it: a high, narrow ship captain's land berth, in a decent street in Battersea not far from the river.

The woman who answered the door was just as she had expected her to be: small, plump, dressed in black, hair rolled up with combs, wearing flat, pinched shoes, and with a pointed face as tart as a lemon. Next to the front door stood a wardrobe, in sober coffin oak and brass; the hall smelt of mothballs and dead time.

'Mrs Spode?'

'You'll have to speak up.'

'Mrs—Mrs Spode?'

'That's right,' the woman replied, in stretched vowels that might have been aping her betters.

'I—'

'I've no rooms.'

'No. It's not about that.'

'Isn't it?'

'I don't want—'

The woman surveyed the stranger with a shrewd eye.

'What *do* you want?' she asked in an accent she might have learned from the films.

'I'm—' Helen looked past her, into the long, cramped hall. Dark pictures—like aquatint engravings—hung on wires, a potted aspidistra perched on a stand, a whatnot crowded the awkward corner of the staircase.

'I'm looking—'

'I see.' The woman's tone had softened, but Helen heard its falseness. 'Why don't you come in?'

'I—' Helen shook her head, and couldn't quite keep her voice steady. 'I can't—'

She glanced over her shoulder.

'You're looking for something?' the woman enquired.

'Some—' Helen didn't know how to avoid the woman's eyes. 'Some—*one*. Actually.'

Mrs Spode assimilated the information with only a slight raising of her eyebrows.

'And who might *that* be?' she asked.

Helen dropped her eyes to the black lace on the woman's Edwardian collar.

'Mr Fowler,' she said.

'You'll have to speak up.'

'Mr *Fowler*.'

'Mr Fowler?' Mrs Spode sounded surprised. 'Did you say?'

'Is—is he here?'

'Gracious, no!' She exclaimed as an actress might.

'This is where he lives?'

Mrs Spode hesitated.

'Once,' she said. 'Once he did.'

'When?'

'Oh, it's months ago.'

Helen felt her face about to crumple.

'I thought—'

'Then you thought wrong,' the woman said. 'Didn't you?'

'Where—do you know where—'

Mrs Spode fastened one of her famous appraising front door looks on the stranger.

'At least,' she said, 'it wasn't in Burma.'

'What d'you mean?'

'Awful place. "That's not a posting, Mrs Spode," he used to tell me, "it's a sentence".'

'He—he went—?'

'Oh, they all *went* in the end. That place is just a graveyard—'

'I don't—I don't understand—'

Mrs Spode's sly considering look was replaced by another: puzzled, even concerned.

'No,' she said, in the more recognisable accent of these parts. 'No, you don't, do you?'

Helen stood on the step shaking her head.

'We got the news. Lost his life, did our Mr Fowler. Joined his Maker. Some weeks back.'

Helen's eyes grew wide. They jellied like a fish's, and Mrs Spode flinched.

'They say—' The woman chased after the words. 'They say we're like the country and its money, dear. We're living on credit, on borrowed time. What do *you*—'

She held out her hands.

'You've turned quite pale, dear. Come in, won't you?'

Helen felt the touch of the hand on her elbow.

'They say there's lots doing it.' The proprietor of Pandora's leaned his elbows on the counter. 'Changing their names, their identities. Thought *you*'d gone too, moved on. Gone to live somewhere else. Disappeared. But folks disappear now just walking along the streets.'

When she looked down she glimpsed silver on the woman's wrist, beneath the tuck of her cuff.

'I—'

Helen reached out for the railing behind her. Her feet retreated down the steps without her bidding.

'I can't,' she said. 'I can't. No.'

She stared up at the woman, then turned away and started running, heels stabbing—still stabbing—on the loosened paving stones.

She didn't look back.

*

She ran on.

Across the river, in Dolphin Square, a car stopped at the opposite kerb, some fifteen or twenty yards away. An owl was hooting, hours too soon.

She stopped for breath. She recognised the man who was climbing out of the driver's seat. He was an authority on French 'plein-air'-ism, another habitué of the house in Kent she used to visit with her father, which he'd told her was going to be so famous one day. Sometimes the man had come to Monmouth Square for earnest, high-minded conversations over dinner. A few days before their own tragedy he'd been involved in a car accident: her father had read her the account from the newspaper in the shelter beneath the back garden.

Now he looked ruddy and well, and was laughing at some remark his colleague had made.

She caught a glimpse of the second man emerging from the passenger seat—the back of his head—and it was as much as she needed to know. In profile he drew himself upright in the gathering, owl-haunted dusk of Dolphin Square, miraculously whole and repaired.

'Sometimes hours. Sometimes minutes.'

'But she can—'

'No, she can't hear.'

'Are you sure?'

'Every day I see it. I know what the end's like when it comes.'

'Poor kid!'

'And all her life before her.'

Their careless laughter floated up into the trees; it caught and snagged in the tangle of branches, and put the discomfited owl to squeaky, urgainly flight.

*

Helen pushed on the door. She saw the proprietor standing behind the counter. She smiled: a weary smile, she knew, and defeated.

Rain was dripping from her, but she couldn't think what she was supposed to do about it.

She crossed to the table. She dropped on to a chair; its feet screeched beneath her on the floor. She laid her elbows on top of the table.

'Thought you'd gone,' the man said.

She looked up.

'Gone?' she repeated. 'Where?'

The man rolled up his sleeve. 'Moved on,' he said.

She nodded.

'Yes,' she said. 'Yes. I might.'

The man rolled up his other sleeve.

She cleared her throat. 'I think—'

The man gave her a knowing look. 'Time for a change?' he asked her.

She moistened her cracked lips.

'Perhaps,' she said.

It was hot in the room. The man seemed flushed; the dome of his head shone.

'Perhaps,' she repeated.

'What's that?'

'I—Perhaps—'

'I always know,' the man said.

There was a pause. Helen listened to the silence: like a deep fissure opening, a fault in the linoleum, a rime without reason.

'Do you?' she replied.

'I've an eye for it,' the man said.

An eye, not an ear.

'A third eye?' she asked.

The man's brow furrowed.

'Come again?' he said.

Helen didn't know how to reply.

'Yesterday I was cold,' she told him. 'Yesterday seems a year ago.' She undid two of the buttons on her coat.

'I'm not now,' she said. 'Cold. Hardly at all.'

The man placed his hands flat on the counter.

'Maybe—'

She repeated him, without much interest. ' "Maybe"?'

The man nodded at a tea cup and saucer.

'There's tea,' he said.

She considered.

'Chrysanthemum tea?'

The man's brow corrugated again.

'What's that?' he said, as if he couldn't hear her properly.

She wondered where the heat was coming from.

'No,' she said. 'No, I don't think so.'

She placed her hands on the table in front of her and turned them palms upwards.

'You see, I didn't disappear,' she said, speaking quietly, with a degree of confidence even. 'You see? They said the pavements couldn't hold my weight.' She tried tracing the life line on her palm but lost track of it. 'There are air pockets under the ground,' she told him, if he was really listening to her. 'London's riddled with them.'

'People're changing their names, their identities. Their natures, maybe.'

'They've found a statue of the sun god, from Roman times. He's smiling.'

'Anything—anything's possible nowadays.'

Helen looked across the room. She saw, on another table, a newspaper: she recognised the word *Times*, and her eyes set as the man continued speaking.

'There's more queer things than you and me'll ever make head or tail of—'

She stood up, crossed to the table, and picked up the newspaper. She pulled out a chair and sat down. Tiredly she laid the paper flat. She quickly scanned the 'Personal' columns. At the bottom of the page she found the same advertisement, ringed this time with red ink instead of black.

'A LONDON GENTLEWOMAN REQUIRES THE DOMESTIC SERVICES OF A YOUNG LADY TO ACT AS HER CONFIDENTIAL SOCIAL SECRETARY.'

She folded the newspaper over on itself. She looked across the room, towards the window, and saw the woman in the good-ish coat, newly come down in the world, with the set of a medieval anchorite to her features.

The woman seemed haggard, unwell, but she was gamely smiling. Helen couldn't bring herself to smile.

Behind the woman she saw another face peering in: an old man's. She remembered the old man who'd spoken to her in front of the vanished house in Rawlinson Gardens.

She pushed the chair back. The heat was torturing her.

'I can't,' she said. 'I have to go now.'

She glanced over at the proprietor, who was wiping his brow with a handkerchief.

The room felt like a hothouse.

*

'Maybe—'

She couldn't breathe under the glass. She glanced over her shoulder, to the terrace of the hotel. Her father might reappear at any moment.

The frond of a plant brushed her forehead and she started.

'I'll write,' he said.

Her breath seemed to be gathered up into a ball inside her chest. The chrysanthemums blazed orange and gold.

'You—'

'I can write to you. Your father—'

'I'll—we've a maid—'

'I didn't think I'd—I didn't imagine—'

'No.'

'It was to be a holiday. A break.'

'How—how can you breathe in here?'

'This is nothing. Not like—out there, I mean.'

'What—what'll happen?'

'I just try to survive. If I can. If that's mine to decide.'

'I could pray for you.'

'If you believed?—that it works?'

She shook her head.

'I—it's so hot,' she said.

'I couldn't think of anywhere else—'

'He won't find us.'

'No.'

'What to say, I mean,' she said. 'It's too hot—to know—'

'This is fine.'

'Words, though. They don't—words to say—'

'Don't think too hard, don't try. It's all right, really.'

'Words just go—round and round, I mean. Oh—'

'Put them on paper. Away from here—'

' "Away from here"—?'

'You'll think about me, Helen?'

'I'll think about you,' she said. 'I'll—think about you, oh yes.'

'Sometime—'

' "Sometime",' she repeated.

'We'll—'

She nodded.

'It'll be over,' he said. 'For better or worse.'

'When?'

'Nothing lasts for ever. Our lives are finite.'

She nodded.

'And our minds,' he said. 'For better or worse. So everything has its natural end.'

*

She walked along wet, unlit streets, away from Pandora's, as far as she could possibly get.

She didn't recognise where she was. Except that she was in an unknown city. Every so often a voice spoke at her shoulder.

'Are you all right, lovey?'

'Know where you're going?'

She didn't look back.

'*Someone*'s in a hurry!'

She didn't know what she was running from, or where she was heading. The journey was the all.

At some point she passed a hot chestnut man at a spitting brazier. The image and the moment fixed in her head and she carried it with her, through the evening streets shiny with rain: the red coals glowing and spitting sparks. She remembered the hurdy-gurdy player, and the man in ARP uniform who'd gruffly pointed her in the direction of Michaelmas Passage, where it was that her problems had begun in earnest.

She was hot and cold. Dark was coming on and she found herself in a part of the city she felt she should be able to identify but couldn't, not quite. There was a three-sided square of tall houses painted white and, in the centre, a garden enclosed by railings.

She crossed the road. A sign hung on a gate: 'PRIVATE—DO NOT PASS BEYOND THIS POINT'. She passed beyond it.

Dusk was taking away the edges and outlines of objects. Everything seemed to be on the point of vanishing. She had the notion that the most significant thing she could see was the pond, and also what was in it: a battered model yacht floating on the leaf-clogged surface of the water. Stepping closer she saw that its mainsail was torn.

It started to rain just as she was satisfying herself that the yacht had never been hers, but another child's. She hurried for the cover of some trees and stood trying to shelter as the shower turned heavier. The gravel danced, a sheet of rain driving across the street shone blue by the moon; the papery, raspy leaves on the branches above her head crackled as if there was loose-flying electricity in the air.

The worst passed. Then the trees began to drip. She jumped as some drops fell on to the back of her neck. All the dark space about her seemed to be dribbling water, like a cave.

It was too much for her nerves. She ran forward.

Her feet felt as if they were on sand, not gravel. She couldn't hear the scrunching of the chips.

With the sizzle of the rain in her ears, she darted towards the gate. She pulled it back—it rattled open—and she toppled out on to the street.

Beyond the end of the square she saw traffic and she made for it.

The road when she got there was broad and still busy with life. People hurried past under umbrellas; car tyres splashed on the wet tarmacadam; an ownerless umbrella rolled along the gutter on the other side. An officious-looking ARP warden stepped in front of her as if he didn't see her and almost caused her to lose her balance and fall.

She held on to a lamp-post, looking about her for a taxi cab, up and down the street. The luxury and the expense of a taxi was of no consequence to her now.

One sped towards her, but carrying a fare. She spotted another one, travelling in the opposite direction, but it was also occupied.

As she stood at the kerbside the rain came on again. She looked down at her shoes: her feet were sodden. Her stockings were sticking to her legs and her hair hung limp and straight. She felt desperate: at the end of her long, frayed tether. Enough was enough . . .

She started walking by moonlight and didn't realise she was walking until she sensed another presence trailing hers. She turned her head.

A car with its headlights on full was drawing up beside her. And, just as brazenly, another car behind it.

She stared, not really surprised any more.

She heard the voices and the laughter. Someone called out to her from the second car.

'Miss Wilmot!'

Then someone else.

'Quo vadis?'

A hand with black lacquered nails fluttered from the open window. Helen made out the face beneath the silver turban.

'I *thought* it was you, Miss Wilmot.'

'Sadly at a loss, I fear,' the man who'd played the violin said from the front. 'Poor thing.'

'I—I saw your photograph,' Helen heard herself saying. 'In—in the newspaper. Beside your—'

But that didn't matter now.

The back door opened. An elegant hand with thin fingers and long pared nails painted black reached out for hers.

She took hold of the hand. The fine fingers were perfectly cold.

She entered and fell on to the back seat between the fur-swathed lady and the poetic young man, who gathered up the folds of his black velvet cape.

'We are bound for a party, Miss Wilmot,' the lady explained.

'Penny ice and cold meat.'

(She smelt perfume like balm on two sides of her: bergamot and attar of roses.)

'A party in the country.'

'Join us for the ride,' the famous violinist said.

'We are a ravenous horde—'

'Ignore Howard, my dear—'

'Meet our driver, Miss Wilmot,' the violinist said.

A face looked back; Helen could just see it belonged to a pleasantly smiling young man with thinning hair.

'I'm James,' he introduced himself. 'James Saunders.'

'James has come up from Bristol,' the famous Charles Castell explained. 'Friend of dear old Lavinia's.'

'How lovely for us!' the lady with the turban said, adjusting her fur cape. 'First James, and now Miss Wilmot. A very fetching pair of travelling companions for us—'

'How—how did you—'

'How did I know it was you?' the lady asked, reading her mind. 'Why, no gas-mask box, my dear!'

James Saunders winked to the new passenger in the driving-mirror.

'I—I don't think I'm—dressed—for a party,' Helen said.

'Oh, fear not,' the equine young man told her. 'Anything goes whither we are bound. Absolutely *anything*.'

The driver sounded the horn at the car in front, then started the engine.

'Probably the others have gone ahead,' the 'femme fatale' in the silver turban said.

A face under tight grey marcel-waves was pressed against the oval back window of the first car. It seemed to belong to Miss Lazare's West Country friend, but Helen couldn't be sure. The car, though, she recognised *that*: it had gone all the way to Porteous Street searching her out . . .

'People will come whenever they can, Miss Wilmot. Some have got there before us; others will follow, at their own speed. Now, however did I know it would be *this* evening you ventured out without your gas-mask box?'

The lady smiled teasingly.

'Don't look so worried, my dear,' she said, tapping her fellow-traveller's wrist with her cold white marble hand. 'Relax! Enjoy! You'll know people when you get there.'

She smiled. Helen nodded.

The car picked up speed. The city was disappearing into twilight through the windows.

'I was getting rather tired of London anyway,' Helen listened to herself saying.

The young man on the other side of her sighed softly.

'The female of the species isn't spared either—when she's tired of London, she is indeed tired of life. Never were truer words spoken, methinks.'

She nodded again. The fatigue of the day was slowly seeping up from her feet, taking away her sense of feeling in the lower part of her legs, beneath the knees.

'By the time we're there, Miss Wilmot—'

Once upon a time chiming moments would come to her, moments that silvered and sparkled, when the rhyme and reason revealed themselves.

It would happen quite unexpectedly, for no reason. Suddenly she would see that everything about her fitted and belonged, and that she belonged to the whole.

Her eyelids were growing heavy. She felt her body was filled up with soft, heavy sand inside, her legs were rooted tree trunks.

She had the sensation there was nothing now to hold the car back, nothing to make the wheels drag.

Darkness was coming down, on all sides of them, over them and underneath.

She heard an owl hooting.

She wondered who might be there, at journey's end. The prospect of a conclusion gave her vague comfort.

The lady's hand returned momentarily to her wrist. The coldness had gone.

A quiet stretch of road opened up in front of them. Were they in the country already? Travelling east-wards, at a guess.

The other car was nowhere in sight.

Their headlamps drew all life towards them. (There was danger in a naked light, wasn't it said?)

Her eyelids dropped. Her body was starting to slip down the seat. She tried opening her eyes to see into the distance.

The car was gathering speed.

They were travelling faster and faster. Over the hills and far away.

Their headlights shone along the road and, transfixed, Helen watched for the 'X' where they couldn't breach the darkness, the vanishing point.

RONALD FRAME

SANDMOUTH PEOPLE

'A strange, haunting, evocative novel. A very unusual talent'
Margaret Drabble

'A genuine piece of original writing . . . dealing with one day
(St George's Day) in the life of a small but wealthy English
seaside town in the 50s. This is a marvellous picture of England
at a fixed point of time. Mr Frame has caught his characters in a
sort of literary aspic. Ambitious as any literary effort so far this
year and, what's more, a thoroughly good read'
Stanley Reynolds in Punch

'One of our most gifted younger writers'
The Times

'A major new novel. Ambitious . . . he writes stylishly and
wittily and takes a great stride forward with this book. It's also
cleverly plotted and builds up to an unexpected climax'
Susan Hill

'A triumph'
William Leith in The Guardian

'Inventive and persuasive. The success of the novel lies in the
skill with which Mr Frame depicts the gap between appearance
and reality, and his sense that we "can't get away from the
past" make this a compelling novel, one that feeds the readers'
imagination and is likely to linger in the memory when far more
self-assertive and less subtle books have faded'
*Allan Massie, author of AUGUSTUS and
Booker Prize Judge, 1987, in The Scotsman*

MICHAEL CHABON

THE MYSTERIES OF PITTSBURGH

Art Bechstein steps out of the library into the summer of his graduation year, a season that lies between a past full of secrets and a future of hard-won experience.

Art's father wants his son to become a respectable adult, even though his own discreet 'business' is that of a gangster. But Art, not yet ready for respectability, falls in with the exotic, charming Arthur Lecomte, and ricochets between a homo-sexual relationship and an intense affair with a strange and beautiful girl called Phlox. Before long, the world of his new friends and the underworld of his father must collide, with consequences that Art cannot control.

THE MYSTERIES OF PITTSBURGH is a remarkable debut from one of the most talented new writers of recent years.

ROSE TREMAIN

THE SWIMMING POOL SEASON

Selected as one of the Best of Young British Novelists, 1983

'Sharp, eloquent, pure'
David Hughes in The Mail on Sunday

'The lines of love and longing, if you drew them, they'd criss-cross Pomerac like a tangle of wool'

After the collapse of 'Aquazure', his swimming pool construction business, Larry and Miriam Kendal have exiled themselves to a sleepy French village. When Miriam is summoned to her mother's deathbed in Oxford, Larry begins to formulate a dazzling new idea: the creation of the most beautiful, most artistic swimming pool of all.

Around them, Rose Tremain weaves the intricate fabric of the lives of two communities: Miriam's mother, Leni, clever, beautiful and arrogant. Polish Nadia, tortured by the passions of her sad and guilty past. Gervaise the peasant woman – content with her boisterous German lover and confused husband. And the young tearaway Xavier, in love with the virginal Agnès.

'Rose Tremain has the rare gift of an inclusive sympathy towards her characters and the ever-rarer talent among English writers of being able to write with absolute conviction about love . . . we watch enthralled'
The Observer

'Rose Tremain seems impressively mature as a writer . . . It has a particular kind of excellence and is an entertaining book'
Sunday Times

ROSE TREMAIN

THE GARDEN OF THE VILLA MOLLINI

'Talented to the point of rare originality'
Jill Neville in The Independent

'Her talent at its best'
Susan Hill

'Professional, ingenious . . . genuinely witty'
Martin Seymour-Smith in the Financial Times

'A quintessentially English writer – her work has a charm and finesse, a civilised irony'
Robert Nye in The Guardian

'The stories have a strange, fairy tale quality: the simple, beautiful prose, the sense of inevitability, the use of allusion and metaphor to suggest undercurrents of disturbing portent'
Selina Hastings in the Daily Telegraph

'An expert at conveying the kind of apparently inconsequential detail that might be the moment of definition in someone's life'
The Times Literary Supplement

'A skilled writer deftly turning her hand to different situations'
Vogue

'A collection full of gems'
Country Life

URSULA BENTLEY

PRIVATE ACCOUNTS

'Ursula Bentley's brilliant, bustling novel'
The Guardian

B. J. Berkely is a woman full of certainties.

Arriving from the States to spend a year in Switzerland with
her physicist husband, she knows all about the smug, con-
formist, unliberated nature of Swiss society. She knows also
that she represents all that is dynamic, free-thinking and
uninhibited in American culture.

All this and more, B. J. Berkely knows. And when B. J.
Berkely is sure of a thing, she acts. Switzerland – perhaps, in
due course, the whole of Europe – is about to be catapulted
into the twentieth century.

'Compulsive reading . . . Bentley uses her characters as a
dramatist might: when it is not their turn to speak you are none
the less aware that everyone has a part to play'
The Times Literary Supplement

'Ursula Bentley's hilarious PRIVATE ACCOUNTS is her
long-awaited second novel; its deft, gentle caricature matches
the exact timing of its Swiss setting'
New Statesman

'Ursula Bentley has a piercing eye for female frailty and in her
new novel she turns it to hilarious account'
The Irish Times

Current and forthcoming titles from Sceptre

RONALD FRAME

SANDMOUTH PEOPLE

MICHAEL CHABON

THE MYSTERIES OF PITTSBURGH

ROSE TREMAIN

THE SWIMMING POOL SEASON
THE GARDEN OF THE VILLA MOLLINI

URSULA BENTLEY

PRIVATE ACCOUNTS

BOOKS OF DISTINCTION